RAVES FOR
THE BEACH HOUSE

"SO INVITING THAT IT PRACTICALLY READS ITSELF."
—*New York Times*

"TAUT, SPARE PROSE...A DELICIOUS, FAST-PACED READ QUITE WORTHY OF ITS PLACE ON BESTSELLER LISTS."
—*Pittsburgh Post-Gazette*

"JAMES PATTERSON KNOWS HOW TO SELL THRILLS AND SUSPENSE IN CLEAR, UNWAVERING PROSE."
—*People*

"VASTLY ENJOYABLE."
—*Publishers Weekly*

"A SLICK, BREEZY TALE OF MURDER."
—*Florida International Magazine*

"A SLICK AND TIGHTLY CONSTRUCTED THRILLER...AN ENTERTAINING PAGE-TURNER."
—*Roanoke Times* (VA)

"A STIRRING THRILLER FILLED WITH NONSTOP ACTION...AN INVIGORATING TALE."
—*Midwest Book Review*

Please turn to the back of this book for a preview of James Patterson's novel, *The Lake House*.

"PATTERSON'S WORDS PAINT A PICTURE SO VIVID YOU CAN ALMOST SMELL THE GUNPOWDER OR FEEL BOXER'S TERROR....A FIRST-RATE THRILLER."
—*Florida Times-Union*

"PRIME PATTERSON: FIRST-RATE ENTERTAINMENT.... PATTERSON'S RICHEST, MOST ENGAGING NOVEL SINCE *WHEN THE WIND BLOWS.* The story ripples with twists and remarkably strong scenes....But what makes this Patterson stand out above all is the textured storytelling arising from its focus on Boxer's personal issues."
—*Publishers Weekly* **(starred review)**

"RE-ESTABLISHES PATTERSON AS ONE OF THE TOP MYS-TERY-THRILLER WRITERS IN THE GAME TODAY. *2ND CHANCE* is a first-rate thriller."
—*Grand Rapids Press*

"PATTERSON AT HIS BREEZY BEST."
—*Fort Worth Star-Telegram*

"A SOLIDLY ENGINEERED WHODUNIT. BOTTOM LINE: WORTH CHANCING."
—*People*

1ST TO DIE

"TERRIFIC...A GREAT THRILLER....What's not to love about a 'club' formed by four women to catch a psycho killing newlywed couples?"
—*Providence Sunday Journal*

more ...

"I SAT DOWN WITH IT AT TEN ON A SATURDAY MORN-
ING…AND REFUSED TO DO ANYTHING…UNTIL I
DISCOVERED THAT ALL OF THE THINGS I FIGURED OUT
EARLY WERE EITHER WRONG OR NOT QUITE WHAT
I ASSUMED."
> —*Denver Rocky Mountain News*

"PATTERSON BOILS A SCENE DOWN TO THE SINGLE,
TELLING DETAIL, THE ELEMENT THAT DEFINES A CHAR-
ACTER OR MOVES A PLOT ALONG. It's what fires off the
movie projector in the reader's mind."
> —**Michael Connelly, author of *City of Bones***

"THE MAN IS THE MASTER OF THIS GENRE. We fans all
have one wish for him: Write even faster."
> —**Larry King, *USA Today***

"HIS CLEVER TWISTS AND AFFECTING SUBPLOTS KEEP
THE PAGES FLYING."
> —***People*** **(Page-Turner of the Week)**

"DELIVERS A SHARP PUNCH."
> —*Chicago Tribune*

"THAT RAPID-FIRE, IN-YOUR-FACE, YOU'D-BETTER-KEEP-
READING-OR-ELSE FORMAT WILL MAKE YOU FINISH *1ST
TO DIE* IN ONE SITTING (barring World War III, a 9.1
earthquake or the Ebola virus)."
> —*Denver Rocky Mountain News*

"JAMES PATTERSON WRITES HIS THRILLERS AS IF HE
WERE BUILDING ROLLER COASTERS."
> —*Associated Press*

JACK & JILL

"FORTUNATELY PATTERSON HAS BROUGHT BACK HOMICIDE DETECTIVE ALEX CROSS....He's the kind of multilayered character that makes any plot twist seem believable."

— *People*

"QUICK AND SCARY."

— *New York Daily News*

"Captivating....A fast-paced thriller full of surprising but realistic plot twists....CROSS IS ONE OF THE BEST AND MOST LIKABLE CHARACTERS IN THE MODERN THRILLER GENRE."

— *San Francisco Examiner*

CAT & MOUSE

"FAST PACED...THE PROTOTYPE THRILLER FOR TODAY."

— *San Diego Union-Tribune*

"A RIDE ON A ROLLER COASTER WHOSE BRAKES HAVE GONE OUT."

— *Chicago Tribune*

POP GOES THE WEASEL

"CROSS IS ONE OF THE BEST PROTAGONISTS OF THE MODERN THRILLER GENRE, AND ONE OF THE MOST LIKABLE."
—*San Francisco Examiner*

"FAST AND FURIOUS....IN THE PATTERSON PANTHEON OF VILLAINS, SHAFER IS QUITE POSSIBLY THE WORST."
—*Chicago Tribune*

ROSES ARE RED

"PATTERSON KNOWS WHERE OUR DEEPEST FEARS ARE BURIED....THERE'S NO STOPPING HIS IMAGINATION."
—*New York Times Book Review*

"THRILLING...SWIFT...A PAGE-TURNER."
—*People*

"IT STARTS OUT, BANG!...PATTERSON HAS GOT THE MATERIAL DEAD ON."
—*Baltimore Sun*

"PATTERSON MASTERMINDS ANOTHER THRILLER.... Once again, we're left to wonder, how does this man continue to write gripping tales that keep us turning pages into the wee hours of the night until the book is finished, and we're disappointed there isn't more to read?"
—*Oakland Press*

For a complete list of books by James Patterson, previews of upcoming titles, and information about the author, visit JamesPatterson.com or find him on Facebook or at your app store.

THE
BEACH HOUSE

JAMES PATTERSON
& PETER DE JONGE

GRAND CENTRAL
PUBLISHING

NEW YORK   BOSTON

Copyright © 2002 by SueJack, Inc.
Excerpt from *The Lake House* copyright © 2003 by SueJack, Inc.
All rights reserved. In accordance with the U.S. Copyright Act of 1976, the scanning, uploading, and electronic sharing of any part of this book without the permission of the publisher is unlawful piracy and theft of the author's intellectual property. If you would like to use material from the book (other than for review purposes), prior written permission must be obtained by contacting the publisher at permissions@hbgusa.com. Thank you for your support of the author's rights.

Cover design by Mario Pulice
Cover illustration by Debra Lil based on a photograph by Peter Turner / Image Bank

Grand Central Publishing
Hachette Book Group
1290 Avenue of the Americas
New York, NY 10104
www.HachetteBookGroup.com

Grand Central Publishing is a division of Hachette Book Group, Inc. The Grand Central Publishing name and logo is a trademark of Hachette Book Group, Inc.

The Hachette Speakers Bureau provides a wide range of authors for speaking events. To find out more, go to www.hachettespeakersbureau.com or call (866) 376-6591.

The publisher is not responsible for websites (or their content) that are not owned by the publisher.

Printed in the United States of America

Originally published in hardcover by Little, Brown and Company
First International Paperback Printing: March 2003
First United States Paperback Printing: April 2003

Walmart edition (9781455565245): July 2015

10 9 8 7 6 5 4 3 2 1

ATTENTION CORPORATIONS AND ORGANIZATIONS:
Most HACHETTE BOOK GROUP books are available at quantity discounts with bulk purchase for educational, business, or sales promotional use. For information, please call or write:

Special Markets Department, Hachette Book Group
1290 Avenue of the Americas, New York, NY 10104
Telephone: 1-800-222-6747 Fax: 1-800-477-5925

For Pete & Chuck
— *P. de J.*

For Jack, the big boy
— *J. P.*

PETER RABBIT

1

IT'S LIKE DANCING SITTING DOWN. Squeeze —
tap — release — twist. Left hand — right foot — left
hand — right hand.

Everything unfolds in perfect sequence and rhythm,
and every time I twist back the heated, gummy, rubber-
covered throttle, the brand-new, barely broke in, 628-
pound, 130-horsepower BMW K1200 motorcycle leaps
forward like a thoroughbred under the whip.

And another snapshot of overpriced Long Island real
estate blurs by.

It's Thursday night, Memorial Day weekend, fifteen
minutes from the start of the first party in what promises
to be another glorious season in the Hamptons.

And not just any party. *The* party. The intimate $200,000
get-together thrown every year by Barry Neubauer and his
wife, Campion, at their $40 million beach house in Ama-
gansett.

And I'm late.

I toe it down to fourth gear, yank the throttle back again, and now I'm really flying. Parting traffic on Route 27 like Moses on a Beemer.

My knees are pressed tight against the sleek, dark blue gas tank, my head tucked so low out of the wind that it's almost between them.

It's a good thing this little ten-mile stretch between Montauk and Amagansett is as straight and flat as a drag strip, because by the time I pass those tourist clip joints — Cyril's, the Clam Bar, and LUNCH — the needle's pointing at ninety.

It's also a good thing I used to be in the same homeroom as Billy Belnap. As the most belligerent juvenile delinquent at East Hampton High, Billy was a lock to end up on the payroll of the East Hampton Police Department. Even though I can't see him, I know he's there, tucked behind the bushes in his blue-and-white squad car, trolling for speeders and polishing off a bag of Dressen's doughnuts.

I flick him my brights as I rip by.

2

YOU WOULDN'T THINK a motorcycle is a place for quiet reflection. And as a rule, I don't go in for much of it anyway, preferring to leave the navel gazing for big brother Jack, the Ivy League law student. But lately I've been dredging up something different every time I get on the bike. Maybe it's the fact that on a motorcycle, it's just you and your head.

Or maybe it's got nothing to do with the bike, and I'm just getting old.

I'm sorry to have to confess, I turned twenty-one yesterday.

Whatever the reason, I'm slaloming through bloated SUVs at ninety miles per hour and I start to think about growing up out here, about being a townie in one of the richest zip codes on earth.

A mile away on the Bluff, I can already see the party lights of the Neubauer compound beaming into the perfect

East End night, and I experience that juiced-up feeling of anticipation I always get at the beginning of another Hamptons summer.

The air itself, carrying a salty whiff of high tide and sweet hyacinth, is ripe with possibility. A sentry in a white suit gives me a toothy grin and waves me through the cast-iron gates.

I wish I could tell you that the whole place is kind of tacky and crass and overreaching, but in fact it's quite understated. Every once in a while, the rich will confuse you that way. It's the kind of parcel that, as real estate brokers put it, comes on the market every couple of decades — twelve beautifully landscaped acres full of hedges and hidden gardens sloping to a pristine, white sand beach.

At the end of the white-pebble driveway is a 14,000-square-foot shingled mansion with ocean views from every room except, of course, the wine cellar.

Tonight's party is relatively small — fewer than 180 people — but everyone who matters this season is here. It's themed around Neubauer's just-announced $1.4 billion takeover of Swedish toymaker Bjorn Boontaag. That's why the party's on Thursday this year, and only the Neubauers could get away with it.

Walking among the cuddly stuffed lions and tigers that Bjorn Boontaag sells by the hundreds of thousands are a gross of the most ferocious cats in the real-life jungle: rainmakers, raiders, hedge-fund hogs, and the last of the IPO Internet billionaires, most of whom are young enough to be some CEO's third wife. I note the Secret Service men wandering the grounds with bulging blazers and earphones, and I figure there must also be a handful of senators. And scattered like party favors are the hottest one-name fashion designers, rappers, and NBA all-stars the professional party consultant could rustle up.

But don't be too jealous. I'm not on the guest list, either.

I'm here to park cars.

3

I'VE BEEN WORKING at the Beach House since I was thirteen, mostly odd jobs, but parking cars is the easiest gig of all. Just one little flurry at the beginning and end. Nothing but downtime in between.

I'm a little late, so I jump off my bike and get to work. In twenty minutes I fill an out-of-the-way field with four neat rows of $80,000 European sedans. They glisten in the silvery moonlight like metallic plants. A bumper crop.

A parking high point is when a burgundy Bentley the size of a yacht stops at my feet and my favorite New York Knickerbocker, Latrell Sprewell, climbs out, presses a twenty in my palm, and says, "Be gentle, my brother."

The rush over, I get myself a Heinie and a plateful of appetizers, and sit down on the grass beside the driveway. This is the life. I'm savoring my sushi and cheese puffs when a black-jacketed waiter I've never seen before hustles up. With a wink, wink, nod, nod kind of smile, he stuffs a scrap of rose-colored stationery in my shirt pocket.

It must have been pickled in perfume. A pungent cloud hits my nostrils when I unfold it. Shalimar, if I'm not mistaken.

The note itself, however, couldn't be more cut and dried. Three letters, three numbers: I Z D 2 3 5.

I slip away from the house and walk back through the fields of shining metal until I find them on a New York license plate screwed into the svelte behind of a forest green Benz convertible.

I slide into the front passenger seat and start pushing buttons to make myself feel welcome. With a comforting whir, windows drop into doors, the roof parts, and Dean Martin's wiseass baritone pours out of a dozen speakers.

I check behind the visor. Nothing.

Then I fish around in the compartment between the seats. Inside a Robert Marc sunglasses case is a long, thin joint dressed up with a pink ribbon. I spark it up and blow a yellowish wreath across the full moon.

I'm thinking this isn't half bad — getting baked as Dino confides about a French lady named Mimi — when a hand clamps down on my shoulder.

"Hi, Frank," I say without even bothering to twist around in my cushy leather chair.

"Hey, Rabbit," says Frank, reaching through the window for the joint. "Get laid yet?"

Frank is Frank Volpi, chief detective with the East Hampton Police Department and the only cop you're likely to see sporting a platinum Rolex. Then again, Volpi logged two tours of duty in Vietnam before tackling crime in his own backyard. So you could argue that he has it coming.

"You know me, Frank. I don't kiss and tell."

"Since when?"

"Why, gee, since last night with your wife."

This distinctly male excuse for conversation continues until the joint is burning our fingertips. Then Frank staggers off into the fragrant night, and I sit tight with Dino in the Benz.

The phone rings. It's a woman. She whispers, "Peter, did you enjoy your gift?"

"Just what the doctor ordered. Thanks," I say in a return whisper.

"I'd rather you thank me in person on the beach."

"How will I know it's you?"

"Take a flier, Peter. You'll know me when you see me."

I push a few more buttons, chat with a couple of operators who couldn't be nicer, and finally I'm talking to my good pal Lumpke. He's in grad school, getting a Ph.D. in sculpture. Maybe it's not going too well, because Lump sounds cranky.

Of course, it's four in the morning in Paris.

I batten down the Benz and slowly make my way down to the beach. I know I've already told you how outrageously beautiful this place is, but I don't think I've done it justice. Every time I'm here, it amazes me. I'm sure I appreciate it more than Barry and Campion Neubauer do.

As I get closer to the beach, I think for the first time about who might be waiting for me. It wouldn't have been hard to figure out whose voice was on the car phone.

All I had to do was open the glove compartment and look at the registration, but that would have spoiled the surprise.

The thrill of the Beach House is that there's no telling. She could be fifteen or fifty-five. She could arrive alone or with a friend, or a husband.

Rose-colored stationery. Shalimar. Hmmmm. I might know who sent me the note.

I sit down in the sand about twenty yards above from where the waves are breaking. The sloppy remains of Hurricane Gwyneth, which battered Cape Hatteras for a week, just hit the Hamptons this morning. The surf is huge and loud, and sounds pissed off.

So loud that I don't hear them approaching from behind until they're on top of me. The shortest and stockiest of the three, with a shaved dome and Oakley shades, kicks me full in the chest.

The kick breaks a couple of ribs and knocks the wind out of me. I think I recognize one of them, but it's dark and I can't be sure. My panic is growing with each professionally aimed kick and punch. Then the dark realization sinks in that these guys haven't been sent here just to teach me a lesson. This is a whole lot more serious.

I start punching and kicking back with everything I've got, and I finally break free.

I'm running and screaming at the top of my lungs, hoping that someone on the beach will hear me, but the reef drowns out my cries. One of the guys catches me from behind and brings me down hard. I hear a bone snap — *mine.* Then all three of them are whaling on me, one punch or kick landing on top of the next. Without stopping, one of them snorts, "Take that, Peter fucking Rabbit!"

Suddenly, about thirty yards away behind some bushes, a flash goes off. And then another.

That's when I know I'm going to die.

And for whatever it's worth, I even know who my killer is.

Part One

THE SUMMER ASSOCIATE

Chapter 1

EVEN BY THE HEADY NORM of millennial boomtown Manhattan, where master craftsmen paint frescoes on subway walls, the new law offices of Nelson, Goodwin and Mickel were over the top. If the great downtown courthouses around Broadway were palaces of justice, the gleaming forty-eight-story tower at 454 Lexington Avenue was a monument to winning.

My name is Jack Mullen, and as a summer associate at Nelson, Goodwin, I guess I was winning, too. Still, it wasn't exactly what I had in mind when I entered Columbia Law School at the advanced age of twenty-six. But when a second-year student with $50,000 in college loans is offered a summer position at the most prestigious firm in the city, he doesn't turn it down.

The phone started ringing the instant I stepped into my small office.

I picked up.

Female operator on tape: "You have a collect call from Huntsville, Texas, from . . ."

Male voice, also recorded: "The Mudman."

Female operator again on tape: "If you wish to accept, please say yes or push the number —"

"Yes, absolutely," I interrupted. "Mudman, how are you?"

"Not bad, Jack, except maybe for the fact that the state of Texas is pissing its pants at the thought of putting me down like a dog."

"Dumb question."

The surprisingly high-pitched voice at the other end of the line belonged to outlaw biker Billy "Mudman" Simon, and it was coming from the pay phone in Huntsville Prison's death row. Mudman was there waiting for the lethal injection that would put him to death for murdering his teenage girlfriend nineteen years earlier.

Mudman is no saint. He admits to all manner of misdemeanors and an occasional felony during his run in the Houston chapter of the Diablos. But killing Carmina Velasquez, he says, wasn't one of them.

"Carmina was a great woman," the Mudman told me the first time I interviewed him. "One of my best friends in this miserable world. But I was never in love with her. So why would I kill her?"

His letters, trial transcripts, and records of repeated failed attempts to win a new trial were dropped on my desk three days after I started working for the firm. After two weeks decoding every wildly misspelled word, contorted phrase, and hundreds of footnotes painstakingly transcribed in tiny block letters that looked as if they had come from the unsteady hand of a grade-schooler, I was convinced he was telling the truth.

And I liked him. He was smart and funny, and he didn't feel sorry for himself, despite a truckload of reasons why he should. Ninety percent of the convicts on death row were as good as screwed the day they were born, and Mudman, with his deranged junkie parents, was no different.

Nevertheless, he had no enthusiasm for blaming them for what had happened.

"They did their best, like everyone else," he said the one time I mentioned them. "Their best sucked, but let 'em rest in peace."

Rick Exley, my supervisor on the project, couldn't have cared less about Mudman's character or my rookie intuition. What mattered to him was that there were no witnesses to Velasquez's murder and that the Mudman had been convicted completely on the basis of blood and hair samples from the crime scene. That all happened before the forensic breakthrough of DNA testing. It meant we had a reasonable chance to be granted our request that blood and hair samples be taken to confirm that they matched the DNA of the physical evidence held in a vault somewhere in Lubbock.

"I'd hate to get your hopes up for nothing, but if the state lets us test, we could get a stay of execution."

"Don't ever worry about getting my hopes up for nothing, Jack. Where I'm at, insane hope is welcome anytime. Bring 'em on."

I was trying not to get too excited myself. I knew this pro bono project, with the pompous name of "the Innocence Quest," was primarily a PR stunt and that Nelson,

Goodwin and Mickel didn't build forty-eight stories in midtown by looking out for the innocent poor on death row.

Still, when the Mudman was cut off after his allotted fifteen minutes, my hands were shaking.

Chapter 2

I WAS STILL MARVELING at how well the Mudman was bearing up when Pauline Grabowski, one of Nelson, Goodwin's top investigators, stuck her head in my office. To introduce the new recruits to the unique resources of the firm, Grabowski had been assigned to Mudman's case and had spent the past two weeks sussing out things in East Texas.

Grabowski, who was renowned for her resourcefulness and was said to have made as much as a junior partner, carried her reputation lightly. Somehow she'd carved out a niche for herself in this male bastion without being overtly aggressive. She was low-key but straightforward. Although attractive in a captain-of-the-soccer-team way, she did nothing to draw attention to it. She wore no makeup or jewelry, except for earrings, pulled her dark brown hair back in a hasty ponytail, and seemed to wear the same tailored blue suit every day. Actually, I liked her looks just fine.

What gave her such style was the way the simplicity of everything else in her appearance contrasted with her tattoo. Rather than a discreet, dainty turtle or butterfly, Pauline had the indelible mark of the Chrysler Building on her right arm.

It started just below her right shoulder and extended for several inches, to her elbow. It was rendered in a lustrous gold that caught the light bouncing off the spire, and in such detail that it included a winged gargoyle scowling down at the metropolis. According to rumor, it had taken six eight-hour sessions.

When I asked her why she felt so strongly about a skyscraper, her brown eyes flashed as if to say I didn't get it. "It's about people choosing to make something beautiful," she said. "Plus, my grandfather worked on a Chrysler assembly line for thirty-eight years. I figured he helped build it."

Pauline sat on the edge of my desk and told me that Stanley Higgins, the prosecutor in Mudman's case, had sent six men to death row from one little Texas county. He'd retired recently, mainly to a redbrick bar in a working-class section of Amarillo. "According to some nice people who befriended me there, Higgins has a serious drinking problem. Approximately every night, he spouts off about his career as a prosecutor and what he calls 'Higgins's justice.' I should probably make another trip before he parties himself to death."

"Is this what you do all day? Collect voir dire on the enemies of Nelson, Goodwin and Mickel?"

She smiled, and it was hard not to join in with her.

"You can use the Latin if you like, but I call it dirt. There's no lack of it out there, young Jack."

"Not as young as you might think. Mind if I ask what you do in your spare time?"

"Garden," Pauline said, straight-faced.

"Seriously?"

"Cactus, mainly. So be careful, Jack. Besides, I hear you're spoken for. Private investigator, remember?"

Chapter 3

AT 9:20 THAT FRIDAY EVENING, I grabbed my
backpack and descended by elevator, escalator, and
stairs, each a little grittier than the one before, until I
reached a subway platform beneath Grand Central Ter-
minal. The MTA shuttled me west and south to Penn Station, and I high-stepped it over to the track that would
take me to Long Island. I caught the last train out.

Every car would soon be cheek by jowl with frisky
young urbanites headed for the summer's first big Hamptons weekend, but I was early enough to claim a window
seat. I slipped a CD into my Discman and hunkered down
for the creaking three-hour ride to where the tracks of the
Long Island Rail Road dead-end.

Montauk.

Home.

Minutes before the train lurched out, a kid who looked
like a college freshman going home for the summer, all

his dirty laundry and worry squeezed into one huge bag, sank into the seat across from mine.

Five minutes later he was asleep, a dog-eared paperback of *The Red Badge of Courage* hanging perilously from the pocket of his Old Navy tech vest. The book had also been a favorite of mine, and I reached over and tucked it safely back in.

Looking at the kid, who was tall and gawky with one of those mustache-goatees a nineteen-year-old sprouts with anxious pride, I was reminded of all the trips I made back home on that same train. Often I traveled in total defeat. Other times I was just looking to rest and refill my wallet, laboring for my old man's little construction company if he had enough work or, more often when he didn't, repainting the hulls at Jepson's Boatyard. But for five years I never made the trip without a nameless dread of what the future held.

It made me realize how much better things had gotten. I had just finished my second year at Columbia and made *Law Review* the semester before. I'd parlayed that into the associate gig, where I made more in a week than in a summer humping two-by-fours or repainting hulls.

And then there was Dana, who'd be waiting for me at the train. I'd been going out with her for almost a year, but it still amazed me. Part of it was her last name, Neubauer. Maybe you've heard of it. Her parents owned one of the biggest privately held companies in the world, and one of the great summer houses on the eastern seaboard.

I started dating her the summer before, when I was working at Jepson's. She had stopped by to check on her father's luxo-cruiser. I don't know what got into me —

but I asked her out. I guess she liked the rich girl–working boy scenario, and I probably did, too. Mostly, though, I liked Dana: she was smart, funny, centered, and focused. She was also easy to talk to, and I trusted her. Best of all, she wasn't a snob or a typical spoiled rich kid, which was some kind of miracle, given her pedigree.

Eastward ho! The old train rattled on, stopping at all the suburban sprawl towns with their 7-Elevens and Indian names like Patchogue and Ronkonkoma, where my tired college pal got off. Real towns. Not the weekend-tourist villages those on board couldn't wait to cavort in.

I apologize if my yuppie tirade is wearing thin, particularly since I had on the same kind of clothes and my prospects were probably better than most. But one difference between us was that for me, Montauk and the Hamptons were real places, not just a way of keeping a conversation going in a singles bar.

It's where my brother and I were born. Where our mother died too young. And where our octogenarian hipster grandfather showed no sign of slowing down.

Half the passengers scrambled out in Westhampton. The rest got off a couple of stops later, in East Hampton.

When the train finally wheezed to a stop in Montauk right on time at four minutes past midnight, I was the only one left in my car.

And something outside the window seemed very wrong.

Chapter 4

MY FIRST THOUGHT was that there were too many people waiting to meet the train at that hour.

I stepped off expecting to see Dana's Range Rover in the middle of the black, empty lot and Dana sitting cross-legged on the still-warm hood all by her lonesome.

But Dana was standing right there at the end of the well-lit platform, and she didn't seem happy to see me. Her eyes were swollen and she looked as if she'd been crying for days.

More alarming was that my father and grandfather were with her. My father, who never looks all that good these days, was ashen-faced. My grandfather looked hurt and angry, a pissed-off eighty-six-year-old Irishman looking for someone to punch.

Off to the side were an East Hampton cop named Billy Belnap and a young reporter from the *East Hampton Star* scribbling feverishly in a notebook. Behind them the pulsing red bar of Belnap's cruiser streaked the scene with the cold-blooded light of catastrophe.

The only one missing was my brother, Peter. How could that be? Peter had spent his whole life careening from one near disaster to the next with hardly a scratch. When Peter was five, a neighbor found him lying unconscious on top of his bicycle on the side of the road. Our neighbor carried him to our house and laid him on the couch. We were about to call the ambulance when Peter sat up, as if from a nap. That was also the year he kept falling out of trees.

But now the faces on the platform were telling me that my brother, Peter, with his risky combination of carelessness and balls, had run out of lives. He'd driven his motorcycle off the Shadmoor Cliffs, or fallen asleep in bed smoking a cigarette, or chased a ball into traffic and gotten run over like a golden retriever.

My legs went weak as Dana wrapped her arms around my neck and put her wet face against mine. "Jack, I'm so sorry. It's Peter. Oh, Jack, I'm sorry."

After Dana let go, I hugged my father, but it just wouldn't take. He was too far gone into his own pain and misery. We were both mumbling words that couldn't express what we were feeling.

Thank God for Mack, I thought as my grandfather put his arms around me. When I was little, my grandfather had been a large, thickly muscled man. In his mid-forties, he tipped the scales at a Mullen family record of 237 pounds and needed little provocation to throw it around. In the past twenty years, he'd shed more than a third of that weight, but he still possessed enormous hands and big, thick bones, and he embraced me with such shocking ferocity that it almost knocked out my wind.

He clutched me for dear life, and whispered in my ear: "Jack, they say Peter went swimming and drowned. It's the single biggest piece of crap I've ever heard."

Chapter 5

THE MULLENS CLIMBED INTO THE BACK of the police cruiser, and Dana sat up front with Belnap.

As I looked at her through the scuffed-up Plexiglas, she seemed a million miles away. She turned and whispered, "Oh, Jack," then stalled, unable to finish her thought.

Light flashing but no siren, we pulled out of the deserted lot and sped westward through the quiet center of town.

"Last night was the big Memorial Day weekend party," said my grandfather, breaking the awful silence, "and Peter was parking cars as usual. About nine he grabs some supper. But when the party breaks up and it's time to retrieve the cars, Peter's nowhere to be found.

"His absence is noted, but since it's not exactly unheard-of, no one gives it much mind. Two hours ago, Dr. Elizabeth Possidente is walking her rottweiler. The dog starts acting crazy. She runs after him and almost trips over Peter's body where it washed up at the edge of the Neubauer property. He's still there, Jack. I wouldn't let them move the body till you got here."

I listened to my grandfather's low, gravelly voice. To me, it's the most comforting, intelligible voice in the world, but I could barely take in a word.

I felt equally disconnected from the passing scenes outside the window. Plaza Sporting Goods, the Memory Motel, John's Drive-Inn, and Puff 'n' Putt looked nothing like I remembered. The colors were wrong, too bright and hot. The whole town looked radioactive.

For the rest of the trip, I sat on the hump of the transmission between my father, John Samuel Sanders Mullen, and my grandfather, Macklin Reid Mullen, feeling the heartbroken sadness of one and the heartbroken rage of the other. We didn't move, didn't speak. Images of Peter were flashing in my head as though there were a projector there.

Belnap's cruiser finally swerved off Bluff Road and sped through the open gates of the Neubauer compound, where it turned away from the house and made its way slowly down an unpaved road. It stopped a hundred yards from where the surf, whitecapped and furious, pounded the shore. The place where my brother had died.

Chapter 6

THE PLATFORM at the train station had been too crowded. The beach was just the opposite. I stepped unsteadily onto a lovely stretch of moonlit sand. There were no police photographers documenting the scene, no investigators sifting for clues. Only the crashing waves showed any urgency.

My chest was tight. My vision was warped, as if I were taking in this scene through a long, thin tunnel. "Let me see Peter," I said.

My grandfather led me across the sand to the ambulance. Hank Lauricella, a close friend who volunteered for EMS two nights a week, opened the rear door and I stepped in.

There was Peter. . . .

The back of the van was as bright as an operating room, but all the light in the world isn't enough to see your kid brother stretched out naked and dead on a steel gurney. Aside from husband and wife, there's more bad blood between brothers than any other familial pairing. But there wasn't any between us, and that's not rosy, revisionist history. The seven-year age difference, and the even bigger difference in our natures, made us less competitive; and because our mother died so young and a lot of our father died with her, there wasn't much to compete for anyway.

The power of beauty is as absurd as it is undeniable. I stared at his body on the stretcher. Even in death it was obvious why every girl Peter ever smiled at since the age of fourteen smiled back. He looked like one of those Renaissance sculptures. His hair and eyes were jet black. He had our mother's chain of Saint Nicholas around his neck, and in his left earlobe was a small gold hoop he'd worn since he was eleven.

I was so intent on finding some enduring trace of Peter in his face that it took a while to see how battered his body was. When Hank saw it finally register, he silently guided me through the damage. Large bruises on Peter's chest, ribs, arms, and legs; discoloration on his forehead and the back of his neck. Hank showed me the twisted broken fingers and how the knuckles on both hands were scraped raw.

By the time Hank was done, I felt sick to my stomach and so dizzy that I had to grab the rail of the gurney to keep from falling.

Chapter 7

WHEN I FINALLY STEPPED BACK out onto the beach, I felt as if I had spent the night in that ambulance. The train ride from the city seemed like a memory from a previous life.

Dana sat alone on the sand, looking weirdly out of place on her own property. I bent over and she put her arms around me. "I really want to stay with you tonight," she said. "Please let me, Jack."

I was glad she did. I held on to her hand as we followed my father and grandfather back toward Belnap's cruiser.

As we were about to get in, Frank Volpi, East Hampton's longtime chief detective, walked toward us from the direction of the house.

"Sam, Macklin, Jack. I'm sorry."

"Then why aren't you trying to find out who killed him?" asked Mack, staring at him cold and hard.

"At the moment, there's nothing to indicate this was anything but a horrible accident, Mack."

"Have you seen his body, Frank?" I asked softly.

"A bad storm just went through here, Jack."

"You think Peter decided to go for a swim in the middle of work?" I asked. "In this kind of surf? C'mon, *Detective*."

"Peter was kind of a crazy. So, yes, I think it's possible." With the sanctimonious tone of a social worker, he added, "At the same time, I don't think we can rule out suicide."

"Peter wouldn't kill himself," said Mack, taking that possibility off the table forever. "You're an asshole to suggest it."

"Belnap clocked him weaving through traffic at ninety miles per hour just before the party. That sounds like someone with a death wish to me."

"That's interesting, Frank," said Mack, "because to me it just sounds like more of your bullshit." Macklin looked dangerously close to hitting him.

"Are you interviewing anyone?" I asked, trying to intercede. "See if there were any witnesses? There must be a guest list. C'mon, Frank, this is Peter who died here."

"You know the people on that list, Jack. You can't interview their gardeners without a court order."

"Then get one," said Mack, "and how about Barry and Campion? Do they have anything to say?"

"They're extremely upset, of course, and extend their condolences. But they left town on business this morning. I can't see what would be accomplished by changing their itinerary."

"No, I suppose you can't. By the way, Frank, are you

still a detective, or have you graduated to full-time messenger boy?"

Volpi's face and neck flushed red. "What's that supposed to mean, Mack?"

"What part of the question can't you understand?" said my grandfather.

Chapter 8

A YEAR AFTER MY PARENTS ARRIVED in Montauk, my father built the small three-bedroom house halfway between town and the lighthouse. We moved in when I was two, and Peter was born there five years later. Although he'd spent at least half his nights over the past few years at one girlfriend or another's place, he never officially moved out.

This might have been a problem if my mother, Katherine, had still been around, but for a long time it had been a curfewless house of men.

My father and Mack staggered off to their beds as soon as we got in the door. Dana and I grabbed the Jameson and a couple of thick glasses. We climbed the steep, wooden stairs to Peter's old bedroom.

"I'm right behind you," Dana whispered. I reached back and took her hand, held it tight.

"I'm glad."

I was struck again by how spare Peter kept the room. A pale wooden desk and bureau against one wall faced two twin beds. Except for the tiny and oblique detail of a stamp-size black-and-white photograph of the great bebop alto saxophonist Charlie Parker that Peter had taped above his bed, we could have been in a Motel 6.

Maybe Peter kept it that way because he didn't want to think of himself as living there anymore. It made me feel even worse, as if he didn't think that he had a real home anywhere.

Dana put on one of Peter's old Sonny Rollins CDs. I pushed the twin beds together and we stretched out on them. We wrapped our arms around each other.

"I can't believe any of this," I said in a daze.

"I know," Dana whispered, and held me tighter.

The whiskey had unclenched my brain enough to know that nothing made sense. Zero. There was no way my brother chose to go swimming that night. For Peter, staying warm was about the closest thing he had to a religion. Even without the heavy waves, the fifty-degree water was enough to keep him out.

It was even less likely he'd killed himself. I didn't know how he could have afforded it, but he'd just bought a $19,000 motorcycle. He'd waited six months to get the exact shade of blue he wanted, and it had less than three thousand miles on it. You don't wash a motorcycle twice a day when you're contemplating suicide.

On top of that, he was scheduled to do a print shoot the next week for Helmut Lang jeans. He had called at work and told me that one of photographer Herb Ritts's assistants had spotted him at the Talkhouse and had sent him a contract. Peter was trying hard to downplay it, but he wasn't fooling anyone, especially not me.

Dana refilled my glass and kissed me on the forehead. I took a long gulp of whiskey. I thought about how as kids, Peter and I used to wrestle in this room, playing a game called king of the bed. I realized now that half the time brothers wrestle, it's just an excuse to hug each other.

Then I told Dana about a fall afternoon, maybe twelve years ago. I was probably babbling, but she let me go on.

"On Saturdays a group of us would play touch football in the field behind the middle school. That day I brought along Peter for the first time.

"Even though he was about five years younger than anyone else, I vouched for him. Bill Conway, one of the two teenagers who ran the game, grudgingly consented to let him play.

"Anyway, Peter was the last guy taken on our side, and our quarterback never threw the ball anywhere near him all afternoon. Peter was so grateful to be included in the big-kids game, he never complained.

"With the sun fading fast, the game was tied. We were down to our last possession. In the huddle I told Livolsi to throw the ball to Peter. The other team had stopped covering him an hour ago. For some reason, Livolsi actually listened to me. On the last play of the game, he sent all the other receivers one way and Peter the other. Then he dropped back and hurled the ball half the length of the field. Peter was this tiny figure standing all alone in the dusk on one side of the end zone.

"Unfortunately, Livolsi himself was not a future Hall of Famer. His pass was way off. Peter chased after it and, at the last instant, left his feet and stretched out parallel to the ground like some dude in one of those slow-motion NFL films. I swear to you, not one person who was there will ever forget it. Livolsi mentions it every time I see him. Dana, he was *nine*. He weighed fifty-eight pounds. The guy could do anything he ever tried. He could have been anything he wanted to be, Dana. He had it all."

"I know, Jack," she whispered.

"Dana, that wasn't the best part. The best part was the ride home. Peter was so happy, I could feel it. Neither of us said a word. We didn't have to. His big brother said he could do it, and *Peter did it*. I don't care what anyone says, it never gets any better than that. The whole way home we shared that peace and lightness you get only after doing something really hard. Our bikes floated. We hardly had to pedal."

I barely got out the last few words. I started to cry, and once I got started I couldn't stop for twenty minutes. Then I got so cold, my teeth chattered. I couldn't believe I was never going to see Peter again.

Chapter 9

STANDING IN THE FRAGRANT SHADOW of a tall evergreen, a large man with a nasty scar, Rory Hoffman watched as the EMS van led the caravan of vehicles off the beach. As the red taillights snaked through the trees, he clucked his tongue and softly shook his head. What a fucking mess. A disaster of the first order.

His official title was head of security, but he had attended to these delicate matters for so long and with such efficiency that he was referred to as "the Fixer." Hoffman considered the moniker grandiose and misleading. He was more like the maid, or the cleaning service.

And now here I am to clean up this nasty-ass mess.

He knew this wouldn't be easy. It never was. Among the petty insights he'd culled in his tenure was that violence always leaves a stain. And while with skill and diligence you might be able to get the stain out, the effort will leave its own telltale residue. It meant your work was never quite done.

The Fixer left the cover of the trees for the gravel driveway, the white stones pushing through the thin soles of his driving shoes. He snuffed out a laugh at the marketing élan of that one. Need to hawk a pair of shoes so flimsy that you can barely walk in them? Call them driving shoes. Genius. And he was wearing them.

He reached the point where the cars had gotten on the driveway. Then he followed their tracks back onto the sand. Half the beach seemed to have spilled into his silk socks. Under the full moon, the ocean was putting on quite a show. Very Shakespearean, as if the whole planet were caught up in the momentum of the so-called tragedy on the beach.

Although the moon was bright, he flipped on a flashlight and searched among the dunes for footprints. The beaches themselves were public. There was no way you could keep people off them entirely. Although for the most part the NO TRESPASSING signs were observed, you never knew who might have intruded.

The north side looked good. Perhaps tonight would be the exception to the rule. *The scene might actually be clean.*

The first ten yards of dunes turned up empty. Then he saw a cigarette butt, and another. Not good. Very bad, actually.

He had the sense of being watched, and when he closed his eyes his prominent nose picked up the scent of sulfur still hanging in the air from a struck match. *Oh, Jesus.*

Boot-shaped footprints led him to a stand of bushes in

the dunes. Behind them were more prints, and more cigarette butts. Whoever had been there had been camping
out awhile.

He crouched and scooped three of the butts into a little plastic Baggie, the kind cops used — or were supposed to anyway.

That's when his flashlight picked out a crushed bright
yellow box in the sand. Kodak.

Christ, someone had been shooting film!

Chapter 10

THE NEXT MORNING my eyeballs hurt. So did everything else above and below. What didn't actually ache just felt lousy. And that was in the two-second reprieve before I remembered what had happened to my brother.

I rubbed my eyes. That's when I saw that Dana was gone. There was a note taped to the lamp: "Jack, I didn't want to wake you. Thanks for letting me stay. It meant a lot to me. I miss you already. Love, Dana." She was smart and beautiful, and I was lucky to have her. It's just that I was having a little trouble feeling lucky that morning.

I walked gingerly downstairs and took my place at the kitchen table with two grieving old men in bathrobes. We weren't a pretty sight.

"Dana's gone."

"I had coffee with her," said Mack. "She was crying a lot."

I looked at my father, and there was almost no reaction. One look at him in the morning light and it was clear to me he'd never be the same. It was as if he had aged twenty years overnight.

Mack seemed as steady as ever, almost stronger, as if fortified by the tragic turn of events. "I'll make you some eggs," he said, springing from his chair.

It's not that my grandfather wasn't devastated by Peter's death. If anything, Peter had been his favorite. But to my grandfather, life, for better or worse, is a holy war, and he was girding himself for another battle.

He peeled off five pieces of bacon and dropped them in a cast-iron skillet as old and gnarly as he was. Soon the room was filled with greasy music.

That morning I realized that my father had never really gotten over the death of my mother. His heart wasn't in his construction company, and he had no desire to chase the biggest building boom in Hamptons history. He watched his fellow tradesmen move from pickups to Tahoes and leave him in the dust. Not that he cared.

My grandfather, on the other hand, had actually gained momentum as he got older. After retiring as an ironworker in his early sixties, he spent a summer reading and farting around. Then he went back to school and became a paralegal. In the past twenty years he had become something of a legend in courtrooms and firms all over the eastern half of Long Island. A lot of people believed he knew the law better than most circuit judges. He insisted that this wasn't nearly as impressive as it sounded.

His love of the law was half the reason I was at Columbia, and he was immensely proud I'd come that far. Sharing a couple of pints with him at the Shagwong included the repeated embarrassment of his introducing me as "the most overeducated Mullen in the history of Ireland and America." I could see by the way he looked at me that morning, however, that he considered all that hypothetical schoolboy stuff compared to this.

"There is no way Peter killed himself," I said. "Volpi is a moron."

"Or doesn't give a shit," said Mack.

To my father, the issue of how Peter died was almost moot. His last moments would have been less terrifying if it was suicide. To Macklin, it was everything.

"The kid got laid more than God. Why would he kill himself?"

Mack broke three eggs on top of the bacon and let them sizzle sunny-side up. When they started to blacken around the edges, he skillfully worked a spatula under it all and flipped the whole thing without spilling a yellow drop. He let it fry for another thirty seconds before sliding the whole greasy construct onto my plate.

It was approaching summer, but this was cold, blustery, off-season food. It was exactly what I needed. After three cups of black coffee, I pushed my chair from the table and announced that I was going to talk to Volpi.

"You want me to come with you?"

"No, thanks, Mack."

"Well, don't do anything stupid. Keep your head. You hear me, Jack?"

"Listen to him," said my father, "the bleeding voice of reason."

For a second, I almost thought he was going to smile.

Chapter 11

SOMEONE MUST HAVE DRIVEN Peter's motorcycle to the house during the night. It sat in the driveway like a giant lizard warming itself in the sun. It was typical of Peter to go into hock for a rolling sculpture. Even if we got a fair price for it, we'd owe the bank a couple of thousand. But I had to admit, it was a thing of beauty, and the license plate got a smile out of me: 4NIC8. Yep, that was Peter.

I climbed into the old black pickup with MULLEN CONSTRUCTION painted on the door and drove to the small brick building on 27 that houses the East Hampton Police Department. I parked next to Frank Volpi's black Jeep.

Tommy Harrison was the sergeant at the desk. He shook my hand and told me how sorry he was about Peter. "I liked your brother a lot, Jack."

"That's what I'm here to talk to Volpi about."

Harrison went back to get Volpi, then returned a couple of minutes later with a sheepish expression.

"The detective is a lot busier than I thought. He thinks he'll be tied up all afternoon."

"If it's okay, Tommy, I'll wait. It's important."

Forty minutes later the desk sergeant told me the same thing. I walked outside. Then I entered the headquarters of the East Hampton Police Department one more time. Through the back door.

Volpi's office was halfway down the hall. I didn't bother to knock.

The detective looked up from a *Post* spread out on his lap. The foam of his latte covered the tips of his mustache. In East Hampton even the cops sip cappuccinos.

"No rest for the weary, huh, Frank?"

"I take enough shit in this town without having to take more from you. Get the hell out of here! Get lost."

"Give me one reason why Peter would go swimming in the middle of his shift, then I'll let you get back to 'Page Six' and your mocha blend."

"I already told you. Because he was a stoned-out little punk."

"And why would he kill himself? Peter had it all going for him."

"Because his best girl was screwing his best friend; because he was having a bad hair day; because he was tired of hearing what a saint his older brother was. You wanted one reason. You got three. Now go away!"

"That's it, Frank? Accident, suicide — who cares? Case closed."

"Sounds pretty good to me."

"When are you going to stop acting like a rent-a-cop for the rich, Frank?"

He jumped out of his chair, stuck his face in mine, grabbed my shirt, and pushed me hard against the wall. "I should kick your ass right now, you piece of shit."

I didn't delude myself about Volpi's ability to back up his words, but the way I felt, maybe then wasn't the best day to get in the ring with me. Even Volpi sensed it. He released his grip and sat down.

"Go home, Jack. Your brother was a good guy. Everybody liked Rabbit, including me. But he drowned."

"Bullshit! That's total crap, and you know it. Frank, if you're not interested in looking into this case, I'm sure the press will be. Considering all the boldface types at the party that night, *Newsday* will be interested. And the *Daily News*. Maybe the high and mighty *New York Times*."

Volpi's face hardened. "You really don't want to do that."

"Why not? What am I missing here?"

"Trust me on this one. You just don't. Leave it alone, Jack."

Chapter 12

I WAS FEELING A LITTLE NUTS, so I drove back out to the scene of the crime. The surf was down considerably, and it was *still* too rough for my brother to have considered swimming in it. Then I checked in on my father and grandfather. They were doing so bad, they were both in bed by 9:30. Dana had left a couple of messages for me.

I didn't get to the Memory Motel until after ten. By then almost every charter member of our highly exclusive club of born-and-bred townies was crowding a small round table at the rear of the bar.

Let me introduce you.

At the back of the table, under a chipped mirror, was Fenton Gidley. Fenton grew up four houses down from us, and we'd been best friends since before we learned how to walk. At six-three and 245 pounds, Fenton was a little bigger than he had been back then. He was offered a boxful of scholarships to play college football — Hofstra, Syracuse, even Ohio State. He took over his old man's fishing boat instead, heading out alone from Montauk Point for days at a time to hunt giant swordfish and tuna, which he sold to the Japanese.

On his left sat Marci Burt, who has planted and shaped shrubs for Calvin, Martha, Donna, and a handful of other less-fashionable multimillionaires. She and I were an item once — when we were thirteen. On Marci's right sat Molly Ferrer, who taught fourth grade and moonlighted for East Hampton's Channel 70. Like Fenton, Marci and Molly were former classmates of mine at East Hampton High School.

Everyone at the table was sporting a surprisingly trendy coif, thanks to the man with almost no hair sitting opposite them — Sammy Giamalva, aka Sammy the Hairdresser. Sammy, who was five years younger than the rest of us, was Peter's best friend. Growing up, Sammy spent so much time at our house that he was like a member of the family. He still was.

When I arrived at the Memory, they each got up to lay a hug on me, and before I emerged from their warm, sad embraces, the final member of our crew and the most sincere person I know, Hank Lauricella, walked in.

Lauricella, a full-time chef and part-time EMS volunteer, was the one who got the call about Peter's body on the beach. The small, scarred table now held my five most dependable friends on the planet. They were as angry and as confused about Peter's death as I was.

"*Accident,* my cute behind," said Molly. "As if Peter, or anyone else, would go swimming in the middle of the night in that surf."

"What Volpi's *really* saying is, Peter did himself," said Sammy, the first openly gay person any of us ever knew. "We all know *that* didn't happen."

"Right. All this time we thought he was having more fun than the rest of us combined," Fenton said. "He was actually crying himself to sleep."

"Then what did happen?" asked Marci. "Nobody would want to hurt Peter. Maybe slap him upside the head a couple of times."

"Well, something sure happened. Except for Jack, none of you saw Peter's body," said Hank. "I sat next to Peter in a space smaller than this table for four hours that night. He looked like he was stomped to death. And Frank Volpi never even looked at him. Never stepped inside the ambulance."

"Volpi doesn't want to go near it," said Fenton. "He's scared shitless it goes right back to the folks who own him and the rest of this little village of ours."

"So maybe we all have to start asking around. Talk to anyone who might know something," I said. "Because obviously no one else cares."

"I'm for that," said Molly.

"I know just about everybody who worked at the party that night," said Fenton. "One of them must have seen something."

"And *moi*," said Sammy. "I'm really good at poking around for dirt."

We held up our beers. "To Peter."

Chapter 13

THE TABLE SUDDENLY FELL SILENT. The change couldn't have been more pronounced if we had been union workers plotting a strike and someone from management had just stuck his head in the door. I turned and saw Dana at the bar.

Actually, the Memory isn't much of a bar. It's not much of a motel, either. Eighteen rooms with unobstructed views of John's Drive-Inn and the Getty station. Its one claim to notoriety is that back in the days when there were these big round black things known as records, a rock 'n' roll band by the name of the Rolling Stones stayed there once and wrote a song about it. The record it's on, *Black and Blue,* came out in 1976, and the cover is tacked on the wall along with the copy of the notes from the recording session.

> We spent a lonely night at the Memory Motel,
> It's by the ocean (sort of),
> I guess you knew it well.

To be fair, the Memory also has a pretty great sign — the name spelled out over the entrance in jet black Gothic type. In any event, Dana, even dressed as she was that night in old blue jeans and a T-shirt, stood out as much as if Mick Jagger himself had shimmied in. I got up and went to the bar.

"I thought you might be here," she said. "I called your house a bunch of times. I had to go into New York this morning."

We found two seats at the end of the bar next to a middle-aged man doing a beer and a shot. He had an old St. Louis Cardinals hat pulled down low over his face.

"They really like me, don't they, Jack?" Dana said, and snuck a look at my friends.

"In their own quiet way."

"I'll go if you want me to. Really, Jack. I just wanted to make sure you were okay. Are you?"

"Nope. That's why I'm glad you're here." I leaned in and kissed her. Who wouldn't? Her lips were so soft. Her eyes weren't just beautiful, they showed off how whip smart she was. I think I'd had a crush on Dana since she was about fourteen. I still couldn't believe that the two of us were together. My friends hadn't given her a chance yet, but they'd come around once they got to know her.

I emptied my wallet on the bar, waved good-bye to the crew, and escorted Dana out of the Memory. Instead of walking toward the street and her gleaming SUV, she led me away from the curb under an overhang to the end of the stone walkway.

Then Dana fumbled with a key until room eighteen lay open before us in all its splendor and possibility. "I hope you don't mind," she whispered, "but I took the liberty of reserving the honeymoon suite."

Chapter 14

WHAT THE FIXER REALLY WANTED was a Tanqueray No. Ten martini with a twist. By the time the bartender at the Memory stopped ignoring him, he had lowered his sights to a Budweiser and a shot of tequila.

By then he had found an empty, torn red-leather stool at the center of the bar, and with his vintage St. Louis Cardinals cap pulled down, he sipped his Bud and *watched*.

An occasional twist of his head gave him a view of the plotting mourners at the back table. Their faces were so sincere and open that he wondered how he and they could be members of the same species.

After a while he started working his gaze around the table, gauging who would give him the hardest time. The unshaved guy in the old jean jacket had the most size, about six-three and 250 pounds, he estimated. And he carried himself like an old ballplayer. The bitch who had arrived in the maroon Porsche looked tough. And, of course, Mullen could be dangerous, particularly in his current state. He was undoubtedly the smartest in the group, and the boy was *hurting*.

By the time the Mouseketeers were done drinking, laughing, and crying, he'd been sitting on the stool for almost three hours and his butt was numb. He watched Lauricella and Fenton leave in Lauricella's van, and Burt tear off in her Porsche. He was about to follow Molly Ferrer home for a little reconnaissance when he saw Dana and Jack slink out of the bar and into the darkness. "A hundred-million-dollar girl in a sixty-dollar-a-night motel," he muttered.

Dana Neubauer and Jack Mullen. Sooner or later, he was going to have to fix that, too, no doubt.

Chapter 15

PETER'S FUNERAL was the worst day of my life. For a week I wandered around in a daze — hollowed out, unreal, a ghost. When I went back to work, Pauline Grabowski came by to say how sorry she was about Peter's death, and I got a sweet condolence call from Mudman on death row. As for everybody else at Nelson, Goodwin and Mickel, it was strictly business as usual.

Every night after work, I went back to my apartment on 114th Street, two blocks south of Columbia. My roommates had left for the summer, and I lay on my mattress, the only piece of furniture left, and listened to the Yanks lose three in a row on a tiny transistor radio I had had since I was twelve.

Friday night I hustled down to Penn Station and caught the last train out. Dana wasn't waiting in Montauk as I had hoped for the entire three-hour trip out there. Since the track stopped barely two miles from my house,

I decided to hump it instead of calling home for a ride. I figured the walk would do me good.

In fifteen minutes I put the darkened windows of Montauk's three-block downtown behind me and climbed the long, steep hill out of town. The night was full of stars, and the crickets were noisier than the traffic. I wondered what had happened to Dana.

I walked by the stone ruin of the historical society and the stark-white sixties architecture of the town library, where I'd often stopped on my way home from school.

Peter and I had covered this stretch at least a thousand times, and every single crack in the pavement looked familiar. We'd walked it, run it, skateboarded it, and biked it in every extreme of Long Island weather, sometimes with Peter propped precariously on my handlebars. And although we weren't allowed to, we'd often hitchhiked. On account of all the carless Irish kids who come over every summer to pump gas, change sheets, and bus tables, Montauk is one of the last places left in the country where drivers still routinely pull over for strangers.

I walked off 27 onto Ditch Plains Road and made the sweeping turn by the beach parking lot. My father's pickup was in the driveway. I guess Mack wasn't done fleecing the pigeons in his weekly poker game.

If I was up when he got back, he'd dump his winnings on the kitchen table and I'd join him in a Rice Krispies nightcap.

All the lights were out, so I lifted the sticky garage door as quietly as possible and entered through the kitchen. I grabbed a beer and sat in the cool, pleasant dark. I called Dana, but all I got was the answering machine. What was that all about?

I sat in the darkened kitchen and thought of the last time Peter and I were together. Two weeks before he died, we had dinner at a trendy restaurant on East Second Street. We polished off two bottles of red wine and had ourselves a gas. Christ, he was such a happy kid. A little crazy, but good-natured. It didn't even bother me when the waitress wrote her phone number on the back of Peter's neck.

For some reason, I found myself thinking about my pro bono case at the office, the Mudman — his life on death row in Texas. What Peter and Mudman had in common was the minuscule regard that the powers that be had for their lives. The government valued Mudman's so lightly, they wouldn't bother to make sure they were executing the right man. And Peter's murder was so trifling, it didn't require solving.

My thoughts were suddenly shattered by a loud crash directly overhead. *What the hell?* Someone must have broken in through Peter's window and toppled over his dresser.

I grabbed the skillet off the top of the stove and sprinted up the stairs.

Chapter 16

THE DOOR TO PETER'S ROOM was shut, but the sound of moaning came from inside. I pushed against the door, met some resistance, then crashed through, stumbling over the outstretched legs of the body on the floor.

Even in the dark, I could see that it was my father.

I switched on the lights. He was in trouble. He was sick. Obviously, he'd collapsed and fallen, which had made the loud racket. He twisted violently on his back as if he were fighting someone only he could see. I hooked one arm under his neck and lifted his head off the floor, but like a child having a night terror, he couldn't see me. His eyes were aimed inward at the explosion in his chest.

"Dad, you're having a heart attack. I'm calling an ambulance." I ran for the phone. By the time I got back to him, his eyes were even more dilated and the pressure on his chest seemed worse. He couldn't take a breath.

"Hang on," I whispered. "The ambulance is on the way."

The color drained from his face, and he turned a sick, ghostly gray. Then he stopped breathing, and my father's eyes rolled up into his head. I held open his mouth and breathed into it.

Nothing.

One, two, three.

Nothing.

One, two, three.

Nothing.

Tires screeched in the driveway and there were loud footsteps on the stairs, then Hank was kneeling beside me.

"How long has he been like this?"

"Three, four minutes."

"Okay. There's a chance."

Hank had the portable defibrillator lifepack with him. It was in a white plastic box about the size of a car battery. He hooked up my father, then threw the toggle that sent electrical current into his chest.

Now I was the one who couldn't breathe. I stood over my father, numb and disbelieving. This couldn't be happening. He must have come up to Peter's room to reminisce.

Each time Hank threw the switch, my father went into spasm.

But the line on the electrocardiogram showed no response.

After the third jolt of electricity, Hank looked at me in shock.

"Jack — he's gone."

Part Two

THE MURDER INVESTIGATION

Chapter 17

MY FATHER'S FUNERAL was held forty-eight hours later at St. Cecilia's. Close to a thousand year-rounders squeezed into the squat stone chapel or stood just outside it for the Monday service. No one was more surprised by the size and intensity of the outpouring than I. My father was reserved and modest, the opposite of a hail-fellow-well-met. Because of that, I always assumed he'd been unappreciated. That wasn't the case.

Monsignor Scanlon recounted how, at sixteen years of age, John Samuel Sanders Mullen left Ireland and traveled alone to New York City, where he found a spot with relatives in an already crowded Hell's Kitchen tenement. Macklin and my grandmother couldn't make it across for another three years, and by then my father had dropped out of school and apprenticed himself to a carpenter. Even after his parents arrived, he was the family's only means of support for several years — "a sixteen-year-old boy working eighty-hour weeks. Can you imagine?" asked the monsignor.

Five summers later Sam and his new wife, Katherine Patricia Dempsey, were looking for a Sunday's respite from the asphalt furnace. So they rode the Long Island Rail Road as far as it would take them. Stepping off, they found a little fishing village that reminded my father of the one he'd left behind in County Claire. "Two weeks later," said the monsignor, "Sam, full of a young man's love and ambition, pulled up roots for the second time in eight years and moved out to Montauk for good."

I often wondered why my father showed so little zeal for the Hamptons gold rush. Now I saw that by the time he arrived at the end of Long Island, he was far more concerned with appreciating what he had than lusting for more.

"Since the Mullens arrived in this town," continued Thomas Scanlon, "I've had many happy occasions to visit them in the house on Ditch Plains Road that Sam built. Sam Mullen had all a man could ask for — a lovely home, an even lovelier wife, an honest business, and in young Jack and Peter a pair of handsome sons who were already two of the brightest lights in our village. Peter was the town's most gifted athlete, and Jack was showing the academic promise that would eventually take him to Columbia Law.

"But then," the monsignor said, "catastrophe blindsided the Mullens. First came the much too early death of Katherine Patricia from cancer. Last week the still unsatisfactorily explained death of Peter Mullen, a blow that unquestionably contributed to Sam's death Friday night.

"To see the hand of God in any of this is obviously beyond our limited knowledge. I only offer what I know to be true. That this life, however short, and it's almost always too short, is precious beyond measure."

Mack, Dana, and I sat in the front row. Behind the three of us, the room shared a cathartic sob — but Mack and I were dry-eyed that morning at least. To us, this wasn't divine mystery, it was murder. Whoever had killed Peter was also partly responsible for my father's heart attack, or at least his broken heart.

As the monsignor continued over his parishioners' tears, I felt the grip of my grandfather's hand on my knee. I looked into his ravaged face and bottomless Irish eyes.

"There's a couple of mysteries of this precious life," he whispered, "that you and I are going to get to the bottom of, whether God in heaven chooses to throw in with us or not."

I put my own bony Mullen hand on his and squeezed back hard enough for both of us to know that a pact had been made.

Somehow, someway, we were going to avenge Peter and my father.

Chapter 18

IF YOU THOUGHT IT WAS A NEAT TRICK squeezing a thousand full-bodied mourners into a church built for two hundred, imagine the human gridlock when the same crowd arrived on our doorstep at 18 Ditch Plains Road.

Shagwong ran the bar and Seaside Market did the food, and for six hours the entire population of Montauk wended its way through our half a dozen small rooms. I believe that every single person who ever had any contact with my father or brother in the past twenty years walked into our living room, took my hand, and looked into my eyes.

Teachers and coaches going back to kindergarten showed up and described Peter's unlimited potential at this sport or that subject. As did the merchants who had kept my father in hardware and bacon sandwiches. The politicians, of course, were out in full force. So were the firemen and cops; even Volpi and Belnap showed their faces.

Despite how badly things had panned out for the Mullens in Montauk, it was impossible not to feel enormous affection for its unpretentious residents. People give a shit about their neighbors out here.

Nevertheless, after a couple of hours, all the faces ran together. I guess that's what funerals are for — turning grief into a blur. In that way, they're diverting.

Dana finally left about seven. She's not much of a drinker, so I understood. And I appreciated that she knew I had to be there and drink with my old friends and relatives.

All my friends were there. After the bulk of the guests left, we gathered in the kitchen. Fenton, Marci, Molly, Hank, and Sammy — the same crowd that had been there for me that night at the Memory.

We had all been working on Peter's case, the situation, or whatever the hell you wanted to call it. Fenton had been lobbying hard with the Suffolk County medical examiner, an old girlfriend of his, that Peter's death not be treated like a routine drowning. I had talked to contacts at the *Daily News* and *Newsday* about possible stories, or at least coming out there to talk to somebody about what really happened that night.

"People are talking," Sammy reported about his A-list clientele. "They're starting to feel some heat at the Beach House, too. The Neubauers already canceled a party for the weekend of the fourth. Out of respect, no doubt."

We all applauded ourselves. Big deal, right, we'd gotten them to cancel a goddamned party.

Not all the news was good. Three nights before, Hank

had walked into Nichols Café, where he'd been head chef since it reopened, and was fired on the spot.

"No reason or explanation," said Hank. "The manager handed me my last check and said good luck. For two days I was going nuts. Then a waitress spelled it out for me. Nichols is owned by Jimmy Taravalla, a venture capitalist worth a couple hundred million. Taravalla is tight with Neubauer. He's a frequent guest at parties. According to my friend, Neubauer called Jimmy, Jimmy called Antoinette Alois, the manager, and that was that. *Hasta la vista.* Put down the *chalupa.* Go directly to the back of the unemployment line."

"It gets scarier," Molly said. "I've been doing some asking around about the party, right. Then, the other night, somebody was following me. It was a black BMW. Tonight I saw the same car parked outside my house."

"That's so weird," Marci spoke up. "The same cretin was following me. It's creepy."

"Hang on to your privates, boys and girls," said Sammy. "The empire is starting to strike back."

It was after midnight before the last mourner gave me a last damp hug. Then it was just me and Mack in the brightly lit kitchen. I poured two whiskeys.

"To Jack and Peter," I said.

"To you and me," said Macklin. "We're all that's left."

Chapter 19

I AWOKE WITH A HANGOVER the morning after my father's funeral and wake. About eleven, I decided to go see Dana, partly to apologize for not paying enough attention to her the day before, but mostly I needed someone to talk to. I knew that her parents were still out of town; otherwise, I don't think I could have gone to the house.

What can you say about the "summer cottage" that the Neubauers had already turned down $40 million for? Is it real, or is it Manderly? I could never drive onto the property without thinking about how much Dana loved the house and the twelve acres it sits on. What's not to love? A grand Georgian-style house surrounded by apple orchards? Two glorious pools — a reflection pool for the mind, a lap pool for the body? A formal rose garden? The English-style garden? A circular drive in front of the house that looked as though it were built for vintage cars, and vintage cars only?

I rode Peter's motorcycle up close to the garage, cut the

engine, and parked in an unobtrusive spot. Even though I had an open invitation to the house, I suddenly felt weird just being there. I tried to shake off the feeling, but it wouldn't shake.

I heard a splash in one of the pools.

I could see the "north pool," as the family called it, the lap pool, and suddenly I stopped walking. My stomach clutched.

Dana was climbing out of the pool and she had on a kick-ass suit that I'd told her was my personal favorite. Beads of water glistened on her skin and the black Lycra of the string bikini.

She tiptoed across the ornate, hand-painted tiles of the deck to one of several cream-and-royal-blue-striped chaise longues. She smiled as she drank in the warmth of the sun.

I couldn't believe my eyes. Propped comfortably on the chaise was none other than Frank Volpi. The sickening thing was that Frank looked none the worse for the wear and tear of his very demanding detective's job. He was as relaxed and tanned and toned as Dana was.

Dana was still smiling as she went and sat next to him on the longue. She laid her water-chilled hands on his stomach, and he playfully grabbed her wrists. He pulled her on top of him, and she covered his mouth with hers. As they kissed, all I could see was the back of her blond head and his hands untying the strings of her suit.

I wanted to look away, to get the hell out of there, but before I could actually move, the kiss ended.

Then Dana looked over Volpi's shoulder, and I was pretty sure she saw me before I skulked off to the Beemer and headed back where I belonged.

Chapter 20

I DROVE AROUND FOR A WHILE — fast, too fast for the winding, crowded side roads of eastern Long Island. I was feeling really bad now, not for myself — well, hell, *yeah, for myself.*

By the time I got home, it was past four. The house was still a disaster from the day before. I figured I'd better clean up before Mack had to do it.

A note was stuck in the screen door. My heart sank. I grabbed the envelope and opened it.

The stationery was rose-colored and I could smell perfume all over it.

The note said — *IL8400. The Memory.*

That was enough. I'd gotten messages like it before. Dana wanted me to meet her at the Memory Motel. She was waiting there now. The letters and numbers were the license plate of her Mercedes SUV. The note, the perfume — it was pure Dana.

I shouldn't have gone over to the Memory but — what can I say? — I went. Maybe deep down, I'm a hopeless sap. Or maybe I'm too romantic for my own good.

Dana was there. What was worse, she knew that I would go. She was so sure of herself. Well, maybe I could change that.

I pulled open the passenger-side door and leaned inside. The Mercedes still smelled new. It also smelled of her perfume.

"Sit down, Jack. We need to talk," she said in the softest voice. A slender, manicured hand patted the seat.

"I'm fine where I am," I said. "I'm good."

"It's not what it looked like, Jack."

I shook my head. "Sure it is, Dana. While I was riding around the past couple of hours, it all came together. I saw you and Volpi talking at my house yesterday. Then you left around seven or so. Amazingly, so did Volpi. You'll have to fill me in on the rest."

Dana somehow managed to look angry at me. "He came to our house this morning, Jack. Not last night. Said it was about the investigation, but he brought his bathing suit. That's Frank."

"So you invited him to have a swim? One thing led to another?"

Dana shook her head. "Jack, you can't believe that I'm interested in Frank Volpi."

"Dana," I said, "why were you making out with him? It's a fair question."

"Hey, Jack, let me tell you something that I learned from my father — *life isn't fair.* That's why he always wins. It's how the game is played. And Jack, it *is* a game."

"Dana —"

She waved me off, and it struck me that I had never really seen that side of her. "Let me finish. I know my timing is dreadful, but I've been thinking about this for weeks. I guess it's why I didn't come and pick you up on Friday night. Jack, I need space. I really need time to be by myself. . . . I'm going to Europe for a couple of months. I've never done that before. The European thing."

"Oh, yeah, me neither," I said. "Run away from my problems."

"Jack, don't make this any harder than it already is. It *is* hard for me." Then tears started to run down her cheeks. I couldn't believe that all this was happening. It almost seemed too bad to be true.

"So, Dana," I finally said, "is Volpi going to Europe with you?"

I didn't wait for an answer. I slammed her car door and walked away. I guess we had just broken up.

Chapter 21

I COULDN'T SLEEP THAT NIGHT because I couldn't stop the bad thoughts and images crashing through my head. I finally got up and cleaned the mess from my father's funeral. About five in the morning I went back to bed.

On Sunday I made the hour-and-a-half trip to the BMW dealership in Huntington. I figured Peter got financing directly from the dealer, and I hoped that if I showed up with the bike and told them what had happened, they might offer fair market value.

The only salesman in the place was a burly, ponytailed guy in his mid-thirties, and I watched him expertly direct a retired couple to a full-dress silver Tourer.

"Bags!" said the salesman, introducing himself once he'd loaded up his prospects with brochures. "Although I don't know what I can possibly do for you since you already got the prettiest, baddest, and best engineered form of automotive transportation in the world parked right out front. Believe it or not, I delivered the same sucker to a handsome kid from Montauk not six weeks ago — same midnight blue paint, same custom black Corbin seat."

I explained that it wasn't a coincidence, and Bags extended an arm and squeezed my shoulder. "That's awful. Listen, man, you'll get a lot more for it by putting an ad in the *New York Times* and selling it yourself."

"All I'm looking to do is pay off the loan," I told him.

Bags's eyes grew wide, and they were large to begin with.

"What loan? You don't owe a dime on that sweetheart."

At his cluttered desk, he pulled out the paperwork from the sale. "Here we go. Peter wrote me a check for nineteen hundred dollars for the ten percent deposit," he said, showing me a copy. "He paid the rest in cash."

Although Bags may have felt that he was delivering good news, he could tell that I didn't see it that way. "Listen, if a dude walks in with the money, I'll sell him a motorcycle. I'd even sell one to a Republican if I was having a bad month," he guffawed.

The check was written on a bank six exits up the Long Island Expressway in Ronkonkoma. I knew where it was. When we were kids my father's truck broke down just outside it, and we spent half the night in a service station there. We loved the name so much, it became family lore.

Ten minutes later I was back in Ronkonkoma for the second time in my life, sitting at the desk of the Bank of New York branch manager, Darcy Hammerman. She'd been expecting to hear from me.

"Peter named you as the sole beneficiary, so the balance is yours. I might as well cut you a check now, unless you want to open an account here in Ronkonkoma. I didn't think so."

She opened a photo-album-sized checkbook and, in her careful banker's hand, filled one out. She stamped FOR DEPOSIT ONLY on the back.

Then she carefully ripped the check out of her book and slid it over to me. It was for $187,646.

I read the six numbers in disbelief. My eyes started to blink. I hadn't felt that bad since, well . . . the day before. *What in hell had Peter done?*

Chapter 22

I NEEDED A FRIEND TO TALK TO, and I knew where to find one. I even had an appointment.

Sammy Giamalva was nine when he matter-of-factly told my brother that he was gay. By the time he was eleven, he knew he wanted to cut hair. Probably because of that precocious self-knowledge, Sammy, despite being one of the smartest kids at East Hampton High, was never much of a student.

At fifteen, he dropped out altogether and started working at Kevin Maple's. He spent his first six months sweeping up hair. Then he got promoted to shampooing. Six months later Xavier quit in the middle of an appointment, and Kevin gave Sammy a shot at his own chair. The rest, as they say, is Hamptons hairdressing history.

But Kevin milked him dry, booking him for ten or eleven heads a day, and after a while Sammy's gratitude was replaced by resentment. Three months ago he quit and opened Sammy's Soul Kitchen in his house in Sag Harbor.

Sammy had been cutting Peter's hair for free on Sundays and, in a weak moment at the funeral, offered to grandfather me on the same sweet deal. I made an appointment on the spot, and after driving back from Ronkonkoma, I pulled into his driveway.

Sammy greeted me with a big hug, then led me to an Aeron chair facing a huge gilt mirror.

"So what did you have in mind?" Sammy asked after my rinse.

"At these rates, I'll leave it up to you. Express yourself."

Sammy set to work, falling into an easy four-beat rhythm of snip and move, pause and touch. My hair fell in clumps on the black and white tiles. I let him work in silence for several minutes before I dropped the question whose answer I'd been dreading the whole ride back.

"Was Peter a drug dealer?" I was studying Sammy in the mirror.

He didn't even look up from my coif-in-progress.

"Hell, no. He bought them."

"Well, how the hell could he end up with a new Beemer and one hundred eighty-seven thousand dollars? Can you explain that?"

Sammy stopped cutting. "Jack, just let it go. Nothing good will come from this."

"My brother was murdered. I can't let it go. I thought you wanted to help."

Sammy gently massaged the back of my neck. "All right, Jack. Here's the truth. Peter was the hardest-working boy in show business." He cleared his throat, then spoke softly. He sounded like a father belatedly telling his kid where babies come from. "One way or another, every last one of us out here earns their keep servicing the rich. That's how it is, Jack. Well, Peter serviced them a little more literally than the rest of us."

I was starting to feel a little sick. And scared. I almost got up and left in the middle of the haircut. I loved my brother. But I wondered if I'd ever really known him.

"He got paid for sex? Is this what you're telling me?"

Sammy shrugged. "It wasn't like he had an hourly rate, Jack. But he was doing some of the richest women in the very expensive free world and doing them rather well. I thought you knew. I thought that Peter told you everything. I guess he didn't mention that one of his ladies was your potential mother-in-law, Campion Neubauer. I think another might have been Dana. But, Jack, that was before you two started going out."

Chapter 23

AFTER I LEFT SAMMY'S, I stopped at a bar called Wolfies. It's located in the same beautiful wooded part of East Hampton where Jackson Pollock used to paint and drink and drive into trees.

I ordered a black coffee and a beer and sat at the bar, thinking about my day and what to do next. I finally plucked a wrinkled scrap of paper out of my wallet and called the number on the back.

The crisp voice at the other end belonged to Dr. Jane Davis. I hadn't seen or spoken to her in ten years. But in high school we had become pretty good friends, when to everyone's amazement, this shy National Merit Scholar hooked up with my fisherman pal, Fenton Gidley.

Jane, the class valedictorian, won a full scholarship to SUNY Binghamton, then went on to Harvard Medical School. Through Fenton, I'd learned that she spent the next couple of years doing a residency in Los Angeles and running a trauma unit at an inner-city St. Louis hospital before burning out. She was now the chief pathologist for Long Island Hospital and chief medical examiner of Suffolk County.

Jane had another hour in the lab, but said she could meet after and gave me directions to her house in Riverhead. "If you get there first, could you take Iris for a little walk?" she asked. "The keys are under the second-to-last flowerpot. And don't worry, she's a sweetheart."

I made a point of getting there early, and Iris, a sleek, pale-eyed weimaraner, was beside herself with gratitude. She may have been the size of a Doberman, but Iris was a lover, not a fighter. When I opened the door, she jumped and yelped and skated round the wooden floor on slippery nails.

For the next fifteen minutes she yanked me around the tiny subdivision, peeing on its invisible canine boundaries. That pretty much bonded us for life, and we were sitting contentedly shoulder to shoulder on the front porch when Jane's blue Volvo pulled in.

Inside her kitchen, Jane poured dry cereal for Iris, coffee for me, and a glass of tawny port for herself. In the past decade, her beanpole gawkiness had turned into athletic grace, but she had the same force field of intelligence.

"There's been a little dip in Long Island's output of suspicious deaths lately," said Jane. "So I've had a lot of time to spend with Peter." She pulled at Iris's translucent ears and looked at me intently.

"So what did you find?" I asked her.

"For one thing," said Jane, "Peter didn't drown."

Chapter 24

JANE REACHED into a battered leather knapsack and dropped a folder labeled "Mullen, Peter 5/29" on the table. Then she pulled out a clear plastic sleeve of color slides and held one of them up to the kitchen light.

"Take a look at these," she said, squinting. "They're photographs of cells I scraped off the inside of Peter's lungs. See the shape and the color at the edge?" The pictures showed a cluster of small circular cells about the size of a dime and tinted pink.

Jane removed a second set of slides. "These are from the lung tissue of a man who got pulled out of Long Island Sound five days before Peter. The cells were nearly twice as large and much darker. That's because the drowning victim struggles to breathe and inhales water into the lungs. Cells like Peter's are what we find in bodies dumped into the ocean *after* they've stopped breathing."

"How did he die, then?"

"Just what it looks like," she said, carefully tucking the slides back in their sleeves. "He was beaten to death."

She reopened the fat manila folder and grabbed a stack of black-and-white prints. "I know you saw Peter that night on the beach, but the cold water holds down the swelling and limits the discoloration. In these, I have to warn you, he looks a lot worse."

Jane handed me the pictures. Peter's shattered, misshapen face was unrecognizable. It was all I could do not to look away. On the beach his beauty was largely intact. In the photos, his skin was an awful gray. The bruises made him look like a human punching bag.

Jane dug deeper into her pile and fished out the X rays. They documented the assault in terms of fractured bones. There were dozens. With the tip of her pen, she singled out a clean break at the top of Peter's spine.

"This is what killed him," she said.

I shook my head in disbelief. The anger that had been building for the past two weeks was getting impossible to control.

"So what do you have to do to prove someone was murdered, pull a bullet out of their head?" I asked in disgust.

"It's a good question, Jack. I sent my initial report to the East Hampton Police Department and the district attorney's office two weeks ago and I haven't heard a thing."

I cursed out Frank Volpi all the way back from Jane's. He had the reports on Peter and he hadn't done a goddamned thing. He was still talking about a drowning, a suicide. How the hell could they cover up something like that? Who was I up against?

When I got home late that night, Mack was snoring on the living-room couch. I slipped off my grandfather's glasses and shoes, spread a light blanket over him, and tucked him in for the night. I couldn't bear to wake him and tell him what I'd found.

Then it hit me. I went into the kitchen and called Burt Kearns, the reporter from the *East Hampton Star* who'd slipped me his number at my father's funeral. Ten minutes later Kearns stood at the door with a tape recorder and two reporter's notepads.

"Christ," I said, "you're faster than Chinese food."

Chapter 25

KEARNS MUST HAVE WORKED right through the night. When I went to the front porch to get the Star, I saw that the shit had really hit the fan. Finally. It was all over the front page. A thirty-six-point, four-column headline with the same question I'd been asking: HOW DID PETER MULLEN DIE?

Beneath it was everything I had unloaded on Kearns in the kitchen the night before: from the absurdity of Peter's, or anyone's, choosing to go swimming that night to the overwhelming and so far ignored evidence of a vicious beating. The story also broadly hinted at the possibility of an affair between Peter and Campion Neubauer.

Running throughout the extensive story was a guilty-sounding chorus of "no comment," "did not return repeated phone calls," and "refused to respond" from Detective Volpi and the startled representatives of Campion and Barry, and Mayflower Enterprises. The power couple was still on the road working to smooth over the Boontaag toy company takeover, and apparently Peter's death didn't justify a simple change in their itinerary.

The aggressive reporting was supported by a righteous editorial calling for an inquiry into Peter's death. "The failure of the East Hampton P.D. to question Barry and Campion Neubauer about a death which took place on their property while the victim was working at their party is ludicrous." It concluded, "This is a disturbing reminder of the often glaring inequities in our criminal justice system."

I read the story through once, then I went and got Mack and read it to him. "It's a start," he snorted.

For the next week the story roiled the East End like a summer storm. You couldn't walk into a restaurant or shop without hearing charged suspicions being aired. Of course, Fenton, Marci, Molly, Hank, Sammy, and I were doing our share to keep Peter's story on people's minds. What had started as a quest for me was turning into an obsession.

The news coverage didn't stop with our local weekly. *New York* magazine sent a reporter and a photographer, and two New York TV stations ran nearly identical segments with a trench-coated reporter treading the moonlit beach where Peter's body washed ashore.

One evening I received a call from Dominick Dunne, the reporter-novelist whose daughter had been murdered years ago and who had emerged as a crusty talking head during the O.J. marathon. "My editors at *Vanity Fair* are begging me to do this story," he told me, "but I hate the Hamptons in the summer."

"I do, too, but you should do the story anyway. My brother was murdered."

"You're probably right. I'm sorry if I was flip. In the meantime, I just wanted to tell you not to let the bastards get away with it." He reminded me of Mack.

At Nelson, Goodwin and Mickel, I threw myself into the Mudman case. The injustice of his scheduled execution and the cover-up of Peter's murder had become connected in my mind. I prepared a two-hundred-page response to the judge's reaction to our latest request for DNA testing in Texas. The senior associate glowed and said it was the best work he'd ever seen from summer help.

No wonder. It was why I had wanted to be a lawyer in the first place.

Chapter 26

FENTON GIDLEY WAS BAITING LINES on the deck of his boat when the Fixer pulled up alongside in a twenty-foot Boston Whaler. He cut the engine and called to the burly, sandy-haired fisherman who happened to be Jack Mullen's best friend.

"Hey, Fenton. How they biting?" the Fixer asked in a snotty, wise-guy voice.

Gidley looked up and saw this big guy with a scar on his cheek. He didn't have time for idle chitchat. "Do I know you, buddy?"

The Fixer pulled out a 9mm Glock and pointed it at Gidley. "I think you're going to wish that we had never met. Now, I want you to stand up real slow. Hey, he follows instructions. Good, I like that in a punk loser. Now jump in the fucking water, Gidley. Jump — or I'll shoot you right between the eyes. It would make my morning."

Fenton jumped off his boat, went under briefly, then

bobbed to the surface. He was wearing shorts, a faded Hawaiian shirt, and work boots. He needed to get the boots off.

"Leave the boots on," the Fixer said. He leaned over the edge of the Whaler and stared down at Gidley. Then he smiled.

"You're going to die out here today. More precisely, you're going to drown. Want to know why?"

Gidley was obviously smarter than he looked. He was paying close attention, searching for some way out. But there was no way out.

"Peter Mullen's murder?" he said. He was already having trouble staying afloat. The water was choppy and cold, and the boots were a bitch.

"Peter Mullen wasn't murdered . . . ," the Fixer said. "He drowned. Just like you're going to drown. I'm going to stay right here until you go under for the last time. That way, you don't have to die alone."

And that's what the Fixer did. He kept the gun on Gidley and watched him with only mild interest. He drank a Lipton iced tea out of the bottle. His eyes were cold and flat, like a shark's.

Gidley was a strong kid, and he really loved life. He didn't go down the first time until almost half an hour after he jumped into the water.

The second time was only a few minutes later. When he fought his way back to the surface, he was coughing up seawater and foam, choking on it.

"Peter Mullen drowned," the Fixer called to him. "You understand that now? You getting a feeling for drowning?"

Fenton finally started to cry, but he wasn't going to

beg this bastard for his life. It wasn't much satisfaction, but it was something.

Fenton went down again and immediately took a big gulp of salt water. His chest felt as if it was going to explode this time. He pulled off his boots — what the hell — and let them go to the bottom. Then Fenton came up for the last time. He wanted to kill the fucker, but it looked as though things were going the opposite way.

Fenton couldn't believe what he saw when he struggled to the surface this time. The Whaler was pulling away.

"You owe me one, Fenton," the bastard shouted over the engine noise. "You owe me your stupid life."

Fenton got the rest of the message, too — *Peter Mullen had drowned. That was the way it had to be.*

Fenton floated on his back for a while, until he was strong enough to swim to his boat.

Chapter 27

THE FIXER was having a busy and productive day.

Looking downright mellow in baggy shorts, oversize T-shirt, and St. Louis Cardinals cap pulled down to his Ray-Bans, he lazily pedaled his rented bicycle down Ditch Plains Road. As he passed number eighteen, he gave it a long, hard look, then released his grip on the handlebars and rolled serenely by.

"Look, Ma, no hands," he said to the cloudless afternoon sky.

A couple of yards later, he swerved into the packed lot of the East Deck Motel and stood his bike in the motley row lined up at the break in the dunes.

Then, with a tube of lotion and the latest Grisham in hand, a big yellow beach towel slung over his shoulder, he backtracked toward the house on Ditch Plains, affecting the exaggerated shuffle of a recreating yuppie. Now came the tricky part.

Two doors down from the Mullen place, he cut across the lot where a big new house was going up and headed toward Ditch Plains Beach. But then, as if realizing he'd forgotten something, he turned toward the Mullens' rear door.

He pulled a flexible ribbon of steel out of his deep-pocketed shorts and probed the lock. When the first two attempts failed to produce the telltale *click,* he realized the goddamned door wasn't even locked.

That's a sign, he thought as he let himself inside. *Don't be too creative.* For the next half an hour he followed his own advice, scouring the drawers, the cabinets, and the bookshelves. But the obvious places didn't yield what he was looking for. Ditto for the clammy crawl space and the tiny attic.

He was starting to sweat. The fucking house wasn't air-conditioned. He checked behind every picture on the wall and peered into the sleeves of old Beatles and Kingston Trio LPs. Then he went through the closets, which were jam-packed with Mullen memorabilia.

Where the hell did you hide it, Peter?

This is important, you miserable little fuck. People could die — including your Mouseketeer pals. Even your hotshot brother.

So where the hell is it, you little dead fuck?

After another thirty minutes he was in such a foul humor, he was sorry to see Mack's old Datsun pull into the driveway. After all, if the old geezer had stumbled on him midsearch, he would have had no choice but to kill him.

Maybe he ought to do him anyway. Let the town spill a few more tears for those poor afflicted Mullen boys.

No, spontaneous mayhem was for amateurs. He'd already caused enough trouble for one day.

He waited by the deck until he heard the garage door squeaking upward, then slipped out the back and hustled toward the beach.

Goddamn you, Peter. Where the hell did you hide the salami, pal?

Chapter 28

ON WEDNESDAY MORNING in New York, I was tucked inside my tiny office by eight o'clock. Everything that could possibly have gone wrong seemed to have. The phone rang. Even before I picked up, I muttered, "Uh-oh."

It was Fenton, calling from the island.

"Hey, man, good to hear your voice," I said.

"Yeah, well, hold that thought," he said. Then he told me what had happened the day before alongside his boat. By the time he was finished, I wanted to rush back to Montauk, but what the hell good would it do?

"You have any idea who he was?"

"I'd bet anything he's one of the bastards who killed Peter."

After I finished telling Fenton to cool it, and to be careful, I sat at my desk and felt like the powerless person I was. Sammy was right. The empire was striking back. And my friends were feeling the brunt.

The bright spot in my day happened between 9:35 and 9:37. Pauline Grabowski, the private investigator, peeked into my office and held up a bag from Krispy Kreme.

"I bought two glazed and I'm only eating one," she said, and smiled.

"You sure?" I smiled back.

"Positive. You okay? Gonna save the Mudman out in Texas today?"

"I hope so. Thanks for the thought. And the sugar hit."

"*De nada,* young Jack. It's only a doughnut."

My best friend had almost drowned, and I was eating a doughnut and flirting. It wasn't right. But what are you going to do?

Midmorning I got a call from William Montrose's executive assistant, Laura Richardson. Montrose, the most senior partner and chairman of the management committee, wanted me upstairs. I reminded myself that if I was about to be fired, the ax wouldn't be wielded by the mighty Montrose but by some anonymous hit man in HR.

Even so, it didn't take the metallic taste out of my mouth.

Chapter 29

THE ELEVATOR OPENED on the forty-third floor, and I crossed the threshold into corporate paradise. The beautiful Laura Richardson was waiting. A tall, regal African American woman whose lustrous skin outshone the mahogany-covered walls, she beamed as she led me down a long corridor to Monty's corner office. The whole floor was enveloped in an otherworldly quiet and calm.

"Don't worry, I've never gotten used to it myself," said Montrose about the panoramic view from his thirty-foot wall of glass. He and fellow partner Simon Lafayette sat on matching black-leather couches. Behind them stretched Manhattan from the UN Plaza to the Williamsburg Bridge. The iridescent tip of the Chrysler Building burned right at the center. It reminded me of Pauline Grabowski and her amazing tattoo — among other things.

"You know Simon," said Montrose, nodding in his direction. He didn't ask me to sit.

On one wall were photographs of his wife and five children. The black-and-white pictures conveyed the gravitas of official royal portraits. That he had procreated was so abundantly a statement in itself.

"I was just telling Simon what terrific work you've been doing on the Innocence Quest. Top-drawer all the way. Everyone seems to think you're very special, Jack, not only someone who will be offered a job here but partner material."

Now his smile vanished and the silver-blue eyes narrowed. "Jack, I lost my own brother a few years ago, so I have a little idea of what you're going through now. But I also need to tell you something you obviously didn't know, or you wouldn't have acted as you have been lately. Barry and Campion Neubauer and their company, Mayflower Enterprises, are very important clients of this firm.

"Jack, you're right on the cusp of something special here," said Montrose, gesturing out toward the metropolis. "Jeopardizing it won't bring your brother or father back. I've been there, Jack. Think it through. It's all very logical, and I'm sure you understand. Now I know you're busy, so I appreciate your taking the time to have this little chat."

I stood there immobile, but as I struggled to come up with exactly the right response, Monty turned his attention to Simon. I found myself staring at the back of his head.

Our meeting was over. I'd been dismissed. A few seconds later the lovely Laura walked me back to the elevator.

Chapter 30

AS I WAITED FOR THE ELEVATOR, I hated myself about as much as a twenty-eight-year-old can. Which is a lot. Finally it arrived, but when the doors reopened on my floor, I couldn't move.

I stared down the long corridor that led to my office and imagined the twenty-year death march, which if I was lucky and a big enough scumbag would lead back up to forty-three. No one walked by, or they might have called security. Or maybe the company nurse.

I let the elevator doors close without getting out. They reopened on the marble lobby.

With enormous relief, I continued outside onto sunny, sooty Lexington Avenue. For the next two hours I walked the crowded midtown streets, grateful for a place in the anonymous flow. I thought about Peter, my father, and the warning that Fenton had gotten. Then it was Dana and Volpi, the Beach House — the evil empire obviously extended to the offices of Nelson, Goodwin and Mickel. I'm not too strong on conspiracy theories, but there was no denying the connection between a lot of recent events.

My walk took me east to a small park overlooking the East River. Technically, I guess, it was the same river that bisected Montrose's view, the one he dangled in front of me like a family heirloom. I liked it better down here. I leaned against a high black railing and wondered what I should do. The Chrysler Building in Montrose's office had reminded me of Pauline. Since I was just about the only one left in the city without a cell phone, I dropped a quarter at a noisy corner pay phone and asked if she'd meet me for lunch.

"There's a cute little plaza with a waterfall on Fiftieth Street between Second and Third," she said. "Pick up whatever you want to eat and meet me there. What do you want, Jack?"

"I'll tell you over lunch."

I headed there immediately. That meant I got to see Pauline nimbly weaving through the packed sidewalk, her head down and her dark brown ponytail brushing her classic blue suit. Despite everything that had happened that morning, I couldn't help smiling. She didn't so much walk as glide through the crowd.

We found an empty bench against the wall, and Pauline unwrapped a chicken sandwich on twelve-grain. It was a big sandwich for such a slender woman. She knew it, too.

"Aren't you going to eat? Is that how you keep so trim — *starvation?*"

"I'm not all that hungry," I said. I recounted my visit to the top of the world as she listened and ate. Her eyes expressed sympathy, then outrage, and when I told her about Monty's amazing view of her tattoo, a little mirth.

The city is full of women who with imagination and style can make a little beauty go a long way. Pauline did her best to downplay hers. But with the light on her face, there was no concealing it, and it took me by surprise.

She already knew about Neubauer's relationship to the firm and had done a little inquiring of her own. "Personally, I don't like Barry Neubauer. He can charm birds out of trees, but he gives me the creeps. Mayflower has an account with the most expensive escort service in the city," said Pauline. "It's not all that unusual for certain corporations. The service is like a co-op, Jack. You need letters of recommendation, there are interviews, and you have to maintain a balance of fifty thousand. That's all common knowledge.

"The next part isn't," she said. "Two years ago one of their A-list escorts drowned when she supposedly fell off a yacht during a moonlight sail with Neubauer and his friends. The body was never found, and Nelson, Goodwin and Mickel handled the matter with such panache, it never made the papers."

I stared at the cement and winced. "What's the going rate for a dead escort these days?" I asked.

"Five hundred thousand dollars. About the same as a one-bedroom. The girl was nineteen." I looked into her eyes as she finished off her sandwich and wiped away the crumbs.

"Pauline, why are you telling me this?"

"I want you to know what you're getting into, Jack. *Do you understand?*"

That's when it hit me, and I couldn't help what I did.

"Pauline, help me on Peter's case," I blurted out. "Work on the good side for a change."

"It doesn't sound like a good career move," said Pauline. "I'll think it over." Then she got up and left. I watched her walk all the way to Third, and then she disappeared into the thick midtown stream of pedestrians.

Chapter 31

"WHAT I'M LOOKING FOR," insisted Rob Coon with contagious excitement, "is not another lovely, formal English garden but a full-on maze where you go in one end and get lost for a few days before finding your way out."

Marci Burt and her potential gold mine of a landscaping client, sitting in one of the sunny front booths of Estia, sipped their lattes and let the deliciousness of the concept sink in.

Coon, the thirty-year-old scion of the country's first family in parking garages, explained the source of his inspiration. "I rented *The Avengers* the other night. Except for Uma, it blew. But the maze rocked."

"It would be a fabulous project," said Marci, and flashing dollar signs notwithstanding, she meant it. "Ideally, you would design it in such a way that you could keep changing the course so no one would get bored."

Coon beamed. "Very cool," he said.

The two fell into an enthusiastic discussion about the hardiest strains of evergreen, landscape libraries, possible models. They were talking about the need for a research junket to Scotland when Coon stopped mid-sentence.

Detective Frank Volpi and two other men in dark suits had entered the popular Amagansett restaurant. Coon's eyes followed them to their back booth.

"You know them?" asked Marci.

"The tall guy with a beard is Irving Bushkin. A lot of people consider him the best criminal attorney in America. If I ever kill my wife, he's the first person I'll call. I believe the guy to his left is the Suffolk County district attorney, Tim Maguire."

Coon didn't recognize Volpi, but Marci did and realized the meeting might have something to do with Peter's death. "Bob," said Marci, "this is the most exciting assignment I've ever been considered for. But I need thirty seconds to make a phone call."

That's when she called me at the office and I called Kearns at the *Star.* Less than five minutes later there was a screech of rubber out front and Kearns stood, mike in hand, in front of Volpi's table.

"What brought you to town?" Kearns asked Irving Bushkin, and although there was no response, he continued, undeterred. "Who's your client? Does your visit have anything to do with the investigation into Peter Mullen's death?"

Small and round, with fat, freckled hands, Kearns doesn't look like much, but he has balls. According to Marci, he peppered them with questions until Volpi threatened to arrest him for harassment. Even then he pulled out a camera and snapped a quick picture of the famous visitor and his pals.

But that wasn't even the best part. After Kearns left, Megan, the waitress who'd taken their order, came out and informed them that there'd been a mix-up. "I'm afraid we're all out of the pasta special," she said.

"It's ten past noon," protested Volpi, but the waitress just shrugged.

There was considerably more grumbling before the three changed their order to cheeseburgers and a turkey club. The new orders were barely in when Megan returned with more bad news. "We're all out of that, too," she said. "As a matter of fact, we're plumb out of everything."

At that point, Volpi, Irving Bushkin, and District Attorney Tim Maguire stormed out of the restaurant. Half an hour later Marci got a handshake deal to build what promised to be the only bona-fide English garden maze in the Hamptons. At least for a week.

Chapter 32

FOR MUDMAN'S SAKE, and I suppose because I wasn't quite ready to ditch my whole legal career yet, I returned to Nelson, Goodwin and Mickel and spent all Friday working on the latest appeal. In the morning I re-reviewed his court records and was outraged by the minimal effort of his court-appointed attorney.

I had lunch with Pauline, who told me she was still thinking about my offer to work for the good guys. I don't know what else we talked about, but suddenly it was three o'clock and we hustled back to the office. Separately.

For the remainder of the afternoon, I drafted a response to the judge in Texas. If I may say so myself, it was persuasive. It was after eleven that night when I e-mailed a copy to Exley.

Even though I felt okay about my day, the moment I got back on Peter's bike and pulled down the visor of his blue Arai helmet, I began rewinding my life like a depressing old video. Soul-searching wasn't a real good idea right then. I couldn't come up with too many selfless or generous acts in my life.

Of course, I had no trouble coming up with bad stuff. The most damning incident that came to mind had occurred seven years before. It was at Middlebury, when I was a twenty-one-year-old senior. Peter was thirteen at the time. It was winter break and he had come up to spend a long weekend with his big brother. One night we borrowed my roommate's car to get some Chinese food. On the way back to the dorm, a local cop pulled us over for a broken taillight. He was being a bastard, and he decided to search the car.

It occurs to me now that on that particular night, the cop was playing the part of the townie and we were the little rich shits. That's why he didn't stop until he was holding up a skinny marijuana cigarette between his fingers. I explained that the car belonged to my roommate and that we had no idea there was pot in it. But he ignored me and drove Peter and me to the station to book us for possession.

When we got there Peter said that the joint belonged to him. I did nothing to refute it. Peter called it a no-brainer. I was planning to go to law school. He had no intention of even going to college. I was an adult. He was a minor, so they couldn't do anything to him.

But, of course, that's what made what I *didn't* do so much worse. What a goddamned role model I was for my kid brother.

I remembered the exact moment when the cop turned

to me and asked if it was true that the pot belonged to Peter, and I just shrugged.

Remembering the incident again on Peter's bike was a bad idea. It felt as if a white-hot current were running through me. It was all I could do to stay on the Long Island Expressway. A week after the arrest in Vermont, the case got thrown out for an improper search. I never told him how wrong I'd been. Whatever Peter had done to get himself murdered, maybe I'd helped put my brother on the slippery slope.

Chapter 33

IT WASN'T QUITE TEN on Saturday morning when I awoke to the pleasant sound of a woman's laughter. Macklin was laying on the blarney charm with a trowel. Judging by the way the lovely laugh kept interrupting his tales, a trowel was barely big enough.

As I walked down the stairs, I wondered who young and pretty enough to inspire Macklin's A game might actually be visiting us on a Saturday morning.

When I eased myself into the kitchen, Pauline Grabowski smiled up at me from the table. She looked as comfortable as if she'd been coming over for chats with Macklin her whole life.

"We have a visitor," said Mack, "who admits to being a friend of yours. And she's so lovely, I'm not even holding that against her."

"I didn't think you went for women with tattoos."

"Me, either," said Mack, dumbfounded. "For eighty-six years I've been living a lie."

The way Pauline chuckled, I could tell she was already taken with Mack.

"Please don't encourage him," I said. "It's worse than feeding the animals at the zoo."

"Good morning, Jack," she said, interrupting our routine. "You don't look so great."

"Thanks. I had a rough night at the shop. But even if I don't look it, I'm at least as happy to see you as Mack is."

"Well, have some coffee. It's out of this world. We've got work to do."

I filled a huge mug and took it outside to the back porch, where Pauline sat beside me on the top wooden step. After my long night, her unexpected presence felt almost angelic, and she looked so starkly beautiful in her Crunch T-shirt, cutoffs, and red Converse sneakers, I had to remind myself not to gawk.

"Here's to working for the good guys. Hope it isn't a huge mistake on my part."

Pauline pulled out two pieces of paper with a long list on each. "This is everyone who attended the Memorial Day weekend Beach House party," she said about the slightly longer one. "And this is everyone who worked there."

A third of the way down the second list was "Peter Mullen — valet" and our phone number. "How'd you manage to get these?" I asked her. "I've been trying, and striking out. There's a lot of paranoia right now."

"I've got a friend who's a very talented and unscrupulous hacker. All he needed was the party planner's e-mail address and the name of her web site."

There was an awkward pause. Despite my best efforts not to, I was gawking at Pauline.

"Why are you looking at me like that?"

"I guess I'm a little surprised you decided to do this," I said.

"Me, too. So let's not look a gift investigator in the mouth."

Chapter 34

"LET'S START WITH THE HELP," Pauline suggested. "The ones you haven't already spoken to, anyway."

The first phone call to bear fruit was to one of Peter's fellow car parkers, Christian Sorenson, whose fed-up girlfriend picked up after a dozen rings. "According to Christian, he's at the Clam Bar washing dishes," she said, sulking over the phone. "That means he's probably somewhere else."

The Clam Bar is a pretentiously unpretentious little shack right on 27, halfway between Montauk and Amagansett. The service is minimal and the decor nonexistent, but something about the vibe and the old classic reggae tapes they play has turned it into an institution. In August you can wait an hour to spend forty dollars for lunch.

Pauline and I were lucky to find seats at the counter,

and we ordered a couple of bowls of chowder. It almost felt like a date.

I spotted Sorenson bent over the sink, and he eventually came out of the kitchen in a sodden apron and latex gloves.

"I don't think you want to shake my hand," he said.

I introduced Pauline, and she explained that we were trying to find out a little more about what happened to Peter that night at the party. Christian was glad to help. "I was working the party all night. I was a little surprised the police never called."

"That's part of the reason we're here," I told him. "They're treating the whole thing like an accident-suicide."

"No way," said Christian, "but maybe the cops are afraid someone heavy is involved with whatever happened to Rabbit."

"Well, if the police had called," asked Pauline, "what would you have told them?"

Sorenson folded his muscular arms and told his story. This was where it got interesting.

"First of all, Peter got there late as usual, so the rest of us were kind of ticked at him. But, as usual, he worked his ass off, so we weren't. Then, just before he disappeared, I saw Billy Collins, who was a waiter that night, slip him a note."

"How do you know it was a note?" asked Pauline.

"Because I saw him open it and read it."

"Ever ask Billy Collins about it?" she asked.

"I've been meaning to, but I haven't run into him."

"You know where we could find him?"

"The last I heard he was an assistant pro at Maidstone.

He's supposed to be a stud golfer, trying to play the mini-tour or something, and basically I think they just let him practice."

"Sounds like a pretty good deal," I said.

"Not half as sweet as this," he said, holding up ten rubber fingers.

"Thanks a lot, Christian," said Pauline, "and by the way, your girl sends her love."

"Really?"

Chapter 35

"I'M IMPRESSED," I said as Pauline and I made our way outside to her car.

"It's what I do, Jack. And sometimes even pros get lucky. There were eight guys parking cars that night. We just happened to find the one who saw something. So where's Maidstone? Am I dressed for the joint?"

I'd lived out there my whole life, but until that afternoon I'd never set foot on the hallowed grounds of the Maidstone Country Club. Then again, I wasn't alone. The Maidstone, built on the Atlantic and laid out like an old British links course, isn't exactly a community outreach program.

As snooty as Maidstone can be, it's an easy party to crash. No rent-a-cop out front. Not even a gate. A couple of visitors in a twenty-year-old Volkswagen can putter right up to the huge stone clubhouse, park their own car, and start walking toward the driving range. And if you carry yourself as though you've got a God-given right to be there, no one will say boo.

I don't know if you've ever been to a country club like Maidstone, but there's this feeling of medicated calm, as if the whole place, from the well-seeded sod to the cloudless sky, has taken a Vicodin, then washed it down with a martini. I could get used to it.

Billy Collins was easy to spot. He was the one hitting one perfect five-iron shot after another. He was also the only golfer on the range.

"Hey, Jack. Can you believe this place?" he said, still gripping the club and pointing at the idyllic landscape with his elbows before sending another ball sailing out over it.

"This is one of the best tracks on Long Island, but so many of the members are ancient, or have other vacation houses, that the course is empty half the time."

"So how's your game?" I asked.

"Shite," said Collins, striping another perfect iron.

Pauline purposely stepped a little closer to Collins so he had to stop hitting balls. "We want to talk to you because Christian Sorenson said he saw you hand Peter a note. It was just before he disappeared that night at the Neubauers'." I liked the way Pauline talked to people. She didn't try to act tough, or falsely flirtatious. She didn't act at all.

"There was definitely something weird about it," said Collins, putting down his club.

"What do you mean?"

"The note was pink and perfumed, but it was given to me by a guy who was hanging with another guy."

"You know them?"

"Nope. Based on their physiques, I thought they might have been Neubauer's personal trainers. But they didn't have the perfect posture, the bouncy energy. And they weren't working the room, trying to hustle up a couple of zillionaire clients. Plus, they were old. Maybe forty."

"Why didn't you call the police?" Pauline asked.

"The day Peter's body was found, I called Frank Volpi three times. But he never returned my calls."

Chapter 36

DUSK SOFTENED THE SKY as we pulled out of Maidstone and drove down Further Lane, one of the town's toniest addresses. It's the kind of street where a $5 million house stands out for its modesty. Only West End Road, with Georgica Pond and estates like Quelle Barn and Grey Gardens, rivals it.

"Outside Detroit," said Pauline, "in Birmingham and Bloomfield Hills, there are some posh enclaves where the auto execs and Pistons and Red Wings live, but it's nothing compared with this. When I was a kid, we used to go out to Birmingham to look at the Christmas lights."

"Nobody has any idea how over the top and ridiculous it gets out here. These people buy ten-million-dollar houses and then tear them down."

One mansion blended into the next, and as tasteful as the homes were, there was something odd about the neighborhood. It looked colorized, a very upscale suburbia, with Ferraris instead of station wagons, and every messy trace of children airbrushed out.

"Strange times we live in," I said. "Everyone believes they're just a couple of breaks from being rich. I think it's something they put in the water."

"I buy Lotto tickets every week," said Pauline. "And I drink bottled water."

The conversation drifted back to Peter's murder and the investigation.

"Actually, I called all of my friends off the case," I told her.

"Why did you do that, Jack?"

I told Pauline what had happened to Fenton on his boat, how Hank had gotten fired, and that Marci and Molly had been followed.

Pauline merely nodded. "Remember what I told you about the big leagues, young Jack."

"I'm twenty-eight, Pauline."

"Uh-huh," she said, nodding. Then she reached into her shoulder bag and pulled out a small revolver. "Ever shoot anybody? Ever get shot at?"

"Did you?" I asked her.

"I already told you. I'm from Detroit."

I watched Pauline's merry eyes concentrating on the road and her hair whipping around in the breeze, and I realized the only honest thing for me to do was to shut up and smile. Because sitting next to Pauline was making me happy. Simple as that.

"Stay for dinner," I said, "and I'll introduce you to Sam's Pizza. On a good day, it's right up there with John's and Lombardi's."

"High praise, but I have to get back. Maybe another time."

"Artichokes and bacon, the yin and yang of pizza toppings?"

"You're persistent."

"Actually, when it comes to women, I tend to discourage pretty easily."

"Maybe it's time you get over that."

Chapter 37

MY BIKE — I guess it's mine now — was still parked in front of the house. After Pauline dropped me off, I stood beside it and watched the orange taillights of her car recede toward Manhattan.

It felt too early to hunker down for the night. And I was a little hurt that Pauline had turned down my invitation for dinner. I liked her, and I thought she liked me. Of course, I'd thought that Dana was rather fond of me, too. So with no particular place to go, and no one to go there with, I threw a leg over the Beemer and pointed it west.

Just beyond town, I turned onto Old Montauk Highway, a well-traveled road full of roller-coaster humps and dips, which had offered Peter and me our first taste of genital titillation. We'd dubbed it "the Weenie Road" because if you're going fast enough as you crest the hills, that's where you feel it.

That night I thought of both Peter and Pauline when I

twisted back the throttle and caught some air. *Long live the Weenie Road,* I thought.

Too soon, I was back on 27, ripping past condo time-shares and trendy restaurants. Every time I got on the bike I was getting a little better at it, learning how to lean into turns, mastering the rhythm of clutch lever and throttle. Maybe a little of Peter was rubbing off.

When I swerved off 27 onto Bluff Road, it occurred to me that I was probably following the same route that Peter had on his last night. It didn't feel like a coincidence.

The Neubauer estate was less than a quarter mile up the road. When I saw the open gates, I braked unconsciously and swerved between them. A hundred yards later I cut the engine and the lights. Then I coasted down the gentle grade toward the beach.

I stashed the bike in the thick brush of the last dune, took off my sneakers, and sat on the cool sand just out of reach of the tide.

Everything about the scene echoed the night they brought me to look at Peter's body. The moonlight had the same powerful wattage. The surf was about as high and as loud.

As I pondered the scene, the tide slithered up the beach and grabbed my heel. I recoiled in shock. No one who wasn't covered in white fur would go swimming in the middle of the night in that.

Next thing I knew, I was stripping off my clothes, bellowing like a madman, and running headlong toward the surf.

No one would go in the water without a really good reason — would they?

Could Peter have done it? Then seemed like as good a time as any to find out.

The water was frightening, bone-aching cold, and it was a full month warmer than when Peter had supposedly drowned. In three steps, my feet and lower legs hurt. But I kept running through the slop of the first wave. I dove under the collapsing crest of the next.

In a kind of shock I swam furiously from the shore, counting out thirty strokes. When I stopped, I was well past the breakers. The safety of the beach looked a mile away.

For what felt like minutes but was probably less than thirty seconds, I bobbed in the moonlit swells. I took deep, slow breaths, and my body adjusted somewhat to the cold.

Peter wouldn't have done this. Hell, no. Peter hated to be cold . . . besides, Peter loved Peter.

I could control my breathing, but I couldn't control my brain. I was up to my neck in the big black ocean, getting scared.

I began to swim back toward the beach as desperately as I'd left it. Halfway there, numbed by the merciless cold, I let myself slip too far forward on a curling breaker.

Suddenly the ocean fell away and I was tumbling in black space. I felt a beat of terror-filled nothingness. I kept reaching out. Then the waves swept me back again. I was lost in a black swirl. I felt as if I were being buried alive. I couldn't breathe. Over and over again the waves pounded me like falling concrete from a collapsing building. They beat me against the shell-covered floor.

Somehow I remembered that you have to stop fighting

back. I grabbed my nose and concentrated on holding my breath. Seconds later, I resurfaced, wildly gulping air.

I wasn't prepared for the second wave. It was smaller, but it was the one that really nailed me. I took a lungful of water down with me. If I hadn't thought about all the shit Mack would have had to listen to about my killing myself, too, I might have given up. The waves seemed to have taken on a life of their own. They felt like half a dozen battering rams. I hung on, one second at a time, until the ocean finally spat me out and I crawled onto the beach.

Even though Jane Davis had told me my brother didn't drown, I had to prove it to myself.

I guess I had. *Peter hadn't gone swimming that night. My brother had been murdered.*

Part Three

THE INQUEST

Chapter 38

VERY EARLY on a Monday morning in August, I rolled over in my Montauk bed and sighed contentedly. Once in a blue moon, Mack gets it into his head to make a "proper breakfast," and all it took was one semiconscious breath to know that downstairs Mack was knee deep in it.

I scrambled down the stairs and found him hunched over the stove. His attention was focused on the four gas-burning rings. His arms were moving as furiously as Toscanini's when conducting on the stage of Carnegie Hall.

I inhaled the greasy bouquet and watched the master at work. Mack had much too much frying to oversee for me to risk saying a word at this delicate moment. In a motley armada of pots and pans, bacon, sausages, blood sausages, potatoes, mushrooms, tomatoes, and red beans were noisily building toward a simultaneous finale of pleasure. I brought out the jams, started squeezing the oranges, and, when he gave me the signal, pushed down the toast.

Five minutes later the stovetop symphony was done. In an excited rush of plucks, scoops, and tilts, a generous allotment from each pan was transferred to two dinner-size plates. The two of us sat down and began silently mixing the reds, yellows, blacks, and browns to our genetically determined liking. It felt as if mere seconds had passed before the last slices of toast were going into the toaster for the final cleanup operation and we were reflectively sipping our Irish breakfast tea.

"God bless you, Mack, this was better than sex."

"Then you're doing it wrong," he said, washing down a marmaladed crust with a big sip of tea.

"I'll have to keep practicing," I promised as I poured him another cuppa, then headed to the front porch for the paper. I read it before coming in and dropping it down beside his well-smeared plate. I'd known this was coming — but now it was official.

"Feast your eyes on this."

I looked over Mack's old bony shoulders and read the big, beautiful headline one more time: MURDER INQUIRY SET INTO SUSPICIOUS DEATH OF MONTAUK MAN. Then we wolfed down the story with the same rapt attention that we'd given our breakfast.

For the first time in two months, I felt celebratory. I pumped the air with a fist. We were too full to jump, so I scampered to the liquor cabinet, and at seven in the morning, with the feast still settling in our bellies and minds, we did a shot of the good stuff.

"Here's mud in your eye, Jackson," Mack said.

"Do you realize what we've done," I said excitedly. "We've shocked the goddamned system."

"The goddamned system is a clever old whore, Jack. I'm afraid all we did was piss it off."

Chapter 39

AT WORK THAT WEEK, I kept my head down. Literally. I figured if no one saw it popping out of my office, no one would think to lop it off. I don't recommend it as a long-term career strategy, but at that point I wasn't thinking long-term about Nelson, Goodwin and Mickel, or anything else.

Since we still hadn't gotten a response regarding the Mudman, it left me plenty of time to contemplate the upcoming inquiry.

Early on Thursday morning Pauline called and asked me to meet her for lunch. She said it was "important," and Pauline tends not to exaggerate. She suggested an out-of-the-way place on First Avenue, in the Fifties, Rosa Mexicana.

When I arrived, I saw her at a table in a back corner. As usual, she wore a dark suit and had her hair in a ponytail. And as usual, she looked great. But she also looked anxious, or maybe in a hurry.

"You okay?" I hadn't seen her in almost a week, and I'd missed her. Streetwise Pauline seemed rattled. I had an awful feeling she was about to tell me that working on Peter's case had been a big mistake and she'd finally come to her senses. Maybe she had been threatened.

"The more I look into Neubauer's file," said Pauline in a whisper, "the nastier it gets."

"Nastier than throwing young women off yachts?"

"I've spent more time than I can spare doing a background check on him. I went all the way back to when he was still in Bridgeport. Bridgeport is not exactly Greenwich and four-acre lots. It's gangs and housing projects.

"In 1962 and again in 1965," Pauline continued, "when Neubauer was in his early twenties, he and a guy named Bunny Levin were arrested for extortion."

"He has a criminal record? That's great."

"It isn't great. In both cases all charges were dropped when the key prosecution witnesses suddenly changed their testimony. One witness disappeared completely."

"So we can't use any of this in the inquiry?"

"That's not my point, Jack."

"If you want to quit, Pauline, please just tell me. You've already helped me enormously. I understand what you're saying to me about Neubauer."

Her face twisted and I thought she was almost going to cry. But she just shook her head. "I'm talking about you, Jack. Listen to me. These people make problems disappear."

I wanted to lean over and kiss her, but she looked

spooked enough already. It didn't seem like a good idea.
I finally reached under the table and touched her hand.

"What was that for?" Pauline asked.

"For giving a shit."

"You mean for caring, Jack?"

"Yes, for caring."

Chapter 40

PAULINE HAD NEVER ACTED LIKE THIS in her life. Not even close. As she and Jack stepped out of Rosa Mexicana, she felt flustered and exposed. "I really don't think we should be seen going back to work together," she announced.

Jack held out a faint smile, but Pauline left him standing slightly befuddled as she vanished up the street. Without looking back, she walked west to Third, headed downtown ten blocks, then turned west again, all the way into Grand Central, where a number six train was waiting with open doors.

As soon as the doors closed, her equilibrium returned. Heading downtown always felt good. Making the trip in the middle of the day added a lovely hooky-playing frisson.

She got off the train at Canal and continued downtown

on foot until she pushed through the heavy doors of a former girdle factory on Franklin Street.

An exchange of buzzes got her into an untagged service elevator that opened directly onto a raw loft strewn with a motley collection of artifacts from its owner's eccentric résumé. Pauline walked past a dusty massage table, a cello, and circus stilts, toward the square of light at the far wall.

It wasn't until she got to the very back of the space that she spotted the wavy-haired head of her sister, Mona, bent under the light of her worktable. She was soldering a pin onto a gold circular earring embossed with what looked like hieroglyphics.

Two years earlier Mona had hung up her cha-cha shoes for the security of a career as an avant-garde jewelry designer. In the past few months her earrings, necklaces, and rings, all based on castings of actual Con Edison manhole covers, were flying out of pricey boutiques all over Manhattan and L.A.

Mona didn't notice her visitor until Pauline sat beside her on the bench and rubbed up against her like a friendly Siamese cat.

"So, what's his name?" asked Mona without taking her eyes off the back of a twenty-four-karat gold earring.

"Jack," said Pauline. "His name is Jack. He's great."

"It could be worse," said Mona. "It could be John or Chuck."

"I suppose. He's this guy at work who lives with his grandfather and whose brother was probably murdered. I've known him three months and already he's got me doing things that could cost me everything I have. What's really screwed me up is, I'm more worried about him than me. Mona, I think he actually has a conscience."

"Sounds like you're penis-whipped. Are you?"

"Totally. Except that I haven't even seen it yet. He is a cutie, though. Best of all, he doesn't seem to know it."

"Sounds like you," said Mona. "So, what do you want me to tell you?"

"No point telling me anything. I just need a hug."

Mona turned off her soldering iron, flipped off her gloves, and wrapped her arms around her savvy, street-wise, utterly romantic sister.

"Be careful," she said. "He sounds too good to be true, this Chuck of yours."

Chapter 41

I WAS DOING SOME DECENT LAWYERING on behalf of the Mudman. Actually, the work was a lot like a legal aid defender clinic I had participated in that spring at Columbia. I had a couple of publications from the National Institute of Trial Advocacy spread out on my desk. Also *Fundamentals* of Trial Techniques, by Thomas Mauet, referred to by us law students as "Mauet."

The phone rang and I snatched it up. It was Montrose's executive assistant, Laura Richardson. Damn.

"Bill asked me to see if you could come up," she said.

"It's not really a good time for me," I said. "I'm up to my eyeballs down here."

"I'll meet you at the elevator."

Her call set off the same adrenaline rush as the earlier one. This time I was less afraid of what Montrose had in mind than of how I might react. To get my heart rate down a notch, I slowly walked the full circumference of the floor before getting on the elevator.

"What kept you?" asked Laura as I arrived on forty-three.

Instead of her walking me down the plank to Monty's office, she led me to an elegant little conference room and parked me at a jet black table illuminated by four recessed spotlights. *Now, what is this?*

"It shouldn't be more than a couple of minutes," she said before closing the door. "Wait here." If you've worked in a big corporation, you may have been the victim of this kind of bloodless violence. First you're summoned to an urgent meeting, then met by an assistant who politely asks you to sit and wait.

I did as instructed, but my mind was rioting. *Why am I sitting here with my hands on my lap? Why am I cooperating?* After maybe ten minutes, I couldn't stay in the hot seat any longer. I wandered outside.

When Richardson saw me walking free, I thought she was going to yank an alarm.

"Going to the bathroom," I explained.

A relieved Richardson rearranged her face.

When I returned to the conference room, I saw Barry Neubauer waiting there. Instead of the surprise or shock I probably should have felt, I was kind of teed off. This was actually his first response to Peter's death. "Hello, Jack," he said. "I don't know if anyone mentioned it, but I'm a client here."

Neubauer pulled his custom-made Italian black suit jacket snug across his square shoulders and sat down. I tried to maintain some perspective. He was just another medium-size, middle-aged man, after all, but he was buffed and art-directed. Every touch, from his perfect tan to his perfect haircut to his thousand-dollar silver eyeglass frames, argued for his special status in the world.

"Do you know why I'm here, Jack?"

"You're finally getting around to paying your condolences? That's touching."

He slammed his fist on the table. "Listen, you insolent punk bastard. Obviously, you've got it into your thick skull that I had something to do with the unfortunate death of your brother. So instead of conducting your little amateur-hour investigation, I thought maybe you'd like to talk to me directly."

He hadn't asked, but I decided to sit down, too. "All right. So where do we start?"

"I didn't murder Peter. I liked your brother. He was a good kid, with a nice sense of humor. And unlike Dana's other boyfriends, I actually liked you."

I couldn't keep back a half smile. "That's nice to know. How is Dana?"

"Dana is still in Europe, Jack. A little vacation. Now, you listen to me. The only reason I'm talking to you right now is because of the respect and affection I have for my daughter. Don't be so naive as to believe that you can slander me in the press, trespass on my property, and hack into my colleagues' computers without consequences. Please consider yourself warned, Jack. And this is a friendly warning, because as I said, I like you."

While Neubauer did his power bit, I thought of Fenton treading water with his boots on, Hank out of work, Marci and Molly afraid to drive their cars. When I'd had all I could take, I got up and moved around the conference table faster than he must have thought possible.

I grabbed him in a hammerlock and held his neck so he couldn't move. The summers I'd worked framing houses and laboring in Jepson's Boatyard had made me a lot stronger than his personal trainer was making him.

"You don't think anybody can get to you," I said through clenched teeth. "Well, you're wrong. Do you understand that?" I squeezed his neck a little tighter.

"You're making a huge mistake," Neubauer said, grimacing. He was in a little pain. I liked that.

"No, *you* made a huge mistake. For whatever fucked-up reasons, you involved yourself in my brother's murder case. Facts were covered up. Friends of mine were threatened for trying to get at the truth."

Neubauer began to struggle harder, but I held him firmly. "Let me go, you fucker!" he ordered.

"Yeah, all right," I said, and finally released the son of a bitch.

I started to walk out of the conference room, but then I stopped and turned to Neubauer.

"Somehow, someway, my brother is going to get justice. I promise you."

Neubauer's hair was mussed and his jacket creased, but he had regained most of his composure. "And you're going to wind up like your brother," he said. "I promise."

"Well, Barry, I guess we've both been warned then. And I'm glad we had this little chat."

Chapter 42

I WENT BACK DOWNSTAIRS knowing that I had just blown my summer associate's job, and probably my law career.

I didn't know whether it was worth it, but I didn't think I had a choice. Sooner or later, somebody had to stand up to Neubauer. I was glad it was me.

I tried to call the Island — I wanted to tell Mack what had just happened and ask his advice — but the line out of my office was dead.

"Christ," I whispered, "they're faster than I thought."

Two minutes later the phone rang. My favorite executive assistant from the forty-third floor was on the line.

"I thought my line had been cut off," I told Richardson.

"You just can't dial out," she said. "Tell me, how did someone like you wind up in a place like this?" she asked.

"Clerical error."

"Well, it's been corrected. Mr. Montrose wants to talk to you."

He got on the line. "What happened to that ambitious eager beaver who practically begged for his job?" asked Montrose, warming quickly to the task. "We hold open a door that almost never gets opened for someone like you, and you slam it in our face. The only decent time you put in here was on a worthless pro bono case."

"You're not talking about the Innocence Quest?" I asked. "Exley told me it was the heart and soul of Nelson, Goodwin and Mickel. That would make *me* the heart and soul of the firm."

"You're history, Mullen," said Montrose. Then he hung up.

About five minutes later a pair of burly security guards — one African American, the other Hispanic — stood outside my office. I knew them from the firm's softball team.

"Jack, we've been asked to escort you out of the building," said the shorter, wider of the two. His name was Carlos Hernandez. I liked him.

"We were also told to give you this," he said, and handed me a piece of paper called a Separation Document.

" 'Effective immediately, Jack Mullen has been terminated from Nelson, Goodwin and Mickel for improper use of company time and resources and behavior detrimental to the firm,' " I read.

"Sorry," said Carlos with a shrug.

I wish I could tell you that when I pushed my way through the shiny steel revolving door and stepped out to the street, I felt relieved. Truth is, I was as frightened as Montrose and Barry Neubauer wanted me to be. Suddenly my threats against Neubauer seemed ridiculous and hollow. I knew I'd done the right thing upstairs, so why did I feel like such a fool?

I walked in a daze over to the New York Public Library and the beautiful paneled reading room where I used to ponder my future when I took the train into the city while I was still in high school.

I wrote a letter to the Mudman. I passed along the news that his old prosecutor finally seemed willing to submit the nineteen-year-old evidence from his case for DNA testing. I wished him luck and told him to stay in touch if he could.

I called Pauline from a pay phone, but I got voice mail and couldn't bear to leave a message.

Then I walked across town to Penn Station and crawled home to Montauk one more time. The whole way home I kept trying to solve the same riddle. *What can I do to make this right?*

Chapter 43

FENTON HOISTED HIS GLASS and toasted my sudden exit from the fast lane. "You did good, my son. You've come back down to our level, maybe a little lower."

"We missed you," said Hank. "Welcome back to the real world."

It was Friday night at the Memory Motel. The membership of the Townie Benevolent Association was present and accounted for, and with the date set for the inquiry, there was a certain defiant joie de vivre.

In this group, my unemployment was hardly cause for sympathy. Despite the biggest economic boom in history and the fact that an obscene amount of that money was being frittered away in our backyard, very little was trickling down to us.

As we compared notes, it became clear we were all on

the same blacklist. We weren't paranoid, either: somebody *was* out to get us.

"I've been knocking on doors all over town and can't
get a thing," said Hank. "Even places like Gilberto's,
which I know is hiring, won't touch me."

"Some bastard has been cutting my nets," said Fenton.
"Do you know how hard it is to repair a net? Not to mention that I'm afraid to go out on the boat alone."

"My story is even worse," said Marci, "because it in-
volves me. Two weeks ago this parking-space monger on
Georgica Pond commissions me to build the Hamptons'
first authentic maze. Last night he calls and tells me he's
awarding the project to Libby Feldhoffer. He was told
that if he stuck with me, the planning and zoning board
would never approve it."

"Libby Feldhoffer!" said an outraged Molly. "Her
work is so pedestrian."

"I knew you'd be there for me, sweetheart."

"I didn't want to tell you, but this morning someone
canceled their eleven-thirty at the last minute," said
Sammy to a round of boos.

Under the circumstances, I was almost glad to have finally shed my golden-boy bloom. I drained the dregs of
our pitcher and was on my way back with a refill when
Logan, the Friday-night barkeep, handed me a large
manila envelope.

"For me?" I asked. "From who?"

"A guy dropped it off. Said it was for all of you."

"You know him?"

"I've seen him around, Jack. He tried to order a martini once."

I returned to our table. "We've got mail."

I gave the envelope to Molly, and was refilling mugs when she flung it across the table.

"I don't know if I'm up for this whole thing anymore, Jack. Actually, I'm not. This is creepy. It's way beyond creepy. Will you look at this!"

The envelope held six pictures, one of each of us. Fenton sitting on the deck of his trawler at dusk. Sammy drinking coffee in the Soul Kitchen. Me getting off the Beemer in my driveway. The shot of Hank showed him racing across our lawn with a defibrillator. One of Marci with her maze client, just before she got dumped.

In every photo we were shot alone, and from behind. Just to remind us how vulnerable we were. Molly's picture set the standard. It was an extreme close-up of her asleep in bed. The photographer couldn't have been more than a foot away.

Under each picture were numbers: *6-5, 4-3, 10-1, 3-1.* There was no note.

Chapter 44

ABOUT MIDNIGHT a boisterous pack of outsiders spilled into the Memory. The front of the bar, "our" bar, was suddenly awash with strained smiles, fake laughs, and shrill squawking into cell phones.

"What a dive — I love it!" shouted one particularly enthused newcomer. "Fuck you, too," retorted an in-house wit.

"Check this out," said Marci, pointing to a tanned figure sipping a sea breeze at the center of the clamor. "That's Horst Reindorf."

Reindorf, a former professional bodybuilder, had starred in more than a dozen hit movies. His latest, and Neubauer's first foray into film production, *Intergalactic Messenger Boy,* was being released the next Friday in 25,000 theaters. "And there's Dennis Soohoo, who plays his Tonto-like sidekick," added Marci as the actors posed for a picture.

"I guess *somebody* around here watches the E! channel," said Sammy.

"Like you don't?" Marci snapped back.

"I don't watch it. I live it."

"Someone at the Beach House probably suggested a great little townie bar," I said. "Told them it would be good for a hoot."

Horst Reindorf had taken his sleeveless T-shirt off and was twirling it over his head. Dennis Soohoo had grabbed a cute girl, who happened to be Gidley's young cousin. Thank God, she pushed him away. One of the entourage's female members climbed up on the bar and started to dance.

"If Barry Neubauer is going to mess with us," said Gidley, "it's time we return the favor. We don't crash his parties. He should know enough not to crash ours."

"I don't think that's such a smart idea," said Molly. "Seriously, Fenton."

"I'm sure you're right," said Gidley as he stood and began working his way through the thicket. Hank, Sammy, and I got up to follow. What choice did we have?

We didn't realize that Gidley was preparing to assault the social summit with as much confidence as Sir Edmund Hillary's assault on Mount Everest. To his right, a party photographer was positioning an executive producer for a candid shot with Reindorf and Soohoo. At the last minute, Gidley squeezed into the viewfinder. He threw a beefy arm around the Dorfmeister.

"I can't believe you're here at the Memory!" Gidley shouted. The subtext was, *where you're not wanted!*

"Excuse me," said the photographer, "we're shooting for *Vanity Fair.*"

"We might as well get one of me and my new best friend," said Horst, with his trademark toothsome grin. "You a fisherman? Smells like it."

"Thank you much, Horst," said Fenton. "I am a fisherman. Fourth-generation."

"Somebody get this asshole away from Horst," said one of the studio junior executives.

The regulars knew something was up. The room tightened around the celebs and their hangers-on. "Mr. Photographer, could you take two in case one doesn't come out?" said Fenton. "It's not every day you get a picture of yourself beside the phoniest asshole in all of show business. And a friend of the sleazy Neubauers to boot."

The next couple of minutes were a blur. Reindorf grabbed Gidley by the throat. Fenton, his crazed grin gone, came over the top with an unscripted punch, complete with convincing sound effects. He caught the action hero on the bridge of his nose. *Real* blood spattered everywhere.

"My God, what are you doing?" shrieked a shiny black-clad publicist. "That's fucking Horst Reindorf!" In a gesture that was way beyond the call of duty, she threw herself at Fenton and pummeled him so ferociously with her Palm Pilot that Horst was able to retreat and slip out a side door.

The rest of Horst's party were not as fortunate. When the producer grabbed a beer bottle, I tackled him against the bar and held him there. Then Hank squared off with Dennis Soohoo. Down went Soohoo. The biggest mismatch pitted Sammy against a young studio-executive type. Even though the guy was half a foot taller and thirty pounds heavier, Giamalva floored him with an uppercut that would have made Sugar Ray proud.

Someone might have actually gotten hurt if Belnap and Volpi hadn't charged in with their batons out and once again made the Hamptons safe for civilized society. Volpi rubbed it in by cracking a few skulls, and he seemed to enjoy it.

He didn't hit me, but he did ask with a wink, "How's your girlfriend, Jack?"

Chapter 45

THE FIXER had been standing in the shadows of the Mullen garage for an hour when the beam of Jack's single headlight broke through the mist on Ditch Plains Road. He elbowed his muscular partner as the gleaming blue motorcycle slowed in front of the small house. "Here comes the bad boy now."

He watched Jack cut the engine, lower the kickstand, and pull a deep breath of night air into his nostrils. *That little shit is still savoring his victory,* the Fixer thought. His knot of anticipation tightened as Jack pulled off his helmet, lifted the garage door, and wheeled the bike in. He'd been looking forward to this meeting for weeks.

Now Jack was opening the small door on the side of the garage, and the Fixer was counting down from three. When Jack stepped through it, he walked directly into the Fixer's black-gloved fist.

To the Fixer, a well-timed sucker punch was one of

life's great unsung pleasures. He loved the way it delivered shock and hurt in one exploding instant, and when the Muscle grabbed Jack from behind and pulled him up by his hair, the Fixer could read the pain register as a ten in Jack's eyes. Then he threw another punch at the center of Jack's face.

With his arms pinned behind him and a knee in the small of his back, all Jack could manage was a flinching twist. But it was enough to reduce a direct hit to a glancing blow, and it sent the Fixer stumbling forward until he and Jack stood eye-to-eye in the darkness.

"Give this message to Neubauer. Can you do that for me?" Jack asked. Then he brought his forehead down on the bridge of the Fixer's nose.

The Fixer was leaking blood worse than Jack, which caused him to seriously consider taking out his hunting knife and gutting Mullen in his own garage. Instead, he started working Jack hard with both fists. This was good work, if you could get it.

When Jack stopped moving, the Fixer stopped missing. This greatly improved his spirits. Pretty soon he felt good enough to deliver a message, his words supplying a rhythm to his fury.

"Don't you ever" — PUNCH — "ever" — PUNCH — "fuck with people who are your superiors in every" — PUNCH — "fucking way," he advised.

The Fixer had some more things he badly needed to get off his chest, but by then Jack was close to unconscious.

"As for Mr. Neubauer, you can tell him yourself."

Somehow, somewhere in his consciousness, Jack heard that, and promised himself he would.

But the man with the black driving gloves wasn't quite finished. He pulled Jack's head up by the hair.

Then he whispered in his ear, "Smarten up. Your grand-father's next, bozo. It'll be easy, Jack. He's really old."

Chapter 46

WIN A FIGHT, you think it's the world's most exciting sport. Lose, badly, and you realize what a fool you were. Once I'd peeled my face off the garage floor and done an inventory of the damage, I knew I had to get myself to the hospital.

I was thinking I'd have to wake up Mack or call Hank, but when I got to my feet, I felt I could manage it on my own, which seemed preferable. I did go in and check on Mack. He was sleeping like an eighty-six-year-old baby.

I got the key and drove my father's old truck to the emergency room in Southampton. Even at four in the morning, it took me about thirty-five minutes.

There's not a lot of mayhem at our end of Long Island. Southampton isn't East St. Louis. When I walked into the ER, Dr. Robert Wolco put down his *New York Times* crossword puzzle and turned his attention to my face. "Hey, Jack," he said, "long time, no see."

"Hey, Robert," I managed. "You should see the other guy."

"I'll bet."

"I'd rather not."

He began by very gingerly and thoroughly cleaning my wounds. Then he laid me down under a bright orange light, shot my face full of Novocain, and stitched it closed. The skin on my face felt as if it were being laced up like hockey skates. It took twenty-eight stitches.

Wolco thought that he had done some of his best work and that the scars would heal nicely. I wasn't too worried. I never had the looks in the family anyway. He gave me a plastic tub of Vicodin for my ribs (X rays showed that three of them were cracked) and sent me home. The night, the beating, was one more thing I owed Barry Neubauer.

And I *was* counting.

Chapter 47

THINGS WERE GETTING TIGHT. The inquest concerning Peter Mullen's death was almost there.

On Monday night the Fixer parked about a block down the street from a modest-looking house in Riverhead, Long Island. There was a terra-cotta planter on the porch and an antique weather vane on the garage. Beside the retro-looking mailbox with J. DAVIS painted across it in childlike yellow script, a stone rabbit was perched on its hind legs. *Yikes.*

For this little slice of heaven, the doc spent fourteen hours a day elbow-deep in stiffs, coming up with all sorts of creative theories about how they got that way. Davis's civic-mindedness baffled the Fixer. She could be pulling down a million per in Manhattan. Instead, she was poking around in cadavers.

Why do people do this? Why do they care if someone drowned or got sunk? They probably watch too many movies. Everyone wants to be a hero. Well, guess what, Jane? You're no Julia Roberts. Trust me on this one.

He knew the doc's loyal pooch would be showing the effects of the yummy treat he'd slipped through the brass newspaper slot at the bottom of the door — another corny retro touch — a few hours earlier. She wasn't much of a watchdog now, lying on her side and snoring to beat the band.

The Fixer quietly let himself in, stepped over the dog, and walked up the stairs toward Jane Davis's bedroom.

This, he was thinking, *this is why I get paid the big bucks.*

Jane was sleeping, too. *Yeah, Janie, you do snore.* She lay on top of the sheets in her bra and panties. Not a lot up top, the Fixer noted, but decent legs for a doc.

He sat down next to her on the bed and watched her breathe. *Christ, she sleeps like the dead.*

He touched his hand down between her legs, and that got her up in a hurry. All full of piss and vinegar, too.

"Hey! What the hell? Who are you?" she screeched, and raised her fists as if she wanted to fight.

But then she saw the gun, and the silencer attached to the long barrel.

"You're a very smart woman, a doctor, so you know what this is about, don't you?"

She nodded, then whispered, "Yes."

"There's going to be an inquest soon, and you've already been overruled by one of your superiors. That should make it real easy for you."

Then he did something naughty — the Fixer pressed the barrel of his gun between Jane Davis's legs. He rubbed it around. Well, it worked for him.

"You *owe* me, Jane," he said, and rose from her bed. "Don't make me come back here. Because I'd like to do you. And, Jane, I wouldn't call the police, either. They're in on this, too. Call the police, and I'll be back real soon."

He left her bedroom, and she listened to him walk back downstairs. She finally took a breath. But then she heard the silenced pistol cough once.

She knew what the bastard had done, and Jane was crying as she hurried downstairs.

He was still there in her house, grinning, and he hadn't shot Iris after all.

"You *owe* me, Jane."

Chapter 48

FIRST THEY MURDER YOU. Then they slander you.
That was my "breakfast revelation of the day" when I
spread out the Star beside my omelette at Estia. I sighed,
shook my head, and felt sad again. Sad and really shitty.

Peter was featured in another bold, fourteen-point
headline, but the story had spun 360 degrees out of control. Now we had a second opinion about how Peter died:
POLICE SUSPECT RIVAL DRUG DEALERS IN MULLEN'S DEATH.

The lead paragraph elaborated: "A bitter battle over
turf or a drug deal gone awry are two possibilities that police are pursuing in their ongoing investigation into the
death of twenty-one-year-old Montauk native Peter
Mullen, according to East Hampton Chief Detective
Frank Volpi."

Mack was right. Life is war.

Volpi also said that there was the possibility Peter
Mullen was under the influence of drugs at the time of his

death and that a request had been made for further tests to determine if that was the case. "We have requested tests to detect the presence of cocaine, alcohol, or marijuana in the victim's blood," said Volpi, "and should have them completed in time for the inquiry."

Neubauer's lawyers were employing the same strategy that had worked so well with O. J. Simpson and so many others. Put enough semiplausible scenarios out there and it becomes almost impossible to conclude that there isn't reasonable doubt.

I borrowed the phone and finally got the *Star*'s editor on the line. "Who is feeding you these stories?" I asked. "It's Volpi, isn't it?"

"No one is feeding us anything. We're reporting everything relevant. That's what newspapers do, Mr. Mullen."

"Bullshit. Why don't you try reporting the truth for a change?"

When the two-bit editor hung up, I called again and asked to speak to Burt Kearns, the reporter who'd written the earlier stories.

"You can't talk to Burt Kearns. Kearns was fired three days ago."

Then the editor hung up on me again.

Chapter 49

THINGS GOT EVEN WORSE later that morning. I was on a roll — backwards.

I took one look at Nadia Alper's littered desk and did my best to conceal my alarm. Alper was the assistant district attorney assigned to the inquiry. The condition of her office, tucked away in an upper floor of the former Seaford Town Hall, didn't communicate a high level of organization or readiness. Every inch of her desk was strewn with police and coroner reports, phone books, notepads, cassettes, and crinkled Subway fast-food wrappers.

As she rummaged through papers, tiny columns of dust sifted through the sunlight tilting through the windows.

"I know it's here," insisted Nadia. "I was looking at it a minute ago."

"Are you handling this completely on your own?" I

asked as calmly as possible. Neubauer had a lockstepping army of five-hundred-dollar-an-hour Ivy League attorneys protecting him like a Kevlar vest. Peter, it appeared, had one very young, underpaid, overworked assistant district attorney seeking justice for him.

"I also have a detective who's out in Montauk interviewing people right now," she said. "And no, this isn't my first case."

"I didn't mean to suggest . . ."

"It's my third."

We both bemoaned the fact that so much of the evidence pointing to foul play in Peter's death was circumstantial. Our strongest cards, she believed, were Jane's medical report and the photographs of the battered body. She finally unearthed the missing folder, and we reviewed it together. Attached were copies of the X rays revealing the multiple broken bones and skull fractures and the severed vertebrae, and photographs of Peter's lung tissue.

Having just been worked over myself, I had an inkling of what my brother's last minutes must have been like. It made me feel sick all over again.

Buried somewhere inside the paper pile, a phone rang. As she burrowed for it, her elbow knocked over a coffee cup, and it sent a mocha sluice flowing toward the pictures. Before I could scoop them out of the way, several were stained. Careful dabbing with a paper towel undid the damage, but I felt like taking the pictures and going home.

"What can I do to help?" I finally asked.

"Nothing. You're in law school, Mr. Mullen. We're in good shape here. Trust me."

"All right," I said with a sigh. What else could I say? "I could help, though, Nadia. I'll even fetch coffee and sandwiches."

"What happened to your face?" she finally asked. I could tell that her decision was final and that she was trying to change the subject.

"I got beat up. Quite possibly by the same people who killed Peter. Neubauer did this to me."

"Why don't you press charges?" she asked.

I wrinkled my nose, shook my head.

"It looks like you have enough on your plate already."

Chapter 50

SAMMY GIAMALVA was having the nightmare again, the one in which he is falling and falling, all the time bracing himself for an impact that never comes. It was the third time he'd had it in a week, so in some part of his brain, Sammy knew it was a dream.

He opened his eyes to a completely different nightmare. This one was real.

In the chair beside the bed sat a large man, with the small, mean eyes of a pig. He wore a well-cut black suit. His legs were casually crossed, as if he were a guest at a cocktail party. Instead of a drink, he held a gun, which, like his awful smile, he aimed at Sammy.

"Get up, Sammy," the Fixer said. "I need a haircut."

He jabbed the muzzle hard into Sammy's throat, and nudged him down the stairs to the kitchen. Still training the gun on Sammy, the Fixer settled into the large chair facing the long mirror.

With the fingers of his free hand, he poked around in his thinning, light brown hair. "What do you think is a good length for me, Sammy?" he asked. "If I go real short, I look like a Nazi. I grow it longer, I look like an asshole with a comb-over."

"Shorter is better," Sammy tried to say, but his mouth was so dry that it sounded more like a cough.

"You don't sound so sure, Sammy."

"I'm sure." This time Sammy managed to get the words out. He desperately tried to size up his situation. He was remembering what had happened to Peter. Not to mention Fenton Gidley. This guy matched Fenton's description right down to the scar on his cheek.

"I guess you've already figured out I didn't come all the way out to Fag Harbor just to get a haircut."

Sammy just nodded and began to spread out the white plastic poncho for the haircut. He was trying to come up with a plan. Anything that would keep him alive. The man with the nasty eyes was cocky. Maybe that was something to play with.

"Is it because of what happened at the Memory?" Sammy finally spoke again.

"I've already taken care of that. That was no big whup. I'm here about what happened at the beach."

When Sammy responded with a puzzled look, the man said, "Don't look so sad. All we want are the negatives. There's no point pretending anymore. The game's over. I win. You lose."

The guy in his barber chair delivered these last words with an awful finality. This was worse than Sammy had thought. It wasn't about scaring him. It wasn't about the inquiry at all.

"Go ahead," said the Fixer. "I still need a haircut. And I'll take your advice on the length."

Soon the man's hair was falling like a light snow on the plastic tarp spread out beneath the chair, and despite everything, Sammy fell into the calming, competent rhythm of his work. Snip and move and pull. Snip and move and pull. Forget that this guy had a gun in his hand.

A simple phrase pulsed in his head: *Do something or die. Do something or die.*

Sammy concentrated on his work as if his life depended on it, and when the Fixer leaned forward in his chair so Sammy could pull off his plastic poncho, he couldn't help but be impressed. "Now I know why those rich ladies drive all the way out here."

Do something or die.

"One last spot," said Sammy, tapping him lightly on the shoulder. The man chuckled, then he settled back in his chair. When he looked into the mirror, he saw Sammy's right hand blur across his chest.

Goddamnit, he couldn't believe it. Not this puny little fag. Not here — not like this. Oh, Jesus, no.

The slice of the razor was so fast and clean, the Fixer didn't know for sure if his throat had just been cut until he saw a second pink mouth flap open beneath his chin. Then, as the hairdresser reached from behind the chair and pinned his arms with a strength and fury that was the final surprise of his life, the Fixer watched the life gush out of him.

"Who's going to fix this?" were his last five words.

When Sammy released his hug, the large man slid out of the chair onto the plastic tarp on the floor. Sammy took a deep breath and tried to think this mess through. Fast.

Jesus, he'd killed this guy. Nothing he could do about it now.

Once he made up his mind, he went upstairs and packed. Then he went to the garage and siphoned a couple of gallons of Exxon regular from his car. He wetted down the cottage, corner to corner. Then he tossed in a flaming Zippo.

By the time the first pumper truck arrived, that's exactly what was left of Sammy's Soul Kitchen. Zippo.

Chapter 51

I WAS WORKING UP A FEW NOTES to give Nadia Alper when I heard Mack's bellowing voice downstairs. "Jack, come outside. Your girlfriend's here. Pretty as ever, too."

Pauline was barely out of her car when Mack insisted she stay for dinner. About ten minutes later he announced he was abandoning us "lovebirds" to investigate the various offerings of Montauk's more reputable vegetable stands and fishmongers. "You *are* staying for supper," he told Pauline, and she didn't bother to argue.

Two and a half hours later, as the sun was losing its edge, he made his triumphant return. In one hand he held the first local corn of the summer. In the other, three fat swordfish steaks.

"Sal swears on the soul of his mother that he carved these out of a three-hundred-fifty-pounder this morning," boasted Mack.

After unloading his treasure, he cracked open three beers and joined us on the deck, where we brought him up to speed on Pauline's latest discoveries about Barry Neubauer.

After he listened to the dirt, Mack surveyed our respective strengths in food prep. Then he doled out assignments. I headed to the garage to dig up the old hibachi. He and Pauline disappeared into the kitchen.

Just having Pauline around was making everyone happy. For the first time in years, the place felt like a home instead of a dorm for lost boys.

Mack was particularly euphoric. It was as if someone had slipped him a tab of Ecstasy. Every once in a while he'd wander out from the kitchen just to stand beside me and share his affection as I poked the coals.

"I know you're dying to tell me how much you love Pauline, so why don't you get it off your chest?" I said.

"You should see her working on the salad dressing, Jackson. Madame Curie in cutoffs. I strongly urge you to marry this woman. Tonight if possible."

"I haven't even touched her yet."

"Yeah, well, what's that about?"

"Macklin, can I ask you a personal question, just between us? Mullen to Mullen?"

"But, of course. Please do."

"You think these coals are ready?"

"I talk to you of the longings of the human heart and you ask me about coal. Cook the damn fish, Jack. Show how you can do something right."

"I like her, all right?" I finally said in an exasperated voice.

"That's not good enough, Jack. This one deserves more than 'like'!"

"Mack, I know what she deserves."

Thirty minutes later we all sat down on the back porch to a perfect summer dinner.

Everything turned out just right — the swordfish, the corn, the wine. Even Pauline's salad dressing lived up to the hype.

We were all a little laid-back after the meal. I looked at Mack's ragged map of a face. It seemed to be lit from within, like a lantern. Pauline looked more relaxed and lovelier than I'd ever seen her.

Mack drew out Pauline about her childhood in Michigan. She told us that her old man was a retired Detroit cop, and her mother taught English in an inner-city high school. Most of her aunts and uncles were autoworkers.

"How'd your parents meet?" asked Mack, still persistently steering the conversation.

"My *father* is my mother's second husband," said Pauline. "Her first was this big, bad charismatic dude from the old neighborhood named Alvin Craig. Craig was a drag racer, a brawler, always in and out of trouble with the law, and once when he was drinking, he beat up my mother. The last time he tried to do it, she was five months pregnant with me. She called the cops.

"The cop who arrived at the house was a big tough guy, too. He took one look at my mother and asked Alvin if they could talk outside for a little bit. My parents lived in a tiny row house, and for about an hour Alvin and the cop sat on the stoop out front.

"There was no fighting. No yelling. Neither one even raised his voice. When they got up, my father went upstairs, threw his stuff into two suitcases, and left for good. The cop stayed for coffee, and a few months later my mother had a new husband.

"I might never have known the real story except that one day when I was fifteen and acting like a total brat, I called my father an asshole. My mother was furious. She decided it was time I learned how they met and fell in love. They are a sweet couple, actually."

It was an impossible story to top, so Mack didn't even try. But he offered childhood tales of his own, including the time he and his best mate, Tommy McGoey, hopped a lorry and spent three days walking around Dublin, sleeping under wagons and living on stolen milk and rolls, mesmerized by everything they laid their eyes on. Pauline had inspired him to dredge up stories that were new even to me.

That's the kind of serenely magical night it was, when friendship feels as solid as family, and family as light and untroubled as friendship. I suppose it was too sweet to last. Just before midnight we heard a car door slam in the driveway. Then the sound of shoes scraping on the gravel.

When I turned to look, Dana was walking toward us like a long blond ghost.

"Ah, speak of the devil," said Mack.

Chapter 52

FOR THIRTY EXCRUCIATING SECONDS, the eye contact around the table was as fast and furious as a Kabuki drama.

"Don't all act too excited to see me," Dana said finally. She turned toward the dark-haired stranger.

"I'm Dana. Jack's girlfriend. I think."

"Pauline."

After extending an urgent conciliatory shrug toward Pauline, I turned to my self-described girlfriend.

"Pauline's a very good friend from Nelson, Goodwin and Mickel," I said, and regretted it instantly.

"Where I understand you're no longer employed."

"They offered me a golden parachute."

"So, what do you do there?" Dana asked Pauline. "Are you a lawyer?"

"I'm an investigator," said Pauline, her voice flat and neutral.

"What do you investigate?"

"You sound like an investigator yourself," said Pauline, the warmth and openness of the evening a memory now.

"Sorry, just trying to make a little awkward conversation."

As for Mack, he still hadn't said a word. To make it absolutely clear which side of the fence he was on, he hadn't even looked at Dana. He hadn't looked at me, either, but I didn't have to see his face to know how upset he was, and that he considered this my fault.

Pauline, having sat through enough of this bad soap opera, rose to leave. "Dinner was delicious," she said, smiling at Mack. "So was everything else."

"You were the best part of it by far, Paulie girl," said Mack, standing and giving her a long hug. "Let me walk you to your car."

"You don't have to leave," I said.

"Oh, but I do," said Pauline.

Then she and Mack took off, arm in arm, almost as if Dana and I weren't there.

"Let me walk with you, Pauline," I said. "Please. I need to talk to you."

"No," said Pauline, without turning to face me. "You stay and talk to your girlfriend. I'm sure you two have a lot to catch up on."

Chapter 53

"I HOPE I DIDN'T INTERRUPT ANYTHING," Dana said. Her mouth was in a pout, but her eyes were smiling slyly.

"Yeah, right. What are you doing here, Dana?"

"Well, you can't expect a girl to give up without a fight," she said with one of her more charming, self-effacing smiles.

"You haven't seen or spoken to me in two months. It was your idea, remember?"

"I know that, Jack. I was in Paris. And Florence. Barcelona. I needed some time to think."

"So, Dana, what did you figure out in Europe? That you don't like yourself as much as you thought you did?"

"You've put me in an impossible position, Jack. You, or my father."

"A no-brainer, obviously. Daddy treated you to Europe, right?"

"Sometimes you don't know what you're talking about, Jack. My father is a wonderful man in many ways. He's great to my mom. He's blindly supported me in anything I've ever tried to do. Plus he's my goddamned dad. What do you want from me?" Her filial loyalty actually made me miss my own father.

"So, what brings you here tonight?"

"You," said Dana, staring at me intently. "I missed you even more than I thought I would. You *are* special, Jack."

When she touched my arm, I almost jumped.

"God, you hate me, don't you?" Tears welled in her eyes. "Oh, Jack. Don't you have anything to say to me?"

"I guess you've heard about the inquiry," I said.

Her head jerked back, the blond hair flying.

"I can't believe anyone really thinks my family had anything to do with Peter's death. Do you, Jack? What makes you even think Peter was murdered?"

"His body was covered with bruises, Dana. He was beaten on your beach. I wish you'd seen him."

"A lot of people think the storm could have done that."

I still couldn't quite believe Dana had gone completely over to the other side. Still, I knew it would be insane to share any of the hard work Pauline and I had done over the past two months.

"Dana, you weren't around when I really needed you, and I *did* need you," I told her.

Tears were still running down her cheeks. "I'm sorry, Jack. What do I have to do to prove it to you?"

"You said some things before you left. Then you never called or wrote. Not even a postcard. Now you just show up here?"

She wiped her face. "Jack, let's go someplace. We

could get a room. At the Memory. Please, I need to talk to you."

She reached out and put her arms around me. It felt way beyond wrong. I pulled away.

"I'm not going to the Memory, Dana. I think you should leave."

Dana folded her arms and stared at me angrily. The transformation was quite amazing.

"So who is she, Jack? The bitch who was here before?"

"A very good friend. She's helping me with the case. That reminds me, how's Volpi?"

Dana flinched, then jumped up out of her chair. She wasn't sniffling anymore. Now she was just pissed-off. Daddy's little girl was a lot like Daddy.

Once Dana was gone, I went inside the house, passed a sullen Mack watching the Yankees–Red Sox game, and tried to reach Pauline on her cell phone.

Either she'd turned it off or she wouldn't take my call.

Chapter 54

I TOOK A GUINNESS out to the front porch and watched the late-departing weekenders head back to the city. Soon the Hamptons would be safe again for dreamy-eyed townies. In the meantime, I sat on the cool flagstone and rewound the evening. What a frigging disaster. I even began to wonder if Dana had known Pauline was there. I wouldn't put it past her.

It was getting late, and watching the passing SUVs was like counting sheep. I was fading a little when a police car screeched around the corner against the west-bound traffic.

To my surprise, it turned into our driveway and skidded to a stop. Frank Volpi and a sergeant I didn't recognize hopped out. What the hell?

"Mind if I ask you a couple of questions?" asked Volpi as he reached the porch.

"Does it matter what I think, Frank?"

"Not really. Where have you been tonight?"

"Here. Why?"

"Someone just torched Sammy Giamalva's house to the ground," he said. "Professional. We're pretty sure with him in it."

I felt as if I'd been hit with the kitchen skillet. I thought of the photographs of Sammy in his kitchen — the ones that were dropped off at the Memory. Sammy, with a cigarette in his mouth and a cup of coffee in his hand. It showed a live-wire twenty-three-year-old getting stoked to do something he loved. A portrait of the stylist as a young man.

Then I flashed on the tiny pairs of numbers scribbled in pencil under each photo.

I suddenly realized they were *odds,* and that Sammy's (6–5) were the shortest.

Volpi was still in my face.

"Is there anyone who can confirm you've been here for the last couple of hours?"

"What is it, Frank, you really think I burned down Sammy's house? With my family gone, I'm turning on my friends?" As mad as I was, it was nothing compared to my panic about the danger I'd put my friends in.

"Mind if Officer Jordan and I have a look around?" Volpi asked.

"Actually, I do," I said, but Jordan was already heading for the garage.

"Hey!" I called. "You can't go in there."

I followed and stood beside him as he pulled up the door and swept his flashlight over the cluttered space. The beam moved slowly over the deep blue sheen of Peter's motorcycle.

"That's one pretty scooter," he said with a smirk. "Almost twenty grand, isn't it?"

"What you're doing here is illegal," I said. "C'mon, huh? Get out of the garage."

He bent to open the immaculate little BMW toolbox. What the hell was he looking for?

I stepped forward and grabbed his arm. "I'd appreciate it if you'd leave right now. Get away from the bike."

Jordan came out of his crouch and jumped into my chest, knocking me back into Frank Volpi, who had followed us into the garage. Volpi immediately grabbed my arms. He let Jordan take it from there.

If the first punch didn't rebreak my almost-healed rib, the second definitely did.

"You're under arrest for interfering with a police investigation and assaulting a police officer," said Volpi. He grinned as he cuffed me and dragged me out to the car. He didn't bother to read me my rights, and I got the message: *I didn't have any.*

Chapter 55

"WAKEE, WAKEE."

A tin cup rattling over steel bars startled me from a dream in which I was trying to save Peter and Sammy. I jumped up and frantically scanned the cell. Then I saw Mack's shit-eating grin, the small grease-stained paper bag under his arm, and the old metal camping cup in his hand, which he must have spent all morning searching for.

"Get out of bed, you lazy so-and-so. I just bailed you out."

"Good to see you, Macklin. And thanks for that little prison-riot vignette."

I threw on my clothes, and Paul Infante, the cop who'd worked the overnight shift, appeared in front of the cell. He extended a key attached to his belt by a long, thin chain, and the big bolt toppled over with an echoing clang. He pulled the heavy door toward him, and I stepped back out into the world.

"Jack 'Hurricane' Mullen," said Macklin, clapping me on the shoulder. "Not even six hours in the East Hampton Hilton could break this man."

"Can it, Macklin."

Upstairs, Infante gave me an envelope with my watch and wallet in it, and I signed a summons pledging to appear in court for interfering with a police investigation. The assault charge had been dropped.

"We should go visit Sammy's mom this afternoon," Mack said somberly. "We're the only ones who know how she feels."

"I suppose they're going to say that was an accident, too," I said. "Maybe a suicide." I described the visit from Volpi and Jordan, how unbelievably brazen and cocky they'd been.

"Can they get away with it?" I asked him.

"Sure. Looks like they just did."

As I pulled out of the driveway, I plucked the bag of Dreesen's doughnuts off Mack's lap. There were three inside — dark, soft, and sprinkled with cinnamon. If it's possible, I think spending my first night in jail made them taste even better.

"So, tell me something," said Mack, snatching the last doughnut before it reached my lips, "you still feel like the man who's going to bring the goddamned system to its knees?"

Chapter 56

I WAS ABOUT TO FIND OUT. The inquiry into my brother's death was held in the gymnasium of the Montauk Middle School. They couldn't have picked a worse spot. For years Peter and I used to play Sunday pickup games there. Every Sunday. Walking to my seat with Mack, I could still hear the deep *smack* of basketballs echoing off the whitewashed cinder block.

As I took a seat, I remembered the very first weekend we ever snuck inside the gym as kids. Fenton got hold of a key, and after stashing our bikes in the woods, we crowded around him as he slipped it into the lock. Miraculously, it fit. We stepped through the small side door into the hushed, voluminous darkness more awed than if we'd just snuck into St. Patrick's Cathedral. Hank found the switch, and the entire trespassed interior, with its gleaming hardwood floor and white fiberglass backboards, lit up like a Technicolor dream.

On the morning of the inquest, at least two hundred folding chairs were set up in long rows across the court. The people who sat in them had all been there before, as either graduating students or proud parents, or both.

Marci had saved Mack and me the last two seats in the front row. I looked around and saw Fenton and Molly, Hank and his wife, an incredible number of friends from town. But not poor Sammy Giamalva, of course. We didn't have to wait very long for the action to begin.

"Hear ye! Hear ye!" proclaimed the bailiff who had driven up that morning from Riverhead. "All persons having business before the Supreme Court of Suffolk County, please give your attention to the Honorable Judge Robert P. Lillian."

In his stark black robe, the judge looked like a commencement-day speaker. He entered the gym from the small cafeteria directly behind it and took his elevated seat. Spectatorwise, it may have been a local crowd, but at the business end, the manpower balance tilted heavily in the opposite direction. Sitting shoulder to shoulder at a long, thin table facing the judge were three Nelson, Goodwin and Mickel senior partners, led by none other than Bill Montrose. Sitting behind them, like proud sons, were three of the firm's most promising associates.

At the opposing table sat twenty-four-year-old assistant district attorney Nadia Alper. And four empty chairs. Alper sucked at a jumbo Coke and jotted notes on a yellow pad.

"She doesn't even have a cut man," observed Mack.

Lillian, a short, sturdy man in his late fifties, informed us from his judicial pulpit that although there was no defendant, the daylong inquest would proceed like a juryless trial. Witnesses would be called to testify under oath; limited cross-examination would be permitted as he deemed relevant. In other words, he was God.

Lillian turned the floor over to Neubauer's legal team, and Montrose summoned one Tricia Powell, a blowsy, dark-haired woman in her twenties.

I had never seen Powell before, and wondered where she fit in.

With Montrose's guidance, Tricia Powell testified that she had been a guest at the Neubauers' Memorial Day weekend party. Near the end of the evening she had strolled down to the water.

"See anyone on your walk?" questioned Montrose.

"Not until I got to the beach," said Powell. "That's when I saw Peter Mullen."

I flinched in my seat. This was the first indication in two months that anyone had seen Peter after his dinner break. It sent a ripple of whispers through the gym.

"What was he doing when you saw him?" asked Montrose.

"Staring into the waves," said Powell. "He looked sad."

"Did you know who he was?"

"No, but I recognized him as the man who had parked my car. Then, of course, I saw his picture in the paper."

"What happened that night? Tell us exactly what you saw."

"I smoked a cigarette and started to head back. But as I did, I heard a splash and turned to see Peter Mullen swimming through the waves."

"Did that strike you as unusual?"

"Oh, absolutely. Not only because of the size of the

waves, but also how cold the water was. I had stuck my
toe in and was shocked."

So was I. This woman, whoever she was, was lying
her ass off. I leaned toward Nadia Alper and whispered a
quick message.

When Montrose finished, Alper got up to question
Powell.

"How is it that you know Barry Neubauer?" she asked.

"We're colleagues," she said, cool as could be. I
wanted to go up there and slap her.

"You're also in the toy business, Ms. Powell?"

"I work in the Promotions Department at Mayflower
Enterprises."

"In other words, you work *for* Barry Neubauer."

"I like to think we're friends, too."

"I'm sure you will be now," said Nadia Alper.

The derisive laughter in the gym was cut off by a sharp
reprimand from Lillian. "I trust, Ms. Alper, that I will not
have to ask you again to refrain from editorial asides."

She turned back to the witness. "I have a list here of
everyone who was invited to the party that evening. Your
name isn't on that list, Ms. Powell. Any idea why?"

"I met Mr. Neubauer at a meeting a couple of days before. He was kind enough to invite me."

"I see, and what time did you arrive?" asked Nadia.

"Unfashionably early, I confess. Seven o'clock,
maybe five after at the latest. With all the celebrities, I
didn't want to miss a minute."

"And it was Peter Mullen who parked your car?"

"Yes."

"You're absolutely positive, Ms. Powell?"

"Positive. He was . . . memorable."

Alper went to her desk, grabbed a folder, and approached the bench. "I would like to submit to the court written statements from three of Peter Mullen's coworkers that evening. They state that the deceased got to work at least forty minutes late. Therefore, it was impossible for him to have parked Ms. Powell's or anyone else's car before seven-forty."

The crowd stirred again. The whispers got louder. People were clearly angry. "Do you have any explanation for this discrepancy, Ms. Powell?" asked the judge.

"I thought he parked my car, Your Honor. I suppose it's possible I saw him at some other point in the party. He was very good looking. Maybe that's why his face stuck out in my mind."

There was so much commotion as Nadia Alper returned to her seat that Lillian had to bang his gavel and ask for quiet again.

"Alper's got some brass," said Mack in my ear. "I'd score that round a draw."

Chapter 57

THIS WAS EXCRUCIATING.

I wanted to be the one handling the cross-examination, objecting to Bill Montrose's every sentence, his blasé attitude, even his goddamned blue cashmere blazer and gunmetal gray slacks. He looked as though he was on his way to the Bath & Tennis Club as soon as this trifling matter was finished.

Montrose's next witness was Dr. Ishier Jacobson, who had quit his position as Los Angeles County coroner a decade ago when he realized he could do five times as well as an expert witness.

"Dr. Jacobson, how long did you serve as chief pathologist at Cook Claremont Hospital in Los Angeles?"

"Twenty-one years, sir."

"And in that time, Doctor, approximately how many drowning victims were you called upon to examine?"

"A great many, I'm sorry to say. Los Angeles–area

beaches are extremely active and crowded with surfers. In my tenure, I looked into over two hundred drownings."

Montrose gleamed up at Judge Lillian, then back at Dr. Jacobson.

"So it is no exaggeration to say that this is an area in which you have an exceptional level of expertise."

"I believe I've examined more drowning victims than any active pathologist in the United States."

"And what were your conclusions concerning the death of Peter Mullen?"

"First of all, that he drowned. Second, that his death was either an accident or a suicide."

It's not as if I didn't know how easily expert testimony can be purchased. If the client can afford to, he can always fly in a second opinion to forcefully contradict whatever the prosecution is putting out. The injuncture, the lawyer's artifice, just seems a little different when the murder victim is your brother.

"How do you explain the condition of the body, Dr. Jacobson? Pictures taken of the deceased after he washed ashore indicate that he was badly bruised and there's been speculation that he was beaten."

"As you know, a storm was passing through the Hamptons that weekend. In that kind of surf, a badly bruised corpse is the rule, not the exception. I've examined dozens of drowning victims where foul play was never a question. Believe me, they looked at least as battered as Peter Mullen did that night. Some were worse."

"That's total bullshit," said Hank, leaning over the back of our seats. "This guy is sickening. Bought and paid for."

Montrose continued with the charade. He was sickening, too. "As you know, I asked you to bring some pictures of previous victims to illustrate this point. Could you share these with the court, Dr. Jacobson?"

Jacobson held up two pictures, and Montrose, as if he hadn't seen them before, winced. "Both of the surfers were approximately the same age as Mr. Mullen," he said. "As you can see they are almost as badly bruised as Mr. Mullen, and as I recall, the conditions were not nearly as severe."

Montrose carried the photographs to the judge, who placed them beside the statement he had received from Alper.

"Is there anything else you found in the records that could shed light on his tragic death?" asked Monty.

Jacobson nodded. "The autopsy revealed significant traces of marijuana in his bloodstream, as if he had inhaled one or maybe two marijuana cigarettes shortly before entering the water."

"Your Honor," interrupted Alper, "this shameless effort to taint the reputation of the *victim* has been going on since he died. When does it stop?"

"Please, Ms. Alper," said the judge, "sit down and wait your turn."

"Why might this marijuana be relevant, Dr. Jacobson?" asked Montrose.

"Recent studies have shown that immediately after using marijuana, the risk of heart failure increases dramatically. Add to that a water temperature in the low fifties, and it becomes a real possibility. I believe that's exactly what happened here."

"Thank you, Dr. Jacobson. I have no further questions."

Chapter 58

THIS WHOLE THING was suddenly too much for me to take. If I had been the DA, I would have cross-examined Dr. Jacobson until he was bleeding from every orifice. I would have asked him to tell the court how many days of expert testimony he had billed Nelson, Goodwin and Mickel in the past five years (forty-eight), what his daily rate ($7,500) and per diem ($300) were, and to name his favorite restaurant in New York (Gotham Bar & Grill, most expensive entrée, veal esplanade, $48).

To belabor the point, I'd ask if those forty-eight days qualified him for Nelson, Goodwin and Mickel's pension plan (no), if he got to keep his bonus miles (also no), and if he had ever delivered an expert opinion other than the ones he was paid for (of course not).

Nadia Alper chose not to pursue this hard line of questioning. Maybe she assumed that Lillian would have cut her off. Perhaps she thought that the sooner we got our own expert on the stand, the better. Whatever the reasons, the gym swelled with righteous indignation when she called Dr. Jane Davis to the stand.

At last we were going to listen to testimony that hadn't been bought, and Montauk would hear from one of its own. This was why we had come to this inquest — to hear the truth for a change.

Even Nadia Alper looked in better spirits as she asked, "Dr. Davis, please tell us your role in this investigation."

"I am the pathologist for Huntington Hospital and chief medical examiner for Suffolk County," Jane said.

"So, unlike Dr. Jacobson, you actually examined Peter Mullen's body, is that correct?"

"Yes."

"How many hours did you devote to his examination?"

"Over sixty."

"Is that more than usual?"

"I grew up in Montauk and I know the Mullen family, so I was particularly thorough," said Jane.

"What evidence did you consider?" asked Alper.

"In addition to an extensive physical examination of the corpse, I took multiple X rays, and sampled and compared lung tissue."

"And according to your report, which I have in my hand, you concluded that Mr. Mullen did not drown at all but was beaten to death. To quote from your report, 'Peter Mullen's death was the result of multiple blows to the neck and head with fists, feet, or other blunt instruments. X rays show two completely severed vertebrae, and the level of saturation of the lung tissue indicates the victim had stopped breathing well before he reached the water.' "

"Those were my findings," said Davis, who seemed nervous and now drew a deep breath. "But upon further consideration and soul-searching, and the benefit of Dr. Jacobson's extensive experience, I've concluded that those initial findings were incorrect, that the evidence does point toward drowning. I realize now that my judgment was compromised by my closeness to the family of the deceased."

As Jane Davis delivered this last bit of devastating testimony, her voice was paper thin and she seemed to shrivel up on the stand. She left Alper standing there twisting in the wind. She was speechless. I couldn't believe what I'd just heard, either. Neither could the crowd in the gym. Heads were swiveling everywhere.

"How much did they pay you, darling?" asked a woman whose son had been in Peter's class.

"I hope it was more than they paid Dr. Jacobson," shouted Bob Shaw, who owns the deli on Main. "He didn't have to sell out his friends."

"Leave her alone," Macklin finally spoke from his seat. "They got to her. They threatened her. Hell, can't you see that?"

Lillian pounded his gavel and yelled for quiet, and when that had no effect, he announced a one-hour recess.

In the near riot, Jane Davis had already left the stand. I ran after Jane, but her car was tearing out of the rear lot.

Chapter 59

MACK AND I STAGGERED out of the gym for the recess. At the side parking lot we took refuge on a small bench. I felt as if I'd just taken another beating, only this was worse than the others.

"You've probably learned more in the last two hours than in two years at your Ivy League law school," said Mack. "Unless they're offering tutorials on witness tampering, bribery, and physical intimidation. Maybe they should."

Mack looked out at the lovely August morning and spat between his shapeless black brogans. In a lot of ways this was an idyllic scene. A nice, well-maintained little school, green playing fields up the wazoo. It was the kind of spot TV stations like to send camera crews to on election mornings. Capture the picturesque machinery of democracy at work. Film the local people filing into their small-town gymnasium in their heavy work boots, stepping behind the curtain to cast their votes.

When you come to the same gym on a morning like this, you realize something is going on that isn't pretty, isn't idyllic, and certainly isn't democratic. *It's the Big Lie, the White Noise, the Matrix.*

Marci spotted us on the bench and came over for a smoke. "Those New York City folks don't take any prisoners, do they?" she said, holding out her pack. I shook my head. "Sure? It's a great day for a life-shortening habit," said Marci.

When I was a student looking out at this same parking lot, it was usually empty except for a modest row of cars belonging to the teachers. As I looked now, a Mercedes sedan slowly circled the blacktop. Long and silver with blacked-out windows, it finally stopped twenty yards from us.

Burly, dark-suited men hopped out of the front. They hustled to open the rear doors.

In a flash of long white legs and blond hair, Dana stepped out. She was tugging on her dark dress, and I have to admit, she looked as good as ever. Around the other side of the car came her father. He looked great, too. All-powerful and all-knowing. He took her hand, and with the bodyguards deployed front and back, the two walked toward the gym.

"Why, it's your old girlfriend," said Mack. "I must have pegged her wrong, because here she is to show her support for you and your brother."

Chapter 60

MARCI STUBBED OUT HER CIGARETTE, and we followed the Neubauers and their bodyguards back into the gym. Judge Lillian was attempting to call the room to order. He banged his gavel several times, and the Montauketeers cut off their bitter discussions and trudged back to their metal chairs.

They were just settling in when Montrose called Dana Neubauer to the stand. My stomach sank.

"God in heaven," mumbled Mack. "What could she have to say?"

Dana walked solemnly to the stand. As I said, she looked particularly stunning that morning. In retrospect, I realize she also looked substantial, serious, and totally credible.

"Did you know the deceased, Peter Mullen?" Montrose asked.

"Yes, I knew Peter very well," she said.

"For how long?"

"I've been coming here every summer for twenty-one years. I met Peter and the rest of his family early on."

"I'm sorry to have to ask this, Dana, but were you ever intimately involved with Peter Mullen?"

Dana nodded.

"Yes."

There was some murmuring, but, overall, the room was still reeling from all the other testimony. I knew about Dana and Peter by then, but I hated to hear it in open court.

"How long did the relationship last?" he asked.

"About six months," said Dana, shifting uncomfortably in her witness chair.

Montrose sighed, as if this was as hard for him as it was for Dana. "Were you involved at the time of his death?"

Oh, Jesus, I was thinking, *this just keeps getting worse.*

"We had just broken up," said Dana, looking in my direction. I knew it was a lie. At least, I thought it was. But when I tried to catch her eye, she looked back at Montrose.

"How recently?" he asked. "I know this is hard for you."

"That night," said Dana in a stage whisper, "the night of the party."

"What a wonderful girl you got there, Jack," said Mack without bothering to look over at me.

Dana flashed me another fearful look and started to cry softly. I stared back in awe. Who was this woman on the stand? Was *any* of this true?

"Peter took it really badly," she resumed. "He started acting crazy. He broke a lamp in the house, knocked over a chair, and stormed out. He called an hour later and told me I was making a big mistake, that the two of us had to be together. I knew he was upset, but I never thought that he'd do anything rash. If you knew Peter, you wouldn't have believed it, either. He acted like nothing ever really got to him. Obviously, I was wrong. I'm so sorry about what happened."

Then Dana put her head down and sobbed into her hands.

"Brava!" Gidley called from a few rows behind. "Bravissima!" Then he jumped up and began clapping wildly for Dana's breathtaking performance.

Chapter 61

A GOOD FRIEND OF MINE once spent a summer interning at a New York TV news station. The anchorman liked him and over a beer offered the secret to on-air success. "The whole thing in this business," said the anchor, "is sincerity. Once you learn how to fake that, the rest is easy."

Barry Neubauer followed Dana to the stand. Neubauer's specialty wasn't feigning empathy but projecting CEO-ness. Every detail of his presentation, from the cut of his charcoal suit to the tilt of his jaw to his full head of gray hair, reinforced the message that here was a man who was your superior.

"Mr. Neubauer," Nadia Alper began, "according to a bartender who was setting up at your place the afternoon before the party, you and Mrs. Neubauer engaged in a lengthy and nasty argument. Could you tell us what the argument was about?"

"I do recall a spat," said Neubauer with a shrug, "but I don't remember it as being particularly serious. In fact, I have no clear recollection of what it was about. Probably just pre-party anxiety. I suspect that bartender hasn't been married for twenty-seven years."

"Would it jog your memory, Mr. Neubauer, if I told you that the same bartender heard you say the name Peter Mullen several times in the course of the argument, often with an expletive attached?"

Neubauer frowned as he strained to recall the incident.

"No, I'm sorry, it wouldn't. I can't imagine any circumstances in which his name would come up in an argument between Campion and myself. Peter Mullen has been a friend of the family for as long as I can remember. We consider his death, whatever the exact circumstances, extremely tragic. I've extended my condolences to the Mullen family. I visited his older brother, Jack, at the law firm where he worked and spoke to him at length."

As a witness, Neubauer had what might be described as perfect pitch. His erect posture, steady gaze, deep voice, and slow, thoughtful delivery all combined to create an impression of absolute credibility. To judge his responses as anything less than the truth seemed cynical and conspiratorial.

Alper persisted. To her credit, she didn't seem afraid of him. "Could you recall your activities on the day Mr. Mullen died?"

"I screened some dailies in the morning and played eighteen holes rather badly at Maidstone in the afternoon. Then Campion and I got ourselves ready for the party."

"Could you tell us what you were doing at about ten-thirty that night, the time that Mr. Mullen died?"

"I was in an upstairs den on the phone," said Neubauer, without hesitation. "This I remember very well."

Nadia Alper tilted her head in surprise. So did Mack and I.

"Is there a reason, Mr. Neubauer, why you remember a phone call so vividly yet have no recollection about a fight with your wife?"

Nothing seemed to shake Barry Neubauer. "For one thing, it was a very long call, a little more than an hour. I even remember feeling very guilty about being away from our guests for so long."

"He's just a goddamned caring human being," said Macklin under his breath.

"Do you have any proof of the call?"

"Yes, I've brought a copy of the phone bill. It shows a seventy-four-minute call from three past ten to eleven-seventeen P.M." Neubauer passed the record to Alper.

"Could you tell us who you were talking to, Mr. Neubauer?" asked Alper.

When Neubauer hesitated slightly, Montrose barked, "Objection."

Both attorneys looked toward Lillian.

"Overruled," said the judge. "Please answer the question."

"Robert Crassweller Junior," said Neubauer. The slightest trace of a smile crossed his lips. "The attorney general of the United States," he said.

This final answer drained whatever energy and tension remained in the courtroom. Some spectators got up and left, as if this was an Islander game and the fat lady had just sung. Barry Neubauer's eyes casually roamed the audience. When he found me, he offered up a lazy smile. *Amateur hour is over, boys.*

After a few more questions, Nadia Alper excused Neubauer. Then both lawyers informed the court that they had presented their list of witnesses.

Judge Lillian made a show of adjusting his robes before somberly addressing the court.

"Normally," said Lillian, "I would withhold my decision until the morning. In this case, however, I can't think of anything that requires further reflection. It is the finding of this inquiry court that on May twenty-ninth, Peter Mullen drowned by accident or suicide. This inquest is now completed, and this court adjourned."

Chapter 62

THE COURT ADJOURNED at about 4:40. When I got to the Shagwong, it was five on the nose. I took a seat at the end of the bar and asked Mike to pour out six shots of Jameson.

Without raising an eyebrow, he grabbed two handfuls of glasses and, with practiced precision, lined them up and filled them to the rims.

"They're on me," he said.

"I would have asked for seven, then," I told him. I smiled for the first time that day.

Mike put down a seventh and filled it also.

"I was joking."

"Me, too."

As Mike laid out my full course of Irish medicine, I saw again that smug little smile Montrose flashed me on his way out of the courtroom. It showed more disgust than joy. Why, he seemed to be asking, was I the only one in the room who couldn't understand that justice is neither a mystery nor a crapshoot, but a major purchase? Spend your money thoughtfully and secretly, you walk free. That was the way it was in America these days. Who knows? Maybe it had always been that way.

Over the next hour and a half to two hours, I steadily worked from left to right. I tossed back shots for each bought witness in the parade of perjurers. I lifted a glass to Tricia Powell, no doubt the Mayflower Employee of the Month, and another for the good Dr. Jacobson, the coroner magician from Los Angeles. Or as Mack described him, "a whore with a résumé."

My old honey Dana rated two shots of Jameson. The first for coming all the way back from Europe just because she missed me. The second for her Oscar-worthy performance that afternoon.

Hardly acknowledging anyone around me, I sipped and stewed until my level of numbness nudged ahead of my rage. I think that happened somewhere around my second Dana shot, my fourth in forty minutes.

Although I'm probably not the most reliable witness, I recall that Fenton and Hank came up and each threw an arm around me but, sensing I wasn't up for a group hug, soon left me to my self-medicating. They were just trying to do the right thing.

When I put in my order I'd counted on a toast for Jane Davis, but by the time her turn came, I was more worried about her than angry. On the way back from the bathroom, I stopped at the pay phone and left a slightly incoherent message on her machine.

"It's not your fault, Jane," I shouted over the din, "it's mine. I never should have gotten you into this mess."

That was when I saw none other than Frank Volpi. He was standing in back, waiting for me to get off the phone. "Congratulations, asshole," he said. Then he grinned and walked away before I could get off a shot.

Back at the bar, I toasted Frank. He'd been there for us from the start, and his performance had been flawless. "Volpi," I said, and drank.

Numero six was for Barry Neubauer himself. The river of whiskey had opened up my poetic side, and I came up with a couplet for the occasion. *Barry Neubauer, scumbag of the hour.*

That was meant to be my last, but thanks to Mike, I had one glistening silver bullet left. I was afraid I was going to have to drink to something vague and amorphous like the System. Then I thought of Attorney General Robert Crassweller Jr. Even I had to hand it to Montrose for the way he set up the big punch line with his phony objection. What panache. He had played Nadia Alper like a Stradivarius. What class! What a winner!

After the last toast, the vertical and horizontal on my picture started to wander. In fact, the whole room was spinning. I treated the problem with a couple of beers. Hair of the dog. Then I made a few attempts to leave Mike a forty-dollar tip. He kept stuffing it back in my shirt pocket until I finally stumbled out the door.

Two blocks later I stopped at a pay phone and called Jane again. That awful look on her face wouldn't go away. I was planning to leave a slightly more intelligible version of my first message when she answered.

"It's okay, Jane," I said.

"No, it's not okay. Jesus, Jack. I'm sorry. *I'm sorry.* They came to my house."

"It wouldn't have made an iota of difference."

"So what!" She sounded hysterical.

Four weekenders walked by and got into a Saab convertible. "Jane, you've got to swear to me you won't do anything stupid."

"Don't worry. But there's something I have to tell you. I didn't before, because I didn't see the point. When I did all those tests on Peter, I also did blood tests. Jack, your brother was HIV-positive."

Chapter 63

THE TWO-MILE WALK and the ocean air did me a world of good. By the time I passed the parking lot for Ditch Plains Beach and cut across my damp lawn, I was close to sober again.

It's something I'll always be grateful for. Sitting on the porch and leaning back against the front door in one of my old tattered sweaters was Pauline.

It was about 10:30. The street and lawn were enveloped in a light ocean mist. It's a weird analogy, and I have no idea why I thought of it, but seeing Pauline blocking my path to the door brought to mind Gary Cooper waiting patiently in the street in *High Noon*. Something about her stillness and her "here I am, what are you going to do about it?" smile.

"You're a sight for sore eyes, Pauline."

"You, too, Jack. I watched from the back of the gym today. Then I drove all the way back to the city. Then I drove all the way back out here. Crazy, huh? Don't try to deny it."

"Did you do something awful that made Macklin kick you out of the house?"

"No."

"You just wanted some fresh air?"

"No."

"Am I getting warm?"

"No."

Most no's aren't too good, but these were about as good as no's could be. I sat on the cool flagstone and leaned back against the red wooden door of our house. I touched Pauline's arm. It felt electric against mine. She took my hand in hers, and my mouth went dry.

"But as I was talking to Macklin, something became really clear to me," she whispered.

"What was that, Pauline?" I whispered back.

"How much I care about you."

I looked at Pauline again and did what I'd probably wanted to do for a long time. I kissed Pauline gently on the lips. Her lips were soft and fit perfectly on mine. We stayed that way for a sweet moment before we pulled back and looked at each other.

"That was worth the wait," I said.

"You shouldn't have waited, Jack."

"I promise I won't wait as long for the next one."

We started kissing again and haven't really stopped since.

Now I appreciate that for those of you who have stayed with me this far, there's nothing too surprising about this romantic development. You probably saw it coming. But I didn't.

Not until I walked across the lawn that night. Not because I didn't want it to happen. I wanted it to happen from the first moment Pauline walked into my tiny office. I wanted it so badly, I was afraid to even hope for it.

"You're a good person. And sweet," Pauline said as we hugged on the front porch.

"Try not to hold it against me."

"I won't." She showed me a blanket she'd brought out from the house.

"Let's go down to the beach, Jack. There's something else I've been wanting to do with you for a long time."

Part Four

THE GRADUATE

Chapter 64

THE SUN SPILLING OUT OVER QUEENS and the East River may not be as symphonic as it is rising out of the Atlantic, but it's nothing to sneeze at. Neither was being able to reach out and slide my arm around Pauline as she slept peacefully beside me. I had thought we would be good together, but I had no idea how good it could be. For the first time in my life, I was in love.

At the end of the summer I abandoned Mack in Montauk and moved in with Pauline on Avenue B. Every day for the next five months I rode the subway to the top of Manhattan to complete my requirements for a degree from Columbia Law School.

Although the summer had dampened my enthusiasm for practicing law, I wasn't simply going through the motions. Inspired by rage and disgust, the way some of my classmates were by ambition, I worked harder than I ever had in my life. The inquest left me perversely intrigued with litigation, and I studied *Trial Techniques* by Thomas Mauet as if it were the Bible. I did the same with *Cases and Materials on Evidence* and *Constitutional Law.*

I worked so hard on all my other course work, too, that when the final grades were posted, I learned I'd graduated third in my class.

Although my employment prospects were murky, I figured I'd earned a break. So while some other third-year students were still jostling for associate positions in white-glove law firms or studying for the bar, I was enjoying life in the East Village. It was a good place to cultivate my soul and try to figure out what an angry, overeducated twenty-nine-year-old should do next.

My unsettled state of mind was compounded by a piece of mail I received from Huntsville, Texas. The Mudman had taken me up on my offer to stay in touch. He sent grim news about the prospect of ever getting his DNA analysis for a retrial. Nothing he had told me, however, prepared me for the next letter I got from him.

The execution date had been set.

Chapter 65

THE FIRST TIME I ever saw the Mudman was on a bitterly cold February morning. It was shortly before he was put to death by the state of Texas. We were separated by a Plexiglas window between the viewing room and the death chamber.

Pauline and I had flown to Dallas the morning before, rented a car, and made the three-hour drive to Huntsville. At the last minute prison officials rescinded their permission for a private visit. Since we were on the Mudman's personal visitor list, we were permitted to view the execution.

Along with the great aunt of the victim and an even more elderly prison reporter who sat beside us on the three-plank viewing stand, we didn't see the Mudman until after his wheelchair was rolled into the death chamber just before 8:00 A.M.

The Mudman had been on death row for twenty years.

They'd taken a terrible toll. The last photograph I had seen of the six-three former bouncer was almost twenty-one years old now, and although he was still a huge man and close to three hundred pounds, he was a prematurely old one. His long hair and beard had gone stone white. Degenerative arthritis in his hips had put him in a wheelchair three years before.

As the warden and prison chaplain looked on, a guard placed a pair of reading glasses on the Mudman. Then the guard held a piece of paper level with the Mudman's chest. Although he was somewhat sedated, he proceeded to read.

"This prison and my government," he said in his surprisingly high-pitched voice, "has already taken the best years of my life. This morning they will take everything I have left. They will commit a murder. God have mercy on their souls."

He turned his head and saw me in the front row. He gave me a grateful smile, and it had a gentleness that touched me deeply. I had to choke back a sob, and Pauline grabbed my arm.

The next minutes proceeded with nightmarish momentum. As sheets of freezing rain pelted the corrugated roof, the chaplain read the Twenty-third Psalm. Then guards hoisted the Mudman out of his chair and onto the gurney.

His white-haired frailty, the prison-issue wheelchair, and the practiced diligence of the guards combined to give the misleading impression that we were witnessing a medical procedure that would make a sick man well. That impression was reinforced when an orderly pushed up the white sleeve on Mudman's massive right arm. He found a vein, wiped the area with a cotton swab, and inserted an IV.

When the warden, a surprisingly kind-looking man in

his late fifties, saw that the IV was attached, he raised his right arm. That signaled the release of the first poisonous dose.

Less than thirty seconds later he raised the arm again, ordering the release of the hydrochloride that would end Mudman's life.

The whole time this was going on, Mudman's eyes were locked on mine. In his last letter, he'd asked if I would be a witness to his execution. He wanted me there so that he could look into one pair of eyes he knew believed in his innocence. I had done my best to be worthy of his steely gaze.

In his last minute on earth, Mudman had tried to sing the beginning of an old Allman Brothers song he had loved since he was a kid. *"Going to the country, baby, do you want to go? / Going to the country, baby, do you want to go?"* Somehow, he managed to get it out.

The hydrochloride finally hit him. It knocked the air out of his huge chest as violently as if he'd been punched. He lurched forward so hard against his straps, it sent his glasses flying off his head and onto the concrete floor.

The prison doctor declared the Mudman dead by state-ordered execution at 8:17 A.M.

Pauline and I left the prison in silence. I felt hollowed-out and empty. It was almost as bad as the night I saw Peter on the beach. I felt that I had failed them both.

"That man was innocent," I said to Pauline as we rode back to Dallas from Huntsville. "And Barry Neubauer is a murderer. There has to be something we can do to that son of a bitch. A dose of hydrochloride would be nice."

She reached over and took my hand, held it gently. Then she sang very softly. "Going to the country / Baby, do you want to go?"

Chapter 66

ON A THURSDAY MORNING in early May, I fell into the ruminative routine I'd been honing since I had returned from Texas. I went out and bought the papers, made Pauline some coffee, and kissed her good-bye as she left for her new job at the boutique law firm MacMilan and Hart. Then, after twenty minutes of push-ups and crunches on the living-room carpet, I hit the street.

First, I checked in with Philip K, a former senior magazine editor. He was a recovering heroin addict and now a regular at a methadone outpatient clinic who ran a tidy used-book store from a card table inside the northeast corner of Tompkins Square Park. An aesthete and a snob, Philip sold only books he deemed worthy of being read. Many mornings there would be no more than three or four battered volumes on the table.

That morning, Philip was touting a coffee-stained paperback novel called *Night Dogs*. I gave him his asking price and carried it in my back pocket to a Second Avenue diner, where I started it at the counter with my coffee and matzo brei.

Although unpierced and untattooed, I was becoming an East Villager in subtler ways. I'd acquired a taste for pierogi and blintzes and other sweet Eastern European foods sold in narrow, enduring eateries from Second to Avenue C. I loved the dark local bars whose jukeboxes were stocked with songs I'd never heard before. Mack loved them, too, and every once in a while he'd take the bus and join me and Pauline on a local pub crawl.

Macklin was such a natural hipster, he seemed more at home in the Village than I did. Wearing this funky fedora I'd bought him, he looked like Henry Miller come back from the dead for one last tour of bohemia.

Speaking of fedoras, I was buying my clothes secondhand now. That morning nothing I was wearing cost more than six dollars, so after breakfast and fifty pages of Philip's latest, I decided to wander over to Ferdi's Vintage on Seventh, where I'd made some of my better finds.

I had just started going through the rack of shirts in the back when a little guy with short hair and a goatee, both dyed peroxide white, walked in.

I watched him rummage through the old suits. It made me miss Sammy. He was around the same height and build. He even had the same cocky carriage.

The resemblance was so uncanny that I began to wonder if we didn't all have clones walking the streets in various cities around the world.

The skinny guy must have sensed my gaze because he

turned to face me. I began to sputter an apology when his startled expression gave him away.

"Sammy!"

He threw a punch, and I found myself on the floor, looking up at the tattered tails of old shirts.

Chapter 67

SAMMY WAS ALIVE? He couldn't be. But, goddamnit, he was!

I was up about as fast as I'd gone down. I ran out of Ferdi's and saw him sprinting west on Seventh. He cut south on First and vanished from sight. He was moving as if he'd just seen a ghost, but so was I.

There was a gay bar on the corner, its front window shrouded with dark red curtains. When I opened the door, the light from First Avenue caught Sammy scrambling out the back.

"Sammy, stop!" I yelled. "I have to talk to you."

I started after him through the shadows until I nearly collided with a massive bartender who had nimbly jumped from behind the bar. He was blocking my path.

"I'm just trying to talk to an old friend I thought was dead."

"Aren't we all, honey," he said. "But sometimes we got to take no for an answer."

I turned and dashed back out the front door. Sammy was crossing First, one block south. The shock I'd felt when I first saw him was turning to anger.

I hurried after him. By the time I saw the back of his white head again, he'd slowed to a brisk walk.

I kept him barely in sight all the way up Sixth Street, past the Indian curry parlors, the old Ukrainian church, and a Guatemalan gift shop. Then I followed him across Second and Third, around Cooper Union, and through the punk skateboarders doing ollies in the shadow of the bright anthracite cube on Astor Place.

Now Sammy headed up the canyon of Fourth, his white head bobbing in the swarm of e-commerce worker bees just released for lunch.

Every time he peered back over his shoulder, I dropped to one knee or ducked into a shop. Separated by about a ten-second lag, I crossed Fourteenth by Circuit City, then traversed Union Square, where I nearly lost him in the swarm of chic, black-clad women clamoring for fresh fruit and veggies.

The reality that Sammy was alive was just starting to sink in. What happened at his house that night? Who died in the fire? Why had Sammy run away? And what was he doing in New York?

I put my questions on hold and focused on the back of Sammy's blond head. A block short of Paragon he turned west again. I followed him toward Chelsea, where all the bars are gay and window-front mannequins have shaved heads and hold hands.

At the corner of Eighth and Eighteenth, near Covenant House, I got cut off by movers delivering a pair of Art Deco couches. By the time I maneuvered around them, Sammy had vanished once again.

Chapter 68

AFTER HE LEFT UNION SQUARE, Sammy snuck another backward peek and spotted Jack a little more than a block behind, near City Bakery.

Without changing his pace, he proceeded west. Just before Seventh, he ducked under a low cement stairway and waited for his old townie friend to hustle past.

Once Jack had crossed the avenue, Sammy sprinted uptown. He didn't look back for five blocks. Then he turned west one last time. At the end of the next cross-block was a small park. He found a bench in the corner and stretched out on his back.

For an hour he lay in the shadows as invisible as the homeless. He listened to the whoosh of the cabs shooting up Tenth four abreast and the cries of the toddlers brought into the park and released like pigeons by their large, calm Caribbean nannies.

What were the odds, Sammy was thinking, of seeing

Jack rifling the racks in a used-clothing store in the East Village? About the same as tripping over him in a leather bar? Well, the world was full of surprises, and guess what? Most suck. He'd have to be more careful. Really careful. Lately he'd had the feeling he was being followed.

He cooled his heels long enough for two shifts of nannies to come and go. Then he edged out of the park and walked down Tenth on the leafy seminary blocks. He wandered through the shadow of the train crossing, where even in the early afternoon the leggy, wide-shouldered transvestites were trawling for commuters inclined to take the long way home.

At Eighteenth he turned east past the taxi garages, and minutes later he entered his apartment. He had a sublet in one of Chelsea's block-long housing projects, and his was the only white face in the building. But, as his neighbors put it, it was a nice crib. Where else but the PJ's were you going to get a one-bedroom on the twenty-fourth floor with a little terrace for fourteen hundred a month? In Akron?

He rode the empty elevator up to the twenty-fourth floor and thought about his chance encounter with Jack Mullen. Jesus! Maybe it was an omen to leave town, go to South Beach, and get a chair in an outré salon on Collins Avenue. He got off at twenty-four, which was also his age for three more days, and walked down the endless corridor, the one thing about the building that creeped him out.

As he turned his key in the lock, two men emerged from the space by the incinerator chute. He recognized Frank Volpi. "Jeez, you need a haircut, Frank."

Volpi pushed Sammy's face against the door, and the other asshole kicked him in the side. The second guy was one of the creeps who had killed Peter. Suddenly he knew he wasn't going to make it to South Beach.

Maybe that's why he decided not to give them a goddamned thing. For the next hour, Volpi and the other guy took turns trying to break him, and it was something they had a real talent for. But Sammy stuck to his vow. Maybe out of respect for Peter, or even Jack. They barely got a sound out of him.

Not when they stuck his head in the backed-up toilet. Not when they cooked his hand over the flames of the gas stove. Not even when they took him out to the shiny concrete balcony overlooking Eighteenth Street.

And threw him off.

Chapter 69

THIRTY MINUTES AFTER I LOST SAMMY, I was still wandering through Chelsea in a daze. I finally retreated to a booth in a coffee shop on Ninth. I decided to count my blessings. It had been a while since someone I thought was dead wasn't.

After the coffee, I headed back to Ferdi's. Maybe Sammy had bought some clothes there before. Maybe he used a credit card or left a phone number. Not likely, but it was the only thing I could think of, and I needed to walk.

At the corner of Eighteenth, a young mother sat on the edge of a large cement planter. She was making bird noises and hoisting her infant over her head.

One second it was urban Madonna-and-child bliss. The next, the mother was screaming at the sky, grabbing her baby, and running for her life.

I looked up.

At first I thought a large, black plastic garbage bag had gotten blown out of a high-floor window. As it fell, I could make out the windmilling arms and legs and the flash of white. I think I knew it was Sammy before he hit the sidewalk.

The horrible, moist *whapp* of the impact stunned everybody on the street. For a few heartbeats, Chelsea was far quieter than it ever is on a sunny weekday afternoon.

A white Lexus parked nearby flashed its headlights in panic. Then its burglar alarm began to wail.

A neighborhood kid pedaled over on a shiny BMX bicycle, stared at the crumpled stranger and the red stain flowering beneath him, and raced away. I got there next and had about a minute alone with him. The name on the driver's license in his wallet was Vincenzo Nicolo. But it was Sammy. The bruises on his arms and face looked as bad as those on Peter's body. There were raw burns on his hands. "I'm sorry," I whispered.

A minute later I was only one face in a ring of morbid curiosity. In five, the rubberneckers were three deep. When I heard the howl of approaching police sirens, I slipped back through the crowd and walked away.

I was even glad Sammy had hit me. At least I had the chance to touch him one last time before he died.

Chapter 70

AN HOUR LATER my legs had finally stopped shaking and I stood in the corner of an empty, chained-off lot on Avenue D. I pulled the tarp off the Beemer.

Despite two months of disuse, it started right up. I let it clear its throat, then tooled over to the FDR and left the city. I kept seeing Sammy falling and falling as if he had been up in the air for minutes. The image wouldn't go away. Ever.

I stopped along the way to call Isabel Giamalva. I told her I might stop by, and Isabel said, "Sure, it's been too long, Jack." Three hours later I was knocking on the door of her modest ranch house, a block and a half off Montauk's Main Street. Sammy's mother was still wearing her black slacks and jacket from her waitressing shift at Gordon's in Amagansett. I tried to pretend it was just a social call, but I was having trouble fooling myself.

"How were tips?" I asked, and forced myself to look Isabel in the eye.

"Eh, you know," she said. Isabel was dark haired, petite, small and round in an attractive way. She'd always been good to us — Peter, Sammy, me.

"People start arriving earlier every year. Except for the pashmina shawls, it could have been a Saturday in August. So who's this Pauline that Mack won't stop raving about?"

"I guess he's counting on another generation of Mullens, although you'd think by now he'd have had enough. I'll bring her by sometime. You'll like her, too."

"So what's up, Jack?" she finally said.

I had no intention of telling Isabel what had happened to her son. What was the point? With Sammy's fake ID and a little luck, maybe she'd never have to know. But I told her I was convinced that whoever killed Peter also killed Sammy. I asked if she ever suspected Sammy and Peter of doing anything wrong.

"I really didn't," said Isabel. "Does that make me a lousy mom? Sammy was working since he was sixteen and was always such a secretive kid. I figured it had something to do with being gay and wanting to spare me the details, not that I needed sparing. He never introduced me to any of his boyfriends, Jack. I still don't know if he even had a serious one."

"If he did, I never met him, either, Isabel."

"You're welcome to look around his room," she said, "but there's not much in it."

She led me to the end of a short hallway and sat on the bed while I scanned the shelves and the black Formica table that ran the width of the room. Sammy hadn't lived at home for years. The only vivid trace he left was a stack of *Vogue* and *Harper's Bazaar* magazines. Beyond that were the skimpy remains of an American high-school education: an old French grammar, an algebra text, copies of *A Separate Peace* and *King Lear.*

The other books were photography manuals. Tucked neatly against the wall were books on portraiture, indoor- and outdoor-lighting techniques, the use of telephoto lenses for photographing wildlife.

"I didn't know Sammy was a photographer," I said.

"Yeah. No one did," said Isabel. "It was another thing he kept private. But right up until Peter died he'd come out here one or two evenings a month. Work straight through the night."

"Here? In your house?"

"He built a darkroom in the basement. Must have been five years ago. I've been meaning to put an ad in the *Star* and sell the equipment, but I just can't get myself to do it."

Chapter 71

THE LIGHT WOULDN'T GO ON. The fuse in the basement had blown. Isabel hadn't gotten around to replacing it. So she gave me an old tin flashlight before I descended the steep wooden stairs. I aimed the feeble beam around the moldy-smelling room. I could see the shadowy outlines of an old oil burner, a pair of ancient wooden water skis, and a folded-up Ping-Pong table.

In the midst of these garage-sale remainders, I could make out the darkroom. It ran half the length of one wall and was framed out with two-by-fours and plywood. It was about the size of a large bathroom. A rubber spinning door allowed you to enter and leave without compromising the darkness.

Inside, I moved the flashlight over the long black matte table. It was covered with gray plastic trays leading to a towering multitiered enlarger.

Against the wall were jugs of developer and a tall

stack of unopened boxes of high-quality printing paper. For some reason, I've hated Kodak since about the time they started doing those warm, smarmy TV ads.

I sank into the only chair and beamed the flashlight to the wall. It was covered with cheap paneling that had warped from the moisture. Idly running my light along the seam, I could see that the edge on the left was badly worn and jagged. It had probably been pried off and reattached numerous times.

I slid back the chair and looked under the table. The smell of mold was a lot funkier down there, and the knees of my jeans were soon wet from the shallow puddles.

Aiming the flashlight with one hand, I tried hard to pry off the paneling with the other. I couldn't get my fingers under the edge.

In this cramped, unlit space, the slightest maneuvering was awkward. I put the flashlight down and, steadying myself with one hand, reached into my back pocket for my keys.

I should have just backed out from under the table. As I strained to extricate my keys, a mouse scampered over the back of my hand on the floor. I couldn't even move without falling on my face.

I managed to pull out the keys and was finally able to pry up the splintered edge enough to get a fingerhold. With a good tug the panel popped off. It exposed a musty space between the footings of the cement foundation.

I reached into the darkness and my fingers landed on something soft and damp. I pulled my hand away fast. Maybe it was a dead rat, or a squirrel. It grossed me the hell out.

I aimed the flashlight and could just make out something white. Sucking in a breath, I stuck my hand into the space again.

This time the sodden object didn't feel like a decaying carcass. It felt more like a soggy cardboard box. I grabbed hold of a corner and carefully pulled it out.

I carried my treasure with both hands and made my way in the dark to where I knew the table was. It was a Kodak paper box like those against the wall. Slowly lifting off the lid — it was so damp, I was afraid it might fall apart — I put on my flashlight and saw that it was packed to bursting with developed prints.

On top was a contact sheet crowded with a grid of tiny, seemingly identical images about the size of two postage stamps.

Running my flashlight over them, I saw that in each frame a naked couple was doing it doggie-style. As the flashlight swept across, my eyes seemed to animate the images until they were rocking against each other like actors in a flickering silent movie.

I didn't know the red-haired woman on her knees, but I had no trouble recognizing the man behind her on his.

It was my brother.

Chapter 72

I WALKED UP the steep basement stairs like a scared teenager leaving a drugstore with a copy of *Penthouse*. The pornographic family album was tucked under my arm. Isabel was waiting at the top of the stairs.

"You all right?" she leaned down and asked. "You look like hell, Jack."

"It's the chemicals. All I need is a little fresh air." Then I added nonchalantly, "I found some old pictures Sammy took of Peter. I was hoping I could go through them a little more leisurely at home. They stirred up a lot of feelings."

"Of course, Jack. Keep whatever you like. You don't have to return any of it. But I am going to hold you to your promise of introducing me to Pauline."

Even before I got out the front door, I was jumping out of my skin. I felt hopped-up and weirded-out. But mostly, I was scared.

I thought about the break-in last summer at our house. I figured that whoever had caught up with Sammy was looking for the pictures. And they were prepared to torture and kill to get them. I carefully put the pictures into the bag strapped to the bike's fuel tank. Isabel watched me from the kitchen window.

I raced the quarter mile into town and called Pauline from the first pay phone I saw. "Pauline, don't go back to the apartment," I said. "Go to your sister's. Anywhere. Just don't go there!"

After I hung up, I parked the bike behind the Shagwong and walked the two blocks to the Memory Motel.

I got a room in the back, double-locked the doors, and pulled the shades. If the guys who killed Sammy had spotted me, I might not have much time.

I began emptying the soggy box, one damp print at a time. At the top of the stack were more contact sheets like the one I had looked at in the basement.

I peeled off at least twenty before I got to the first eight-by-ten print.

It showed Peter sitting on the edge of a bed, grimacing unself-consciously into the lens. A fortyish woman straddled him like a jockey.

I began laying out all the prints, one at a time, until every piece of furniture, every square inch of musty broadloom, and every cracked bathroom tile were covered with Sammy and Peter's brilliant career. The glossy prints, still redolent of the development chemicals, captured twosomes, threesomes, foursomes, and one fivesome. There was straight sex and gay sex and bi sex.

Sammy's work was not amateurish. The lighting was good, the focus sharp, and the camera angles explicit.

Sammy had a good eye, and my brother was a talented model. After a while I just couldn't look at any more pictures. I called Pauline on her cell phone. I told her what I'd found and where I was.

At midnight she arrived, and after a long hug, I showed her Sammy and Peter's greatest hits. For a couple of hours, we drank coffee and studied the pictures. When the shock of the content wore off, we realized we had evidence. We really had something here. Like curators preparing an exhibit, we took notes, made lists, and estimated dates.

Then we rearranged them chronologically. We started with Peter looking no older than fifteen and ended with shots that couldn't have been taken more than a few weeks before he died.

In those last few shots, he sat in a hot tub with a gray-haired man and a beautiful blond woman who was topless.

Barry and Dana Neubauer.

I guess she really was Daddy's little girl. Believe it or not, it wasn't the photo of Dana and her father that did it to me, though. It was Peter at fourteen and fifteen. He was a sophomore in high school when it started.

That night the rules changed forever. I called Fenton first, then Hank and Marci. Finally, I called Mack.

In twenty minutes we were all crowded into the same seedy motel room. Before the sun came up, we'd not only vowed to avenge the death of my brother, we had an idea how we might be able to do it.

Part Five

THE TRUTH, AND
NOTHING BUT

Chapter 73

FOR THE AVERAGE single-digit Hamptons million-aire, the start of another summer in paradise is marked by gridlock on Ninety-sixth Street, then a slow crawl on Route 27 and an hour's wait for a twenty-five-dollar pizza at Sam's. For those who fly over the traffic in private planes and helicopters, it starts with the party at the Neubauers' Beach House.

According to friends of Marci's and Hank's who were part of the vast army of suppliers, Barry Neubauer had written his party planner a blank check. With a week to go, she had already dropped a million dollars. Among other niceties, that buys you David Bouley to stir the sauce, Yo-Yo Ma to scrape his Stradivarius, and the inimitable Johan Johan to cut the flowers and fluff up the bouquets. And there's still enough left for champagne served in chilled, ten-ounce crystal stem glasses; a dozen different kinds of oysters; the deejay of the moment, Samantha

Ronson; and a wooden dance floor constructed on the back lawn.

Pauline and I had spent a little cash, too. To find out who was coming this year, Pauline got back in touch with her old hacker pal. He reinvited himself into the party planner's hard drive and plucked out the guest list.

Placing last year's list and this year's side by side offered a peek into the interaction of celebrities and socialites. Among the anonymous rich who made up the bulk of the guests, virtually everyone was invited back. But among the boldface celebs, the turnover was 100 percent. Last year's hip-hop emcee had been replaced by this year's Oscar winners. Last year's fashion designer was supplanted by a more current fashionista. Even if you were an artiste whose stock had managed to soar for another twelve months, you still weren't coming back. Invite the riffraff two years in a row and they might start to feel as if they actually belonged. They don't. To the seriously wealthy, celebrities are only a notch above the help.

As far as I was concerned, the only difference between last year and this year that mattered was that my brother, Peter Rabbit, wouldn't be in the front yard parking cars.

Chapter 74

BUT FENTON GIDLEY WAS.

A week before the party, I sat beside Fenton as he called our fellow townie friend Bobby Hatfield. Bobby has held down the Neubauer party parking franchise for years, so when Fenton told him he hadn't snagged a decent swordfish in months and could use the cash, Bobby gladly added him to the crew.

On that warm but rainy evening at the end of May, Fenton stood alertly beneath the elegant gold-striped awning that had been hastily erected to offer Barry and Campion's guests dry passage from car to door.

For Fenton, he was highly presentable. He wore his dress shoes, his best pair of jeans, and one of the two shirts he owns with a collar. He was also freshly shaved, showered, and deodorized. He looked so good, I was tempted to take his picture and send it to his mom.

In addition to guidance on wardrobe and grooming, I'd

given Fenton a quick tutorial on kissing up to the rich, something I'm ashamed to admit I'd shown an innate talent for. It's not so much how quickly you jump to open their doors or how competently you perform your lackey tasks, I explained. Generally, the superrich aren't looking for excessive subservience or even gratitude. That's embarrassing to them. "What they want," I told Fenton, "is for you to be excited. They want to see that your little brush with money is turning you on."

When Gidley checked in punctually with Hatfield at 7:15 P.M., the first thing he did was examine the guest list. He wanted to make sure that it was the same one he'd studied with me and Pauline and that there were no last-minute cancellations.

At 8:05 the parade of Audis, Beemers, and Benzes started rolling in. Within an hour most of the 190 guests had made their way through the stately oak doors and out to the lovely tented and lantern-lit flagstone terrace.

There, waiters and waitresses in fuchsia blazers designed by Comme des Garçons dispensed sushi and vintage champagne. With their elongated, surly good looks, they could have been moonlighting runway models.

Among the first to arrive was Tricia Powell. Since her perjury at the inquest, Trish's career at Mayflower had taken off. She stepped out of a black Mercedes E430 in a little black Armani dress, stared through Gidley as if he were a smudged pane of glass, and walked inside on Manolo mules.

Neubauer's lawyer and my former mentor, Bill Montrose, was in the second wave. When Montrose's dark green Jaguar rolled to a stop, Gidley wasn't at the head of the line of valets, but he cut to the front.

After giving Montrose his ticket, he steered the car off the driveway and down a gentle slope to one of the two moonlit clearings designated for parking. He tucked the car safely in the far corner.

Before he and his fellow valets took a break, Gidley noted the arrival of several men and women from Sammy's pornographic portfolio. He couldn't help thinking that they looked a lot better with their clothes on.

Chapter 75

SARAH JESSICA AND *MATTHEW* were in attendance. So was *Bill*, who was staying at *Steven*'s place, without *Hillary*. *Richard* was there holding his new baby. It looked as if babies were the hot summer accessory again. *Allen* was there, and so was *Kobe*, but not *Shaq*. *Caroline*, *Patricia*, and *Billy* were there, as well as four principals from *The Sopranos*.

At about eleven, just as the festivities began to lose a bit of their magic, Bill Montrose tracked down his hosts. One last heartfelt hug (Barry) and affectionate peck (Campion), and he beat his retreat.

He worked his way through the resplendent crowd to the rear doors of the house. As soon as Montrose stepped outside, Fenton hopped off the black cast-iron bench beside the driveway and unhooked key number 115 from the board.

Montrose was still fishing for his half of the parking chit as Gidley approached.

"No worries, sir," he told him. "Green Jag, right?"

Montrose winked. "You're good."

"I try, sir."

Gidley hustled back to where he'd parked the Jag only hours before. Whistling the old Johnny Carson show theme, he slid behind the walnut wheel and drove it off the lawn to the front of the house.

"Lovely car," he told Montrose as he climbed out and accepted his five-buck tip. "Have a terrific night."

Relieved to be out of there at last, Montrose yanked off his Hermès silk tie. He punched in a number on his car phone. After a short delay of gentle ringing, the voice of his assistant, Laura Richardson, poured from the speaker.

"Who is it?"

"Laura, it's me," he said. "I'm leaving the Neubauers' right now. Believe me, you didn't miss a fucking thing."

"Bullshit, Monty. You're a bad liar, especially for a professional. Everybody was there, right?"

"Well, I did stand next to Morgan Freeman."

"Don't tell me. He's five-six and smells funny."

"Six-three and fragrant."

"Anyone else?"

"No one you'd know. Listen, Laura, I can't make it tonight."

"Big surprise, Monty. What now?"

"In terms of the divorce settlement and the custody and everything, it's going to look real bad if I'm gone this weekend."

"You mean it's going to look *really* bad if they find out

you've been screwing your black assistant for three years."

Montrose held back a yawn. "Laura, do we really have to do this now?"

"Nope," said Richardson. "You're still the boss."

"Thanks," said Montrose, "because I can't tell you how shot I feel."

When he heard the click, he slapped the dashboard in a rage. "Don't you dare hang up on me!" he yelled. "I don't need this shit."

I took that as my cue to pull off the blanket, sit up in the backseat, and press the barrel of a gun to his neck.

"I guess this isn't your night, Monty," I said when our eyes met in the mirror.

Chapter 76

I GAVE MONTROSE ONLY a couple of seconds to get over the shock. Then I jabbed the barrel of the pistol into his neck one more time. It felt good.

"Turn right at the stop sign," I instructed. "Do exactly as I say, Monty."

He slowed to take the turn and met my eyes in the mirror. It was amazing how quickly he'd managed to wipe the panic from his face and realign his Big Man in the Big World mask. In thirty seconds he'd convinced himself that everything was still essentially under control.

"You realize what you've just done is a kidnapping, or could be construed as such. What the hell do you think you're doing, Jack?"

"Take a left," I said.

Montrose obediently turned onto Further Lane, the moon pursuing us through the branches of the colossal overhanging elms. Amazingly, his confidence was growing. It was almost as if he were back in his long, black-windowed office and all he had to do was push a little buzzer for Laura Richardson to trot in with Security.

"I offered you a view of half of Manhattan," he reminded me. "You screwed everything up. You just don't get it, Mullen."

"You're absolutely right, Monty. I remember it well." I pulled the gun away from his neck, stuck it in his ear, and pulled back the trigger until the hammer caught with a *click*.

"It's a nasty old gun. If I were you, I'd concentrate all my energy on avoiding potholes. Make a right."

Montrose flinched and squeaked, and when I looked in the mirror, he had transformed again.

"Another left," I said, and we turned toward the water, onto DeForest Lane.

"The third driveway on the right."

He dutifully turned the car into the driveway of a low-slung cottage and parked. I gave him a blindfold and told him to tie it himself. His hands trembled about as badly as Jane Davis's had at the inquest.

"Nice and tight," I said. "I want this to be a surprise."

I walked him into the house, spun him around a few times in the kitchen, and took him out back to a raised red-brick patio. Just beyond it, a tall, vintage milk truck was parked on the grass.

I opened the back door of the truck and shoved Montrose in with the three other bound, blindfolded hostages. One was Tricia Powell, a star at my brother's inquest; the other two were Tom and Stella Fitzharding, the Neubauers' very best friends.

I slammed the milk-truck door, leaving the four of them completely in the dark.

Chapter 77

I GOT BACK INTO MONTROSE'S SEDAN, slid back the seat, and readjusted the rearview mirror. I imagined how he must have felt when he looked into it and saw my face. *Glad you're enjoying yourself, Jack.*

I drove Monty's Jag along the back roads until I saw the gates of the Beach House gleaming through the rain-soaked windshield. I lowered the window to inform the gatekeeper that I was picking up a guest. He'd already figured as much and waved me through.

A quarter of a mile short of the house, I turned off the drive and disappeared behind some hedges. I made my way to the field where the car had originally been parked. I backed it into its old space and dropped the keys under the front seat.

There was only one car left in the field. Leaning against it was Fenton. When I got out of the Jag, he clapped me on the shoulder and looked me in the eye.

"It's showtime, Jack," he said. "You ready?"

"Close enough. At least it's a good cause."

"The best."

Fenton slipped out of his red parking jacket. I put it on along with a black baseball cap. I pulled the hat low on my brow, then hurried to the service kitchen, where a swarm of workers were helping themselves to leftover nouvelle cuisine. The room was full of people I'd known since grade school. But in the feeding frenzy no one looked up as I passed through.

Without stopping, I hurried down a dark hallway and up a stairwell to another long corridor, off which were half a dozen well-appointed guest bedrooms.

Dana may never have been my girl, but for almost a year I was definitely her boy. During family functions we'd sometimes slip away to one of those guest rooms. I ran to the end of the hallway and pulled down an aluminum ladder from a trapdoor in the ceiling.

Then I climbed into the attic and pulled up the ladder.

There was a stack of extra mattresses in the corner. I settled down on one, with my backpack as a pillow. I set my watch for 3:15 and tried to get some sleep.

I was going to need it.

Chapter 78

YOU COULDN'T HAVE CREATED a less suspicious scene if you tried. Barely had the sun peeked above the horizon when an old-fashioned, top-heavy milk truck puttered down a gorgeous country lane. It was an image sweetly evocative of an America long gone.

Every half mile or so, the truck would turn into a driveway and roll up to another expensive house. As the motor idled peacefully, Hank hopped out in his blue overalls with the white patch of the East Hampton Dairy sewn on one shoulder. He crossed the dewy grass and went round to the back. He fetched the empties from the tin container by the kitchen door, then returned with three or four cool, perspiring bottles.

The whole thing was a homogenized joke, of course. At the end of the week, nearly every drop of milk got poured down the drain.

But there was something about the waxed cardboard

origami caps and the widemouthed glass bottles with the etching of a cow on the face of each bottle that made the elite clientele feel as down-home as Iowa farmers.

For the next hour the milk truck slowly made its appointed rounds. As it dropped off precious lactic fluid all along the East Hampton shore, it barely kept up with a Rhodesian Ridgeback out for its morning romp.

Finally, in the early-morning light, the truck turned into Bluff Road. Three stops later, Hank drove it through the open gates of the Neubauer compound.

Chapter 79

My Casio went off in sharp, persistent beeps, and my eyes flipped open on a splintery beam slanting down from the ridge of the roof.

I slid to the end of the mattress, set my feet on the loose plywood floor, and breathed deeply.

There's nothing like waking up in the attic of a house you've entered illegally to get the blood flowing. *Oh, man, Jack,* I thought once again. *Is this the only way to get this done?*

When my heart rate slowed, I laced up my sneakers and pulled a flashlight from my backpack. Then, with one hand aiming the light and the other holding on to the overhead beams for balance, I made my way rafter to rafter across the attic.

The huge two-story house, built in the 1930s, faced the water and was laid out like a staple whose sides bulged a little past ninety degrees. When I reached the end of the guest wing, I wriggled through a thicket of beams, turned right, and set out across the main body of the house, which contained the kitchen and living and dining rooms. Just below where I was walking, a forty-eight-seat screening room.

Huge industrial-strength air-conditioning units had been wedged into that part of the attic. I had to maneuver around the metal casings and the thick tangle of plastic tubing piping chilly air into the rooms below.

Up there, however, it was as steamy and airless as a subway platform. By the time I'd crossed over the center part and turned right again over the bedroom suites, sweat was dripping off my nose, splattering softly on the baking wood.

I kept walking until I reached the tiny window cut into the gable of the attic at the end of the house.

It was 3:38. I was five minutes ahead of schedule.

From the window I could see ocean waves hitting the beach in the eerie light. I could see the spot where Peter's broken body had washed ashore.

It was good to be reminded of why I was in that attic.

I counted off fifteen strides, to where I estimated Dana's bedroom would be. When I couldn't find the sliding sheet of plywood I was looking for, I expanded my search three strides in each direction. Finally, I spotted the sliding plywood flooring that opened down into her closet.

Squatting low, I stuffed my flashlight into my backpack and mopped my face and neck with my T-shirt. When I slid the plywood sheet aside, a jet of cool air blew into my face.

Supporting my weight with my palms, I slowly lowered myself into the chilly darkness of Dana's room.

Chapter 80

I FOUND MYSELF in the back of a deep closet between scented rows of designer blouses, dresses, and slacks. I used my flashlight to see. Each shelf was labeled with a designer's name: Gucci, Vera Wang, Calvin, Ralph Lauren, Chanel. I pushed my way through the thicket of Dana's linen, silk, and cashmere to the edge of the slightly open closet door. Fifteen feet away on the bed, Dana lay asleep.

It was time for a judgment call, and I had to make it. The question was whether Dana was directly involved in Peter's murder. By now I knew a fair amount about that night a year ago. I knew Peter had received a perfumed note on stationery that looked like Dana's, and maybe it even was hers. But I was pretty sure that whatever relationship she'd had with Peter had been over before the night he died. She'd lied for her father at the inquest.

So I made the call: Dana was more a victim than a true

accomplice. She might not be the best person, but she wasn't a murderer. She'd been sexually abused by her own father. *Let sleeping dogs lie,* I told myself.

Keeping my eye on the rows of expensive shoes and jeans scattered about, I slid out of her closet, then out of the bedroom. I was in a wide gallery that led to the separate bedrooms her parents had maintained for decades. It was lined with paintings by Pollock and de Kooning and Fairfield Porter, all of which had been done in the Hamptons. The tiny red lights of their alarms blinked in the darkness.

A toilet flushed to my right. I froze against the wall.

Then a dark-skinned young guy in boxers stepped out of the bathroom. *Who the hell is this? What is he doing in this part of the house?*

He looked to be about nineteen, Indian or Pakistani, and at least as handsome as Peter was. In a postcoital cocoon, he padded dreamily toward the guest wing. *Peter's goddamned replacement.*

A few more steps and I was at the threshold of Barry Neubauer's bedroom. The last day — the whole last week, really — had passed like an endless nightmare. Every few hours I found myself doing something, or committing to something, that I knew I shouldn't. I could still turn back. It wasn't too late. It was like one of those suspense-movie scenes where we want to yell, *Don't do it. Don't open that door, Jack.*

I didn't listen, of course.

I took out my starter pistol and nudged open Neubauer's door. My heart was thundering inside my chest. I'd never set foot in the room before. Even in the Dana months, it was off-limits.

The room was spare and loftlike with irregular white

floorboards. By a bay window was a sitting area with a flat-screen TV, a black leather couch, and matching arm-chairs.

It was another five paces to the huge wood-and-steel sculpture of a bed. I could hear Neubauer breathing heavily. It sounded as though he was chewing something in his sleep.

In a kind of a trance, I cautiously crossed the floorboards. He lay sprawled on his back, his hands instinctively shielding his black silk briefs. A ribbon of drool trickled out of the corner of his mouth. Even in my disembodied state it occurred to me that it had the makings of a wonderful portrait of the CEO at rest.

I was afraid that if I watched him any longer, he would sense a presence and open his eyes, so I dropped to a crouch below the level of the bed. I removed a roll of silvery electrical tape from my backpack. My heart was exploding.

Still crouching, I peeled off about a half-foot strip of tape. This was it. I counted three, took a deep breath, and brought the tape down on Neubauer's mouth before he could make a sound. Hard. I pushed down so hard against his whiskery cheeks that the back of his head sank deep into the pillow. I brought my free hand around and pressed the barrel of the pistol to the bridge of his nose.

For a long, hard beat, we were locked in a kind of negative harmony — his shock and rage matched perfectly by mine.

Suddenly, he grabbed for the gun, setting off a struggle. But I was in a much better position. I was also stronger. I ripped the gun away, reared back, and slammed it hard into his ear. Neubauer didn't offer any more resistance. Only his dark eyes showed his anger and hatred. *How fucking dare you?*

I rolled Neubauer over onto his stomach and hand-cuffed him. Then I yanked him to his feet and looped more silver tape around his thighs, limiting his movement to small, hair-plucking hops.

"Good morning," I finally said. "At the inquest you said you had gone out of your way to offer your condolences about Peter. That discussion wasn't very satisfying to me or my family. I've come back to continue it."

Chapter 81

OUTSIDE CAMPION'S BEDROOM, dim light trickled from under the door. I pushed Barry onto his stomach and added another circle of tape above his ankles. I was afraid my scuffle with her husband might have awakened her. It helped that they didn't sleep together.

When I opened the door, I saw that the light was cast by the flickering flames of some two dozen small butter lamps burning at the base of a painting of a multiarmed Krishna. Campion's bedroom looked more like an ashram than a bedroom.

But all the deities invoked couldn't spare Campion from being abruptly awakened by the rip of electrical tape I was about to place across her mouth.

"Good morning, Campion," I whispered. "I'm not going to hurt you."

"Okay" was all she said. She seemed strangely calm, and I realized she was probably sedated.

I let her pull on a terry-cloth robe over her silk night-shirt and grab a pair of sneakers. Then I handcuffed Campion and led her to where her husband lay struggling on the floor.

I pulled Barry to his feet and prodded the couple down the circular staircase to the ground floor.

Halfway there, I heard the sputter of the East Hampton Dairy's only milk truck.

"Your chariot," I told the Neubauers.

We left the estate, but we still had one more stop closer to town. We picked up Detective Frank Volpi.

Chapter 82

THE MILK TRUCK MOSEYED down the glistening country lanes like a squishable, anthropomorphic vehicle in a Saturday-morning cartoon. *Look, boys and girls, it's the friendly East Hampton Dairy milk truck. There behind the steering wheel is Mr. Hank, the handsome, courteous milkman.*

I thought that I might get into the flow after a while, but it hadn't happened. I was feeling numb and withdrawn, and the queasiness in my stomach wouldn't go away. There was a dreamlike quality to the morning. It was hard to believe this was even happening.

Turning left at the end of Bluff Road and right onto 27, the truck drove through a still-dormant Amagansett. Past the closed restaurants and shops, and the battened-down farmers market.

Then it motored through the flat, lunar dunes of Napeaque and into Montauk. Except for a couple of fishermen eating their egg sandwiches at John's Pancake House, it was also deserted.

The engine strained against its heavy load as it climbed the hill out of town. We rattled past the library and the familiar cutoff to my house on Ditch Plains Road.

About a mile short of the lighthouse, the truck turned right. It bounced over a heavy chain that lay unlocked in the dirt between unkempt hedges.

After hopping out to secure the chain behind us, Hank continued up the long, sandy drive until we could see whitecapped waves dancing in the early light.

Only after topping the crest did we catch our first glimpse of a dream house nestled in the dunes at the very edge of the cliff. It was as if Max Kleinerhunt, CEO and founder of everythingbut.com, had been determined to ensure that the sun shined on him before anyone else in North America.

Unfortunately for Max, his stock, which at one time had been selling for $189 a share, had settled in at 67¢ a share. Although he'd already sunk $22 million into his summer house, Kleinerhunt was now far more preoccupied with saving his butt than tanning it. For the past six months the only visitor was the occasional surfer or mountain biker who climbed up from the beach at sunset to catch the view from the endless balconies.

The hot real estate phrase that spring was BANANA, which stood for "build absolutely nothing anywhere near anyone." Max Kleinerhunt had succeeded in that.

Hank pushed a button on the remote control clipped to his visor. A burnished steel door rose out of the dunes, and the truck rolled into an immaculate, subterranean twelve-car garage.

Even before we pulled to a stop, Pauline came running up and hugged me through the open window of the truck. "These were the longest twelve hours of my life," she whispered.

"Me, too," I whispered back.

Behind her stood Fenton, Molly, and Marci.

Chapter 83

MY OLDEST FRIENDS crowded around the back of the milk truck like kids around the tree on Christmas morning. I opened the creaky rear door and hopped inside. I began to remove the tape, though not from around anyone's wrists.

"How dare you treat us like this!" Campion said when I pulled the tape off her lips. "You were a guest at our house."

"And now you're our guest," I told her.

Tricia Powell was next to vent, pointing at the creases and smudges on her black velvet evening gown. She hissed, "This is Armani, you animals." Barry Neubauer remained silent after I removed his tape. I looked into his steely eyes and knew he was too busy plotting to say a word.

Frank Volpi offered up that I was "dead meat," and I found the threat convincing coming from him.

While Fenton and I helped them out of the truck, Marci opened up some beach chairs. Hank wheeled out a serving cart bearing two translucent piles: one, disposable, prewrapped syringes; the other, 100ml plastic vials.

Barry Neubauer continued to glower at me as I shared some good news and some bad news. "In a few minutes, you'll be able to go inside and make yourselves comfortable. But first, this man, who is a trained medical technician, is going to draw blood from each of you, except for Mr. Montrose. I'm not going to explain any of this, so please don't ask."

It didn't go down well.

"Anyone who *touches* me with a needle is going to be sued!" yelled Tom Fitzharding. I remembered the pictures of him and his wife with Peter, when my brother was sixteen or seventeen years old.

I slapped Fitzharding across the face. It made a loud noise and shut everybody up. It felt good, too. I didn't like Fitzharding and his wife, and I had good reasons.

"Once this unpleasantness has been taken care of, you can go inside," I repeated. "You can shower, change, and lie down for a nap. But whether you cooperate or not, no one is going in until this is done."

"You little snot," said Stella Fitzharding.

I leaned in close to her. "I know all about you and Peter. So shut the hell up."

"I need a shower. You can start with me," offered Tricia Powell, sitting down on one of the chairs. She wearily held out her arm.

After that, things went surprisingly smoothly. Hank and Marci carefully drew and labeled 90ml from everyone in the garage. Then the hostages were brought inside and led to the almost completed sports entertainment wing. Foam mattresses were lined up on the floor. There were bathrooms, of course. We even had coffee and rolls. And lots of organic milk.

"Try to get some sleep," I advised. "It's going to be a long day."

Chapter 84

EARLIER IN THE WEEK Marci had gone to the K-mart in Riverhead and rummaged through the discount tables looking for garments to clothe our guests. When the Neubauers and Fitzhardings, Volpi, Tricia Powell, and Montrose lined up for breakfast, they were dressed, well, modestly and inexpensively. The food and sleep had improved their spirits, but their faces were marked by confusion and anxiety. *Why are we here? What now?*

We had given a lot of thought to security and decided to keep it simple. Every door in the wing we were using was padlocked. A few were double-padlocked. Everyone was told they would be gagged and tied down the first time they gave us any trouble, or even made us suspicious. So far, the threat had worked. It also helped that Marci, Fenton, and Hank carried stun guns at all times.

Shortly after breakfast Macklin arrived with a petite, gray-haired woman. The group exchanged more puzzled looks and seemed buoyed by the hope that this would be over soon.

Then, as Macklin and I huddled in the corner, Bill Montrose appealed to my grandfather's better judgment.

"Mr. Mullen, it's very good to see you," said Montrose. "I think you realize that if we're released before anyone is hurt, those involved are likely to fare much better. I can almost promise it."

"You'd know more about that than me," said Macklin as he turned his back on the lawyer.

Nevertheless, the six hostages saw some reason to be hopeful until they were led into a vast oceanfront living room, whose slate floors and redwood beams and jaw-dropping view were the focal point of the house.

That morning, however, the drapes were pulled across the entire expanse of glass. The room was lit by powerful lights that Marci and Fenton had hung from the ceiling.

Montrose muttered, "Oh, Jesus, no."

The sparsely furnished room held a pair of long wooden tables and several beach chairs. Facing them from a foot-high plywood platform was a black leather office chair.

Between the elevated chair and the tables were two more chairs. One held a Bible, the other fronted a small desk. On it was an archaic contraption that looked like a typewriter with a few working parts chopped off.

Behind the raised chair hung two shimmering flags — the Stars and Stripes, and the green, orange, and white of Ireland.

In the midst of the furniture was a rolling tripod holding a TV camera. EH70 was stenciled on the side.

Molly aimed it at our guests as they filed into the

room, handcuffed and grumbling, and sat in the row of beach chairs behind the tables. Each of them looked in shock. Next, the door to the room was locked. Hank stood beside it with a stun gun and a Louisville Slugger.

Then Molly spun the camera around to track Macklin as he walked the length of the room. He stepped warily onto his little stage and sat in the leather chair.

At about the same time, his friend and court stenographer, Mary Stevenson, took her seat in front of the old machine.

To Macklin's right, a homemade sign had been taped to the otherwise pristine white wall.

Molly focused on the simple block letters: THE PEOPLE V. BARRY NEUBAUER.

Chapter 85

THE FIRST REAL DISTURBANCE CAME, not surprisingly, from Volpi. He stood up and yelled at the top of his voice, "This is bullshit!"

Hank ran over from the door with the stun gun held out like a sword. He zapped Volpi, who dropped to the floor, writhing in pain. I thought it was a good lesson for the group to see. I knew that the camera was still focused on the handmade sign. Hank's crowd control was not being broadcast.

"Frank, keep your mouth shut," Hank yelled. "That goes for the rest of you scum, too." I think they all got the point.

Without warning, Molly spun her camera again, this time to aim its merciless eye at me. I stood to my full six foot one, took a deep breath, and stared straight into the lens.

Ever since the cold-blooded murder of Sammy in

Chelsea, I had applied myself in ways I never could have at Nelson, Goodwin and Mickel. I just hoped I was doing the right thing. I had been cramming for this my whole final year at Columbia. And not just by obsessing about Peter's murder and the injustice that followed. I had read and reread *Fundamentals of Trial Techniques* and *The Art of Cross-Examination,* a classic published in 1903 that still held up.

"We're on," said Molly, tapping the red light on the camera. "We're broadcasting. Go, Jack."

"My name is Jack Mullen," I began, my voice cracking slightly and sounding as if it belonged to someone I barely knew. "I was born and raised in Montauk and have lived here my whole life."

No one in the room was half as uptight as I was, but I put my faith in the steady, measured cadence I'd practiced so diligently during lawyering clinics at Columbia. Everything about my tone and bearing attempted to communicate that I was sane, basically reasonable, and worth hearing out.

I also knew that the time was ripe for this. I was pretty sure that a lot of people were angry and upset about what they considered courtroom injustices in the recent past: the Simpson trial, the Diallo verdict in New York City, the botched Jon-Benét Ramsey case, and others in their own cities and towns.

"A year ago yesterday," I continued, "my brother died at a party held at a Hamptons beach house. He'd been hired to park cars. The next day his body washed up on the beach below the property. The inquest held at the end of that summer concluded that my brother, who was twenty-one, died accidentally. He didn't. He was beaten to death. In the next few hours I will prove not only that he was murdered, but why and by whom.

"Sitting at the end of the table to my left is the man who owns the house and hosted the party. His name is Barry Neubauer. He's the CEO of Mayflower Enterprises. You've probably watched his cable channels or visited his web sites or taken your children to one of his theme parks. Maybe you've read about his bigger-than-life exploits in a business magazine or seen a picture of him taken at a celebrity charity gala. But that doesn't mean that you know the real Barry Neubauer.

"You will, though. Far better than you want to, because Barry Neubauer is about to stand trial for the murder of my brother."

"Jack Mullen is going to prosecute me?" shouted Neubauer. "Like hell! Turn that fucking camera off! Turn it off now!"

His outburst was followed by so many others that Macklin had to crack his black walnut gavel for quiet.

"This trial will begin in a few minutes," I finally said to the camera. "We're broadcasting live on Channel Seventy. This short break will give you a chance to call your friends."

Chapter 86

MOLLY TURNED OFF THE CAMERA, and I motioned to Fenton and Hank. We walked over to Neubauer. He held up his handcuffed wrists. "Take them off!"

I ignored the demand as if it had come from a spoiled child.

"It doesn't make any difference to me whether you all participate in the trial or not," I told Barry flat out. "It changes nothing."

He huffed like a self-important CEO. "We're not going to cooperate. So what will that look like on TV? You'll look like a complete fuckup, Mullen, which is what you are."

I shook my head at Neubauer, then took a manila envelope out of my briefcase.

I showed him what was inside, and I showed only Barry.

"This is what it will look like, Barry. And this. And all of these," I said.

"You wouldn't dare," he snarled at me.

"Oh, yeah, I would. As I said, it's your choice. You can offer your side of things. If you don't, that's fine, too. We're going back on the air."

Molly started filming again, and I repeated my introductory remarks. This time a little more calmly and cogently.

"Before this trial is over," I continued, "you'll understand that Barry Neubauer is a killer and that everyone sitting in these chairs contributed to either the crime or its cover-up. Once you've seen what they've done, you won't have an ounce of pity for them. Believe me, you won't.

"The People will show that Barry Neubauer killed my brother himself or hired someone else to do his bloody grunt work. We will also show that along with the means and opportunity to kill Peter, he had one hell of a motive. When you hear the motive, you'll understand everything.

"I fully recognize these aren't ideal circumstances to determine a man's innocence or guilt," I said.

"Oh, really," said Bill Montrose. "That's the first intelligent thing you've said so far, Mullen."

I ignored Montrose. I knew the crucial thing at that point was to keep plowing ahead and not allow myself to be sidetracked. My mouth had become too dry to continue. I stopped and picked up my water glass. My hand trembled so badly, I almost dropped it.

My voice was steady, though.

"If you bear with me, I believe you'll see that this trial is at least as fair as any you might have followed lately. Fairness is all we're looking for here.

"For one thing, Mr. Neubauer will have the benefit of counsel. And not an overworked, underpaid green defender like those assigned to the many indigent defendants who end up on death row. He's the eminent Bill Montrose, senior partner and management committee chairman at a large New York law firm. And since Mr. Montrose is Mr. Neubauer's longtime personal attorney and recently represented him with such success at the inquest, he's extremely well versed in all the particulars. When you consider that Mr. Montrose's adversary will be me, a twenty-nine-year-old barely out of law school, it is, if anything, a mismatch in the defendant's favor.

"Acting as judge in this courtroom will be my grandfather, Macklin Reid Mullen," I said, setting off another round of outrage from Montrose. "The stenographer is Mary Stevenson, a court reporter in New York City municipal courts for thirty-seven years.

"Once again, I realize this is more than a little unusual. All I can say is, watch the trial. Give us a chance. Then make your own judgments. My grandfather came to this country from County Clare, Ireland. He has spent the past twenty-five years working as a paralegal, and he cares more about the law and justice than anyone I've ever come across, including my law professors.

"In any criminal trial, the judge is there not to determine guilt or innocence, but to rule on differences between the lawyers regarding evidence or procedure and to keep the process intact. In this case," I said, staring intently into the camera, "you will be the jury. Macklin is not here to issue a verdict, just to administer the proceedings. And he'll do a great job. That's all I have to say right now. Mr. Montrose will speak next."

Chapter 87

BILL MONTROSE WAS THE ONLY ONE of our guests not wearing handcuffs. He sat there, lost in thought. Then, like any good poker player, he turned to read my face.

I did everything I could to seem oblivious to the crucial importance of the next few seconds. If he was genuinely concerned about the welfare of his client, his course would be clear. But like many highly successful yet relatively anonymous attorneys, Montrose had reached a point in his life where he yearned for some fame and glory to stack beside his cash and real estate. I knew that much about him from my time at Nelson, Goodwin and Mickel. According to colleagues, he'd proclaimed himself a far better trial lawyer than Johnnie Cochran or Robert Shapiro. Bill Montrose had the largest ego of anyone I had ever met. I was counting on it.

I sucked in a breath as Montrose stood. He faced

Molly's East Hampton Channel 70 camera. This was his big moment, too. He wasn't about to sit it out.

"Please don't misunderstand or misinterpret," he began. "Just because I'm standing in front of you for the moment doesn't mean that this proceeding has a shred of legitimacy. It doesn't.

"Make no mistake," he continued after a dramatic pause. "This is *not* a trial. This is *not* a courtroom. The elderly man behind me, no matter how spry and avuncular, is *not* a judge. This is a kangaroo court.

"You should know that justice has already been served in this case. Last summer an inquest was convened to look into the drowning of Peter Mullen. In a real courtroom presided over by a real judge — the Honorable Robert P. Lillian — my client was found to be blameless.

"During that inquest the court heard a witness who saw the deceased dive into a dangerous ocean at high tide, late at night.

"Not one but two medical examiners presented evidence to support their conviction that there had been no foul play. After weighing the testimony, Judge Lillian, in a decision available to anyone who wants to take the time to read it, concluded that Peter Mullen's death, however sad, was no one's fault but his own.

"Apparently, his family is unable to accept this. By taking this unfortunate action, Peter Mullen's brother and grandfather are turning an accident into a crime."

Once again, Montrose paused as if to gather his thoughts. I had to admit that the guy was very good. Maybe it was a mismatch. "Now they are asking you to watch. Please don't! Turn off the set, or turn the dial. Do it right now. Do it if you believe in justice. I trust that you do."

Montrose sat down, and I wondered if we would ever get him to speak again.

Macklin tapped his gavel on the plywood platform below his chair.

"This court," he said, "will recess for ninety minutes to allow the prosecution and defense to ready their cases. I suggest you both get busy."

Chapter 88

FOURTEEN MINUTES INTO THE RECESS, ABC interrupted its coverage of the L.A. Open from Riviera Country Club and cut to Peter Jennings in the Lincoln Center studio of *World News Tonight*. A bold breaking news was superimposed over the screen.

"ABC News has just learned," said Jennings with the most discreet warble in his deep voice, "that media billionaire Barry Neubauer, his wife, and at least three guests were abducted last night following a Memorial Day party at their Amagansett, Long Island, summer home. According to a transmission just broadcast live on East Hampton Channel Seventy, the abductors plan to try Neubauer for the murder of a twenty-one-year-old resident of Montauk. The trial, at an undisclosed location, is set to begin in less than an hour."

As Jennings continued in his clipped Canadian accent, a red square appeared in the upper-right-hand corner of the screen. It showed a simple outline of the end of Long Island and in bold red type, CRISIS IN THE HAMPTONS.

Within minutes, the anchors, or substitute anchors, for both CBS (THE SIEGE OF LONG ISLAND) and NBC (HOSTAGES IN THE HAMPTONS) had tightened their ties and joined the fray. Like Jennings, they would spend the next forty-five minutes authoritatively treading water as their reporters scrambled to catch up with the breaking story.

ABC's first remote was an interview with Sergeant Tommy Harrison in the parking lot behind the East Hampton police station. "Jack and Macklin Mullen," said Harrison, "are well-known, longtime residents of Montauk who seemed to have acted out of frustration about the outcome of an inquest into Peter Mullen's death last summer."

"Does either have a criminal record?" asked the reporter.

"You don't get it," said Harrison. "Except for one minor incident that Jack Mullen was involved in after his brother died, neither has ever been arrested. Not even a speeding ticket."

ABC then cut to the Justice Department in Washington for a live briefing that had just begun with a spokesman. ". . . of the hostages seized in Long Island last night. The five who have thus far been identified are Barry and Campion Neubauer, Tom and Stella Fitzharding, who own a home in Southampton, and William Montrose, a prominent New York attorney."

When the spokesman looked up from his notes, he was peppered with discordant queries: "Why were the hostages taken?" "Why can't you track the source of the broadcast?" "What do you know about the kidnappers?"

He made just one more short statement, then brought the briefing to a close: "The abductors are employing a scrambling device that so far has prevented us from pinpointing the source of the broadcast. To say any more at this point would be counter to our efforts to resolve this situation as quickly as possible."

Then ABC cut away again to the offices of Channel 70 in Wainscott. The twenty-four-year-old station manager, J. J. Hart, stood beside the station's lawyer, Joshua Epstein. Hart stated that he had no intention of complying with the government's gag order. "Our reporter, Molly Ferrer, has pulled off one of the great scoops in television journalism. We have no intention of *not* sharing it with the public."

"The injunction is blatantly unconstitutional," said Epstein. "Monday I'm going to have it thrown out of court. Unless something happened last night that no one's told me about, we still live in a democracy."

"To summarize what we know so far," said Jennings, "we have five hostages, maybe more. The grandfather and grandson kidnappers were apparently unhinged by the controversial death of a family member. And a most unusual murder trial is about to begin. We will have more soon, but right now we're going to pick up the feed from Channel Seventy in East Hampton, where the live broadcast of the murder trial is about to start."

Chapter 89

"THE PEOPLE'S COURT OF MONTAUK," said Macklin in a calm and assured voice, "obliged to nothing but the truth, and having zero tolerance for bullshit, is called to order."

Then he brought down his gavel with a resounding smack.

My grandfather and I acknowledged the sweet significance of the moment by exchanging a quick glance before I called Tricia Powell to the stand. I think she understood the significance of appearing on TV, but maybe not what was about to happen to her. Once she had been sworn in, I began.

"Ms. Powell, I understand you arrived at this season's party in style."

"I guess you mean my new Mercedes."

"It's been quite a turn of events, hasn't it? One summer you're an executive assistant at Mayflower. The next you're stepping out of a forty-five-thousand-dollar sedan."

"I've had a good year," said Tricia Powell with some indignation. "In February I was promoted to director of special events."

"Forgive me for prying, but what were you making last year?"

"Thirty-nine thousand."

"And now?"

"Ninety," she said proudly.

"So, months after you lied at the inquest about seeing my brother dive out into deadly cold waves at Neubauer's party, you're promoted and your salary more than doubles. Perjury served you better than a Harvard MBA."

"Your Honor," barked Montrose.

"Sustained," said Macklin. "Knock it off, Jack."

"Excuse me. Months after you testified that you saw my brother dive into fifty-degree water in the middle of his shift parking cars, your salary increased by fifty-one thousand dollars. Is there anything other than your testimony that made you so much more valuable to your employer?"

"There is, but you wouldn't want to hear about it," said Powell. "After all, it doesn't fit in with your conspiracy theory."

"Please, Ms. Powell. Give me a chance. The court wants to hear your version of things."

"I worked fifty- and sixty-hour weeks. There was no way I was going to stay an assistant for long."

"I believe that's correct," I said, opening the manila folder I held in my hand.

"Ms. Powell, I'm showing you what has been marked People's Exhibit A." I handed her the document.

"Do you recognize it?"

"Yes."

"What do you recognize it to be?"

"That's my six-month evaluation at Mayflower Enterprises. How did you get it?" she demanded.

"That's not relevant just now," I said. "Do you recognize the signature on the bottom of the last page?" I asked, pointing to her signature.

"It's mine."

"Your Honor," I said, looking up at Mack, "at this time, the People offer People's Exhibit A in evidence."

Mack turned to Montrose. "Any objection?"

"I object to these entire proceedings," said Montrose.

"Overruled," snapped Mack. "People's Exhibit A is admitted. Go ahead, Jack."

"I'm going to skip right past the opening section that documents the days you managed to be late or sick, and read from the section titled 'Conclusion — Next Steps.' I think it should give us all a fair idea of the impression you were making on your employer before my brother died.

"Asked to rate your performance from zero to ten in attitude, effort, and overall competence, your three supervisors gave you no score higher than a six," I said. "Here is the final paragraph: 'Ms. Powell has been given a written warning. If her work doesn't improve dramatically in the next few months, she will be terminated.' "

"Well, I guess I made a dramatic improvement," said Tricia Powell.

Chapter 90

BILL MONTROSE was out of his seat in a flash. With his shock of white hair, sturdy body, and abrupt, confident movements, Montrose looked a little like a maestro at Lincoln Center. He stood very still at the front of the room. He evoked the concentration of a conductor waiting for his orchestra to settle down.

"Ms. Powell," he asked when he emerged from his spell, "were you compensated in *any way* for your testimony at the inquest last summer?"

"Absolutely not," said Powell. "Not a penny."

"Were you promised anything by Barry Neubauer or anyone else acting on his behalf?"

"No."

"Was a promotion, a raise, a window office, a personal trainer, or even a new pair of shoes dangled in front of you?"

"No!" said Powell even more indignantly.

"Ms. Powell, Jack Mullen seems to be under the delusion that there's something scandalous about an ambitious and talented person coming to the attention of the CEO. There isn't. You've done nothing to feel the slightest bit apologetic about."

"Thank you."

I rose from my seat. "Does Mr. Montrose have a question?"

"I certainly do. Ms. Powell, let me ask you how it is that you came to be in this courtroom this afternoon. You're not here voluntarily?"

"Of course not," said Tricia. "None of us are."

"Could you tell us how you got here?"

"I was driving home," said Powell, "when a man sprung up from my backseat. He threatened me."

"Were you afraid?"

"Wouldn't you be? I almost drove off the road."

"Then what?"

"He directed me to a house, where I was forced into the back of a smelly milk truck with you and the Fitzhardings."

"How long were you in the truck?"

"Almost seven hours."

"And are you free to leave now?" Montrose asked.

"No."

"If Mr. Mullen will allow it, Ms. Powell, you may return to your seat."

"Thank you."

After Tricia Powell retreated, Montrose turned to face the camera. He was about to make a speech when a look of alarm swept over his face. His jaw actually dropped.

Chapter 91

MONTROSE'S ANXIOUS EYES followed Jane Davis as she strode across the stone floor, her footsteps echoing in the room.

Jane wore black dress slacks and a black blouse, and she didn't appear nervous or afraid, as she had at the inquest. She stared at Montrose, then turned to look directly at Barry Neubauer.

To show his lack of concern, Neubauer flashed a smug smile. To show hers, Jane smiled back serenely.

"The People call Dr. Jane Davis," I announced, and she walked to where Fenton was waiting with his family's Gideon Bible. Whereas at the inquest her hands had trembled, now she seemed perfectly calm. She placed a hand on the Bible's red leatherette cover and swore "to tell the truth."

"Dr. Davis," I said as she was seated, "we appreciate

the potential consequences of your testifying today. We're grateful."

"I want to be here," she said. "No one has to thank me." Then Jane leaned back and took a deep, calming breath.

"Dr. Davis," I began, "could you please review your education for the court?"

"Certainly. I graduated first in my class from East Hampton High School in 1988, and was a National Merit Scholar. I believe I was the first person in over a decade to be admitted to Harvard from East Hampton High, but I couldn't afford the tuition, so I went to SUNY Binghamton."

"Where did you receive your graduate education?"

"I attended Harvard Medical School, then did my residency at UCLA Hospital in Los Angeles."

"How are you presently employed?"

"For the past two years, I have been chief pathologist at Long Island Hospital and also the chief medical examiner for Suffolk County."

"Your Honor," I said, looking up at Mack, "the People offer Dr. Jane Davis as an expert witness in pathology and forensic medicine."

Mack turned to Montrose, who was still in a state of agitation. "I'm sure Mr. Montrose has no objection to Dr. Davis's testimony, as he called her as an expert witness before the inquest. Correct, Counselor?"

Montrose nodded distractedly and mumbled, "No objection."

"Dr. Davis," I continued, "you performed the autopsy on my brother?"

"Yes."

"Dr. Davis, before you came into the courtroom, Ms.

Powell described her abduction before the start of this trial. I was hoping you could share your own experience before the inquest?"

She nodded. "The night before I was to testify," she said, "a man broke into my home. I was in bed, asleep. He woke me and put a gun between my legs. He said he was concerned about my testimony going well. He had been sent to 'coach' me. He said if I blew any lines at the inquest, he would come back and rape and murder me."

For the first time since she'd entered the room, Jane lowered her head and stared at the floor.

"I'm sorry you had to go through that, Jane," I said.

"I know."

"What did you do in court the next day?" I asked. "At the inquest."

"I committed perjury," said Jane Davis, loud and clear.

She continued, "In the course of completing your brother's autopsy, I took twenty-six sets of X rays. I performed half a dozen biopsies and did extensive blood and lab work. Peter had nineteen broken bones, including both arms and both wrists, eight fingers, and six ribs. His skull was fractured in two places, and he had three cracked vertebrae. In several cases the welts of his body showed such perfect fistprints and footprints, they looked like they had been traced on.

"On top of that, Peter's lung tissue was not consistent with drowning. The level of saturation was in keeping with someone who was dumped into the water *after* he'd stopped breathing. The evidence that Peter had been kicked and beaten to death, then dragged into the water, was overwhelming. That Peter Mullen was murdered is as irrefutable as that I'm sitting here right now."

Chapter 92

MONTROSE ROSE FROM HIS CHAIR. The enormous strain was evident by the set of his jaw. I could almost hear him reminding himself that he was the great Bill Montrose.

"Is there such a thing as a fair trial that isn't quite fair?" he asked. "Of course not. But our abductors would have you believe otherwise. 'I know it's not exactly accepted legal procedure,' Mr. Mullen suggests with an apologetic shrug, 'for defendants to be dragged at gunpoint out of their cars in the middle of the night. But give us a chance, we're just ordinary people like you. We've been driven to this because the system is broken, the system is unfair.'

"But that's not how justice works. Certainly not how it's supposed to work according to the Constitution and the laws of our country." Montrose flinched as if he felt a threat to the Constitution as keenly as a physical blow.

"Justice," he continued, "is not about being slightly fairer than your expectations. It's about being fair. Period. And how can there be a fair trial when the prosecution can ambush the defense with a surprise witness like Jane Davis?"

I had heard more than enough of Montrose's rhetoric. If Macklin was going to allow speeches, I was going to give one of my own. "Everyone in this room understands your frustration," I said, rising from my chair. "We were in the courtroom last summer when Dr. Davis, after being terrorized all night, said she believed my brother's death was accidental. Just like you, the young prosecutor, Nadia Alper, was so taken aback, she wasn't prepared to cross-examine.

"But although the tactics you're facing today are almost identical to the ones she faced, there's a fundamental difference," I said, feeling my face redden. "At the inquest, the prosecutor was ambushed by a lie. You've been ambushed by the truth, a truth you've probably known all along.

"You love to go on about what a mockery this trial is, Mr. Montrose. What really galls you is that it's almost fair. After tirelessly defending the rich and powerful for twenty-five years, you've become so warped that anything even resembling a level playing field is offensive. I suggest you get over it."

"All right, that's enough," Mack finally said from his chair. "This court is adjourned for the evening."

Chapter 93

THIS TIME WHEN *The People* v. *Barry Neubauer* adjourned, the newsmaking machinery was stoked and ready to crank. "The Siege on Long Island" was the most ratings-friendly story in years. And it was convenient. Half the reporters and producers who filed stories that evening were already in the Hamptons when the day began.

The instant Channel 70 went black, the dueling anchors began addressing the nation. They rolled out the profiles their networks had thrown together in the past two hours. The country learned how Barry Neubauer had married into one of the East Coast's most prominent publishing families and extended its reach into radio and cable, theme parks, and the Internet. They heard respectful assessments of his vision from rivals like Ted Turner and Rupert Murdoch.

They also learned that his Yale-educated lawyer,

William Montrose, hadn't lost a case in seventeen years. Montrose had cemented his reputation in a Fort Worth courtroom nine years before with his defense of a wealthy rancher who'd killed a tennis pro he wrongly suspected of sleeping with his mistress. Colleagues said Montrose so outlawyered the prosecutor that the state, which had pushed hard for second-degree murder, was grateful to get a thousand-dollar fine for possession of an unregistered firearm.

Then came the deluge about the Mullens. Interviews with prominent townspeople touched on the death of Jack's mother and father and revealed how little the pair conformed to a terrorist profile. "The only reason I'm the mayor of Montauk," said Peter Siegel, "is that Macklin didn't run. And Jack is our homegrown golden boy."

"They're the working-class Kennedys of Montauk," pronounced Dominick Dunne, who arrived in town on assignment for *Vanity Fair.* "The same good looks and charisma, the same Irish Catholic blarney, and the same tragic curse."

The reporting showed how quickly the story had polarized the East End. When a sunburned investment banker getting out of his Porsche in front of an East Hampton wine shop was approached by a reporter, he said, "I hope they get life." He was expressing the prevailing sentiment of the *oberen Klassen.*

The locals saw it differently. They may have couched it in neutral-seeming sound bites like "I just hope everyone gets home safe," but the only ones whose safety they were concerned about were the Mullens and their friends.

"If you know what's happened to this family in the past few years," said Denise Lowe, a waitress at PJ's Pancake House, "you'd understand that this is an American tragedy. It's just so sad. We all love Jack and Macklin."

But it wasn't until nearly midnight, when the news-readers went home and the cable pundits took over, that the first truly sympathetic editorial commentating began to seep out. As has been the case quite often, the voice ahead of the curve belonged to Geraldo.

That night, he broadcast from the bar of the Shagwong restaurant. Moderating the show like a town meeting, Ger-aldo drew out the locals. He encouraged them to gush and reminisce about Mack and Jack.

"One reason that Macklin might be so comfortable in his new role," said Gary Miller, who owned a nursery, "is that unofficially he's been the town judge for twenty years. As a matter of fact, we're sitting in his favorite court right now."

Geraldo also set up a live remote with Chauncy How-ells, dean of Columbia Law School. "Jack Mullen was not a good law student, he was a *brilliant* law student," said Howells. "One of the sharpest I ever taught. Never-theless, he didn't apply for a single legal job. That sug-gests he was planning this for some time, and appreciated the consequences. I have no doubt that for Jack Mullen this was a moral and ethical — and well-considered — decision."

"Make no mistake," said Geraldo in closing, "Jackson and Macklin Mullen are not fanatics or radicals, or even nut jobs. They are people who, not unlike you and me, were fed up by the transparent inequities in the criminal justice system. The only difference is that those injustices hit a lot closer to home for them than for us. They decided to do something about it. Our prayers go out to *everyone* caught up in this tragedy. Good night, my friends."

And as the networks and cable stations turned *The People* v. *Barry Neubauer* into more grist for the mill, the FBI poured into the Hamptons. In their styleless rubber-soled brogans, bad haircuts, and generic domestic sedans, they looked as out of place as someone on food stamps.

Chapter 94

"IF I'M NOT REAL CAREFUL, I could get used to a place like this," said Macklin, running one long, bony finger along the aged mahogany wainscoting that made the room seem as if it had been lifted from a stone manse in some British PBS miniseries. We were sitting in the corner library, just off the more austere space we'd turned into our courtroom. Mack and I parked ourselves on the polished oak floors and sat facing the long, tall window that looked out onto the empty beach. I felt as if I'd just lived through the world's first hundred-hour day.

"I've been thinking about Marci and Fenton and Hank," I said. "We shouldn't have let them get involved."

"It's a little late for that, Jack. Besides, they wanted to be here," said Macklin impatiently. "And I hope you've more in your hand than you showed today."

"How about Jane's testimony?" I asked him.

"It was the best you had. But it didn't implicate

Neubauer. Not in the least. Where's the hard evidence, Jack?"

"You can't skip steps, Mack," I told him. "As Fenning, my old trial tactics instructor, put it, you got to 'build the boat.' "

"Well, build the frigging thing already, and make sure it floats. Now help me up, Jack. I've got to get into my sleeping bag. I shouldn't be talking to you anyway."

I grabbed a huge gnarled hand and pulled hard. While I had him there, I gave him a long, stout hug. I felt I was grabbing a bag of bones.

"Don't get old on me, Macklin," I said. "I need you too much."

"I feel like I've aged ten years in the last ten hours. That's not too good when you start the day at eighty-seven."

Chapter 95

THE LIBRARY HAD ITS OWN BALCONY, and once Mack hobbled off, I slid open the glass door and stepped outside. I knew I shouldn't be out there, but I needed to clear my head. I wanted to think everything through one more time, especially the main reason I hoped we might actually get away with it.

The deck was angled out from the corner of the house. Whether you looked east toward the lighthouse or west toward town, you didn't see another man-made structure. In its vast cold-blooded beauty, a Montauk night can make you feel as insignificant as a fly jammed up on the wrong side of a windowsill. But that night the dwarfing scale was comforting. And the stars were dazzling.

One of the many happy side effects of perspective and clear thinking is that it helps you sleep. I stretched out on the cedar planks, and in seconds I was out.

I was jarred from sleep by footsteps at the end of the deck.

It was too late to run. I sat up and stared blindly into the dark. Maybe the FBI. Some deep, scary voice about to order me to roll over on my stomach and put my hands behind my back.

We had made it clear, I hoped, that we weren't going to harm any hostages. There was no need to shoot me on sight. I almost said out loud, "No need to shoot."

I smelled Pauline's light perfume before I saw her. "Coming back here was insane," I said when she stepped out of the darkness.

But I didn't say it with much conviction. I figured she'd been thinking the same thing I had, that it might be our last night together for a long time.

"So, I'm insane," she said.

"Well, you've come to the right place."

Pauline lay down and leaned into me, and for a few minutes I forgot about everything except how right she was for me. The thought filled me with anguish.

"I didn't mean it, Paulie girl. I'm really glad you came back from New York."

"I know, Jack. So give the girl a kiss."

Chapter 96

AN HOUR OR SO LATER, Pauline and I were still out on the deck beneath the canopy of a thousand glittering stars.

"Did you get the blood work back from Jane?" she asked softly. For a second I was somewhere so far away that I didn't know what she meant.

"Not till tomorrow. Early, I hope. How about you? How'd it go out there in the big, bad world?"

"I did good," said Pauline with her loveliest cat-that-swallowed-the-canary grin. "Real good, Jack. You're going to be happy."

"How many could you track down?"

"Twelve," she said, "out of twelve."

"And how many signed?"

"All of them. Every single one, Jack. They hate that son of a bitch Neubauer as much as we do."

"Looks like I hired the right investigator," I said, and kissed her again.

"You have an eye for talent. Oh, by the way, Jack, you're *famous*."

"Good famous? Or bad famous?"

"Depends on the channel, and the commentator. The guy on *Hardball* says you and Mack should be dragged into the town square and hanged."

"It would make powerful television."

"Ten minutes later Geraldo compared you to heroes in the American Revolution."

"I always felt Geraldo never got the respect he deserves."

"Since when?"

"Since tonight."

"And this weatherwoman on Fox, I think she wants to have your baby."

"Someone should tell her I'm taken."

"Good answer, Jack. You're learning."

"It's true. If there's any baby-making involving me, it's going to be done with a non-weatherwoman with the musical name of Pauline Grabowski."

There was a sweet pause.

"Pauline?"

"What's that, lawyer boy?"

"I love you."

"I love you, too. That's why I'm here," she whispered. "It's probably why we're all here, Jack."

"I love you more than I ever thought I could love anybody. I worship you, actually. You surprise me, in good ways, just about every day we're together. I love your spirit, your compassion, that sweet, funny laugh of yours.

I never get tired of being with you. I miss you terribly when you're away." I stopped and looked into her eyes. Pauline stared back, didn't blink. "Will you marry me?" I whispered.

This time the silence was frightening. I was afraid to move.

I finally propped myself up on one elbow and leaned over her. Her face seemed to be broken into a million shimmering pieces. She looked more beautiful than I had ever seen her.

When she nodded through her tears, the riddle of my life was solved.

Chapter 97

TWENTY-NINE-YEAR-OLD Coast Guard Lt. Christopher Ames sat tall behind the tapered windscreen of his jet-powered Blackhawk 7000 helicopter and felt as if the night were his own private video game. He was on duty, searching for the missing millionaires, but his heart wasn't in it. He didn't much like any of the millionaires he'd met. All three of them.

Eighteen miles northeast of Montauk was Block Island. Ames had spent the day flying back and forth over every square inch. Zilch. He wasn't really surprised.

Now he was racing back to Long Island, hotdogging it slightly, but nothing to get court-martialed for. He took a glance at the speed indicator: 280. Hell, it felt twice that. He was flying less than fifty feet above the cement-hard whitecaps.

At the Montauk lighthouse, Ames juked left and followed the steep, jagged coastline. In the moonlight, it seemed to be crumbling into the surf.

He figured he'd ride the cliffs for a few miles before tacking inland to MacArthur Airport. That's when he spotted the dark, low-slung mansion in the dunes.

He'd been scoping out multimillion-dollar vacation homes all day, but this one was over the top, even by the lofty standards of waterfront real estate in these parts. Sleek and serpentine, it went on forever along the cliffs.

Still, on the first big weekend of the summer, there wasn't a single light on. Strange, and a goddamned waste. *Somebody* ought to be using this spread.

He pulled hard on the stick, and the big bird seemed to screech to a stop in midair. It made him think of a cartoon character who realizes a beat too late that he's just run off the side of a cliff. Then, for the umpteenth time that day, Lt. Ames banked toward the mansion.

In close, he could see that the place wasn't quite finished. He spun around the grassless site like a stock car circling a quarter-mile track. His turbine engine hacked up a dirt cyclone that would settle over everything in its path — from the front porch to the big yellow steamroller at the end of the driveway.

He was about to swerve back and head for the airport when he noticed the mountain bike leaning up against one of the few trees.

He hit it with his 8,000-watt spotlight, and saw a lock hanging open from a back tire.

What have we here?

More slowly now, he circled the place again. He hovered at roof height and beamed his lights along the row of blacked-out windows.

That's when he saw the couple literally under his nose on the deck. Both of them buck naked.

Ames was about to reach for the two-way radio when the woman stood up and turned to face the lights. She was beautiful, and not in a pouting-model sort of way.

For about ten seconds she stood with her hands on her hips and stared up as if she were trying to tell him something important with her eyes. Then she raised both hands above her shoulders and flipped him the bird with each one.

Ames started to laugh, and for the first time all day remembered why he liked America.

I must have something better to do, he thought, *than bust a couple of trespassers for making love in one of the most beautiful spots in North America.* He put the handset back on its cradle, then swung the big bird back toward MacArthur Airport.

He was still smiling about the pretty girl who had flipped him the double bird.

Chapter 98

PAULINE AND I WERE LOST in our own little world, holding hands and watching the surf, when Fenton burst through the French doors to the deck.

"Jack, Volpi's gone!"

"I thought you were doing ten-minute checks? The doors were double-locked?"

"I was, Jack. I swear. He can't be gone more than a few minutes."

Fortunately, Pauline and I were dressed by now. We followed Fenton out onto the beach. We looked up and down the shoreline. *Nothing. No Volpi.*

"He would have headed west, toward the Blakely place. It's the only way that makes any sense," I said.

The three of us sprinted toward the garage and Pauline's car. With Pauline driving, we raced down the long dirt driveway, then turned left toward town.

"It can't end like this," I said.

Pauline, who was already going faster than I would have, put the pedal to the floor. It was a little before two in the morning, and the road was empty. After half a mile she took a hard left toward Franklin Cove.

"Pull over here," I told Pauline. "The shoreline is just over that dune. Either we've beaten him here, or we're fucked."

We jumped out and clambered hand over hand to the top of the dune. My heart was pounding as we topped the crest.

We were too late. Volpi was already a hundred yards past us, chugging through the sand toward a cluster of big houses at the bend.

We took off after him anyway, and quickly began closing the gap. But Volpi, who had just noticed us, was running for his life, and we weren't going to catch him before he got to the first house.

As I struggled through the sand, a gun went off behind me. Fenton and I turned to see Pauline with her Smith & Wesson held out in front of her. Then she fired again at Volpi.

The second shot must have barely missed him.

He stopped in his tracks and raised his hands. "Don't shoot!"

We kept running. Fenton got there first. He lowered his shoulder and 240 pounds into Volpi's chest, sending him sprawling onto his back. In a second we were on him, all the anger and frustration of the past year pouring into our punches.

"That's enough," said Pauline. "Stop it."

But Fenton wasn't through. He grabbed a fistful of

sand and shoved it into Volpi's mouth. Volpi gasped for breath, spat, and sputtered out a few words.

Now I grabbed a handful and pushed it in.

"What happened to Peter?" I shouted in his face. "You were there, right, Frank? What happened?"

He was still spitting out sand and gasping. "No . . . no," he managed.

"Frank, I just want to hear the truth. It doesn't matter what you tell us out here! Nobody will know but us."

Volpi shook his head, and Fenton pushed another handful of sand into his mouth. More gasping and spitting and choking followed. I was almost feeling sorry for him.

This time we gave him a minute to breathe and focus.

Gidley couldn't leave him alone, though. "Now you know how I felt when I got a visit from your friend. He tried to drown me. I couldn't breathe! I was spitting up salt water. How's the sand taste, Frank? Want some more?"

Volpi held both hands in front of his face. He was still choking, trying to clear his mouth.

"Yeah, Neubauer had his goons kill your brother. I still don't know why. I wasn't there, Jack. How could you think that? Christ, I liked Peter."

Jesus, it felt good to hear that — to finally get the truth out. Just to *hear* it.

"That's all I wanted, Frank. The truth. Stop blubbering, you piece of shit."

But Volpi wasn't finished. "You still don't have anything on him. Neubauer's too smart for you, Jack."

I hit Volpi with a short right hand, definitely the best

punch of my life, and he went face first into the sand. "I owed you that, you bastard."

Fenton put his hand on the back of Volpi's head and ground his face in the sand. "Me, too."

At least I knew the truth. That was something. We dragged Volpi's sorry ass to Pauline's car and took him back to the house.

Chapter 99

A FEW HOURS LATER, after Pauline, Molly, and I made eggs and coffee for the group, we all filed back into the courtroom. I wasn't feeling too chipper, but then the adrenaline kicked in and I was okay.

After Macklin smacked his gavel and called the room to order, Montrose rose and launched into another of his pompous speeches, something he must have been working on all night.

I objected, and Mack called the two of us to the bench.

"You know better than this," he said to Montrose. "You should be testifying to the facts, not philosophizing, or whatever the hell it is that you're doing. You, either, Jack. But because of the other restrictions put on you, Mr. Montrose, and in the interest of fairness and getting at the truth, you go right ahead and make your speeches. Just keep 'em short, for God's sake. I'm not getting any younger."

I shook my head and returned to my seat. Montrose took center stage again.

"Our would-be prosecutor delights in recklessly tainting the reputation of my client," said Bill Montrose, glancing my way. I had the sense that he was just warming to the task. "Till now, we haven't retaliated by drawing attention to the sad details of his late brother's life. It seemed inappropriate and, I had hoped, unnecessary.

"Now," said Montrose as if he'd spent the night wrestling with his oversize conscience, "we have no choice. If, in fact, Peter Mullen's death wasn't an accident, which is doubtful, there are people far more likely to have done him harm than Barry Neubauer.

"When Peter Mullen died at the end of last May," said Montrose, clearing his throat, "the world did not lose its next Mother Teresa. It lost a high-school dropout who, at the age of thirteen, had already been arrested for drug possession. You should also know that despite having never held a regular job in his life, Peter Mullen had almost *two hundred thousand dollars* in his bank account at the time of his death. Two months earlier he paid for a nineteen-thousand-dollar motorcycle with an envelope of thousand-dollar bills."

How did they know that? Had someone been following me?

"Unlike our prosecutor, I am not irresponsible enough to stand up here and claim that Peter Mullen was a drug dealer. I don't have enough *evidence* to say that. But based on his background, bank account, and lifestyle, and no other way to explain his wealth, it does beg the question, doesn't it? And if Peter Mullen made his living selling drugs, he would have attracted violent rivals. That's the way the drug world works, even in the Hamptons."

Hearing these phony charges dragged out yet again pushed me out of my seat.

"No one," I said, "claims my brother is a candidate for sainthood. But he wasn't a drug dealer. Everyone in this room knows it. Not only that, they know exactly how two hundred thousand dollars found its way to his bank account. Because it was *their* money!"

"Your Honor," protested Montrose, "the prosecutor has no right to this kind of grandstanding. Even if he is your grandson."

Macklin sat there and nodded.

"If the prosecutor has something to share with the court," he said, "he should cut the crap and do so. He should also be advised that any further unprofessional behavior will not be tolerated in this courtroom. This is supposed to be a fair trial, and damn it, that's what it's going to be."

Chapter 100

AFTER MONTHS OF MY OBSESSING about this trial, studying for it, investigating and gathering evidence, the moment of truth was here. I'd wanted justice for Peter, and maybe I could get it — *if* I was good enough, *if* I could keep my temper and indignation in check, *if* I could actually beat Bill Montrose just this one time. Fair and square.

"I have some crucial evidence to present to the court," I said. "But first, I want to clear up something regarding my brother Peter's drug arrest. It happened in Vermont eight years ago. I was a twenty-one-year-old college senior, and Peter, who was thirteen, was visiting me.

"One night, a local policeman pulled us over for a broken taillight. He came up with an excuse to search the car and found a joint under the driver's seat. That's what happened.

"Knowing that I had just applied to law school, though

I wouldn't actually go to Columbia for a few more years, Peter insisted that the joint was his. It *wasn't*. It was mine. I'm telling you this to set the record straight and to illustrate that while Peter was no saint, he was as good a brother as anyone could hope to have. Nothing I am about to show you changes that.

"Now, if you can adjust the lights," I continued, "the People have a couple of exhibits we would like to share."

Marci scrambled up a small stepladder and refocused a pair of 1,500-watt spots until they flooded a twelve-foot section of the sidewall. Close to the center of the lit area, I taped a large, colorful illustration.

It showed a rosy-cheeked toddler, snug and warm in a reindeer-festooned sweater. The child was surrounded by cuddly stuffed animals.

"This is the cover of last year's Christmas catalog for Bjorn Boontaag, which is now owned by Barry Neubauer. I will read what the catalog copy says: 'Boontaag is the most profitable manufacturer of toys and furniture in the world. The three stuffed lionesses on the cover are the incredibly popular Sneha, Saydaa, and Mehta, sold by the tens of thousands to parents all over the world. Inside this catalog are two hundred pages of children's toys, clothing, and furniture.'

"The People will offer this picture as Exhibit B," I said.

Then I looked around the room like a guerrilla fighter in the eerily serene seconds before firing off his first missile.

"The People will now offer Exhibit C."

Chapter 101

"EXHIBIT C, I HAVE TO WARN YOU, is not nearly as wholesome as the Boontaag Christmas catalog," I said. "In fact, if you're watching with your children now, you should have them leave the room."

I walked slowly back to my table and picked up the portfolio-size envelope. As I did so, I peered at Barry Neubauer, holding his glance until I could see the first shadow of panic in his narrowing eyes.

"The images I'm about to put on this wall aren't warm and fuzzy. They're hot and cruel and in razor-sharp focus. If they celebrate anything, it's definitely not children or family."

"Objection!" shouted Montrose. "I vehemently object to this!"

"Let the evidence speak for itself," said Macklin. "Go on, Jack."

My heart was banging as violently as if I were fighting

for my life, but I spoke with preternatural calm. "Your Honor," I said, "the People call Ms. Pauline Grabowski."

Pauline briskly walked to the witness chair. I could tell that she was eager to play her part, even if it meant implicating herself.

"Ms. Grabowski," I began, "how are you employed?"

"Up until recently, I was a private investigator employed at Mr. Montrose's law firm."

"How long were you employed there?"

"Ten years, until I quit."

"How were you viewed by the firm?"

"I received five promotions during my ten years. I was given performance bonuses each year that exceeded the target bonus by at least one hundred percent. Mr. Montrose himself told me that I was the best investigator that he had worked with in his twenty-five years of practice."

I couldn't help but smile as Montrose squirmed in his seat.

"Now, Ms. Grabowski, what if any role have you played in the investigation of this case?"

"Well, I've done the usual background checks, talked to potential witnesses, collected documents. . . ."

"Directing your attention to Thursday, the third of May, did you meet with counsel at the Memory Motel?"

"Yes, I did."

"What, if anything, did you find there?"

"I found Sammy Giamalva's private collection of photographs. I examined several dozen black-and-white prints."

Now it was about to begin.

I moved in slow motion . . . extracting the photographs inch by inch.

"Ms. Grabowski, are these the photographs?"

"Yes."

"Are they in the same condition today as the day you first saw them?"

"Yes."

"Your Honor, the People offer People's Exhibit C, thirteen eight-by-twelve black-and-white print photographs."

Montrose screamed, "Objection!"

Macklin waved him off. "Overruled. This is relevant evidence that has been authenticated by a qualified witness. I'll allow it."

I held the first photograph with its back to the room and carefully examined it. It still made me sick.

Then I walked to the wall and taped the photograph beside the cover of the Boontaag Christmas catalog. Only when I was satisfied that it was securely attached to the wall, and not the slightest bit askew, did I step aside.

I let Molly zoom in and lock off in tight focus.

The first thing that hit anyone who viewed the photograph was the lurid intensity of the lighting. Even in this well-lit room it burned like neon in the night. It was the kind of light that is pumped into operating rooms and morgues. It froze every vein and follicle and blemish in a nightmarish hyperreality.

Matching the harsh intensity of the lighting were the crazed expressions of the two men and one woman, and the heat of the action itself. They were crowded together at the center of the print as if the woman were on fire and the men were huddling around her for warmth.

Only after adjusting to the glare would anyone notice that the woman between the two men was Stella Fitzharding. The man sodomizing her was Barry Neubauer, and the man on his back beneath her was my brother.

Chapter 102

THE BLACK-AND-WHITE PHOTOGRAPH jolted the room like a powerfully concussive blast that leaves those in the vicinity damaged but unbloodied. It was Neubauer who broke the silence. "Goddamned bastard!" he shouted.

Montrose bellowed, "Objection! Objection! Objection!" as if his client's cry had tripped a mechanical alarm in his throat.

Their ruckus set off Macklin. He was mad, and it showed. "I'll gag the whole room if you don't pipe down. This is evidence, and it's certainly relevant. I'll allow it."

Only when quiet had been restored did I return to the painstaking task of hanging more photos. Reminding myself to take my time to "build the boat," I spent the next five minutes taping up pictures of Peter and various partners. All together I put up thirteen, a pornographer's dirty dozen and just about the saddest family album I've ever seen.

Although there were occasional cameos by unidentified guests, the core troupe remained constant: Barry and Peter, Stella and Tom — the Neubauers' best friends. We definitely had the right people in the room. They had been doing my brother since he was a kid.

There's no denying the disconcerting power of hardcore pornography. After each photograph was secured to the wall, Molly zoomed in for a close-up. She held it for a full ten seconds.

"Turn off the camera!" screamed Neubauer. "Stop it now!"

"Could the prosecutor and I approach the bench?" asked Bill Montrose after speaking to Neubauer. When Mack waved us forward, Montrose said, "Mr. Neubauer has a proposal he believes could end these proceedings. He's asked me to pass it on."

"The People aren't interested," I said flatly.

"What is it?" asked Macklin.

"My client insists on presenting it himself. In private."

"There is nothing of value he can offer this court," I told Macklin. "Let's move on."

Montrose repeated his request to Macklin. "All he wants is ninety seconds, Your Honor. Surely you can spare us that — in the interest of fairness, or whatever the hell this is supposed to represent."

"This court is recessed for two minutes," announced Macklin. "Give the networks a chance to sell some beer."

He motioned for Gidley, then led all four of us into a library equipped with a running track and a ladder to get to the high shelves. Of course, there were no books.

Being in the same room with Neubauer, even with his hands cuffed, was unsettling. He was close to a rage state. He wasn't used to not getting his way. His eyes were dilated, and his nostrils flared. He gave off a feral, vinegary odor that was hard to take.

"Ten million dollars!" said Neubauer as soon as the door shut behind him. "And none of us will cooperate in any criminal proceedings against you, your grandfather, or your friends."

"That's your proposal, Mr. Neubauer?" asked Macklin.

"Ten million dollars," he repeated, "in cash deposited into an account in your name in Grand Cayman in the Bahamas. Plus, no one in your group spends any time in jail. You have my word on it. Now would somebody take off these cuffs? I want to get out of here. You got what you wanted. You won!"

"We aren't interested in your money," I said flatly.

Neubauer flicked his head at me dismissively. "A couple of years ago," he said, "some of my guests got a little carried away. A hooker fell off my yacht. It cost me five hundred thousand dollars. Now another whore has died, and I want to settle my account again. I am a man who pays his debts."

"No, Barry. You're a murdering scumbag. Frank Volpi was good enough to confirm that last night. You can't buy your way out of this, asshole!"

I realized I had gone over the edge. Neubauer's face twisted into the same pre-ejaculatory grimace recorded in some of the pictures. Then he spoke in a freaky whisper. "I liked fucking your brother, Jack. Peter was one of my all-time favorite pieces of ass! Particularly when he was thirteen, okay, Mullen?"

I was leaning on the ladder and Neubauer was straddling the metal track in the floor less than two feet away. The track led straight to his groin. All I had to do was grab the ladder and push hard, but I grabbed control of myself. I wasn't going to let him return to the courtroom looking beaten-up or abused.

"I already know what you did to my brother," I finally said. "That's why we're here. And it's going to cost you a lot more than money, Barry."

"Let's get back to work," said Mack. "It's not polite to keep a hundred million people waiting, and if nothing else, we Mullens have our manners."

Chapter 103

STELLA FITZHARDING didn't fit the profile of a third wife of a New York–Palm Beach billionaire. She was not young or blond or augmented. She was a former professor of Romance languages at the small midwestern college to which her husband had given millions to get his name on the library. If she was embarrassed by her appearance in the graphic display on the wall, she didn't show it. The first time she had screwed my brother, he was fourteen years old.

"Mrs. Fitzharding," I said once she'd been sworn in, "I have the feeling you've seen these photographs before. Is that true?"

Stella Fitzharding frowned but nodded.

"Peter had been using them to blackmail us for two years," she said.

"How much did you pay him?" I asked.

"Five thousand dollars a month? Seventy-five hundred? I forget exactly, but I remember it was the same amount we pay our gardener." She seemed bored by my questions. *Bear with me, Stella. It will pick up soon.*

"Didn't you complain to Barry Neubauer?"

"We might have, except that we found the whole experience of getting blackmailed so deliciously theatrical and, I don't know . . . noir. As soon as the pictures got dropped at our back door, we'd grab them and rush into the den, where we'd pore over them the way other folk look at themselves smiling in front of Old Faithful. It was a game we played. Your brother knew that, Jack. It was a game for him, too."

I wanted to go after her, but I held everything inside.

"Who did you make the payments to?" I asked.

She pointed to the witness table. "Detective Frank Volpi was the messenger boy."

Volpi sat there very calmly. Then he gave Stella the finger.

"So you paid the monthly fee to Detective Volpi?"

"Yes. But when the merger of Mayflower Enterprises and Bjorn Boontaag was announced, Peter suddenly realized how damaging the pictures could be. Instead of a few thousand, he wanted millions."

"So what did you think when my brother's body washed up on the beach?"

"That he had played a dangerous game — and lost," said Stella Fitzharding. "Just like you are, and just like you will."

Chapter 104

"I CALL DETECTIVE FRANK VOLPI."

Volpi didn't move. I wasn't surprised. In fact, I had expected it to happen with more of the witnesses.

"I can question you from here, Detective, if you would prefer?"

"I'm still not going to answer your questions, Jack."

"Well, let me try just one."

"Suit yourself."

"Do you remember the talk we had last night, Detective?" I asked.

Volpi sat there impassively.

"Let me refresh your memory, Detective. I'm referring to the conversation in which you said that Barry Neubauer had two of his goons murder my brother on the beach a year ago."

"Objection!" yelled Montrose.

"Sustained!" yelled Mack. "Mrs. Stevenson, please delete these last two questions from the record."

"I apologize, Your Honor," I said. "The People have no further questions."

"Nice work, Jack," said Volpi from his seat.

Chapter 105

WE BROKE FOR LUNCH and returned promptly after forty-five minutes. I couldn't eat, mostly because I was afraid I wouldn't be able to keep anything down.

The witness I was about to call represented the kind of risk any really good trial lawyer is cautioned not to take. I felt I had no choice. It was time to find out if I was a good judge of human nature, and also if I was any kind of lawyer.

I took a deep breath.

"Campion Neubauer," I said.

A hush fell over the room. Campion slowly got up and walked forward. She looked back at the other witnesses, as if expecting one of them to throw her a lifeline.

Bill Montrose immediately rose from his seat. "Absolutely not! Mrs. Neubauer is currently undergoing treatment for chronic depression. She's been unable to take her medication since this ordeal began."

I looked at Campion, who had already sat down in the witness chair. "How are you feeling?" I asked her. "You okay with this?"

She nodded. "I'm fine, Jack. Actually, I want to say something."

"Not that it means anything to you," shouted Neubauer from his seat, "but the law prohibits forcing a wife to testify against her husband!"

"The so-called spousal privilege," responded Macklin, "can be asserted by either spouse for their own protection. But the privilege only protects statements made by one spouse to another, not the underlying facts. You may testify, Mrs. Neubauer."

A thin smile broke across Campion's lips. I had known her for a long time and had seen her change from a beautiful, free-spirited woman to an extremely bitter one. That was part of the reason I was taking a chance with her now.

"Not to worry, darling," she said to her husband. "No one's forcing me to testify against you. I'm here of my own free will."

After Gidley swore in Campion, I asked if she would go with me to examine a few of the photographs on the wall. She did as I asked.

I pointed to a woman apparently reaching climax in the third picture in the row. "Who is that?" I asked.

"Stella Fitzharding. She's a freak."

"And this younger woman on her knees?"

"Tricia Powell. The young businesswoman doing so well in Special Events at my husband's company."

"And poured between the two of them, my brother, Peter, who was certainly no saint."

Campion shook her head. "No, but he never hurt anybody. And everyone did love Peter."

"That's comforting," I said.

I walked her down the line of photos. I pointed.

"Peter again," Campion said.

"How old would you say Peter was when this picture was shot?"

"I don't know — maybe fifteen."

"No older than that?" I asked.

"No. I don't think so. Jack, you have to believe this — I had no idea this was happening in my house. Not at first anyway. I'm sorry. I apologize to you and your family."

"I'm sorry, too, Campion."

We proceeded down the row. "In each of these next half dozen shots spanning five years, my brother, who in the earliest pictures is no more than fifteen, is being mounted by a much older man."

"That would be my husband, Barry Neubauer," she said, and pointed to the man grabbing the arms of an old beach chair as tightly as he held Peter in the photos.

We skipped several shots, then stopped together in front of the last photograph in the series.

In it Peter and Barry were joined by a third middle-aged man, wearing a studded dog collar hooked to an industrial-strength leash. "The man on all fours," I said. "I'm almost positive I've seen him before."

"Undoubtedly," said Campion. "He's Robert Crassweller, Junior, the attorney general of the United States."

Chapter 106

I ESCORTED CAMPION back to the witness chair. Suddenly she looked younger and more relaxed. She'd even stopped glancing over at Barry for approval, or disapproval. Or whatever it was she got from him.

"You still okay?" I asked.

"I'm fine. Let's keep going."

I gestured toward the wall of photographs.

"Other than the faces and bodies, Campion, is there anything else you recognize in the pictures?"

"The rooms. The pictures were all shot at our house. The house I grew up in. The beach house my family has owned for nearly a hundred years."

"Different rooms or the same one?" I asked.

"Mostly different."

"One thing I can't quite figure out," I said, "is where the photographer hid."

"It depends on the shot, but there are any number of

places. Lots of nooks and crannies. It's a huge old house."

"But how would the photographer know where to hide and be able to get himself there again and again without being detected?"

There was a crash behind me, and when I twisted to face it, Neubauer, having destroyed the card table with his full-stretch lunge, was crawling across the floor toward his wife. As Fenton and Hank pounced on him, a black tomahawk flew across the room, leaving a nasty black mark on the wall six inches from Campion's head. It was Stella Fitzharding's left shoe.

"Your husband and friend seem quite certain you were the one helping the blackmailers, Mrs. Neubauer," I said. Unscathed by either attack, Campion sat on the stand as calmly as when she arrived.

"I was," she said.

"You were blackmailing your own husband, Mrs. Neubauer?" I asked. "But as controlling partner of Mayflower Enterprises, you had more to lose than he did."

"I guess we would have to agree, Jack, that there are some things more important than money. At first I merely wanted to document it," Campion explained. "Have a record of what was going on in a house that has been in my family for a century. But then I couldn't resist the thought of watching my husband squirm."

"Peter didn't know about the blackmailing, did he?"

"He never would have gone along with it. He didn't hate Barry enough. Peter didn't hate anyone except himself. That was his loveliest flaw."

"Wouldn't it have been easier to simply divorce your husband?"

"Easier perhaps, but definitely not safer. As you've noticed by now, when Barry gets upset, people start washing up onshore."

I covered my mouth with a hand and took in a breath. Then I asked my next question, a big one. "Isn't that why you needed pictures even more incriminating than the ones up on the wall, Campion?"

Her back stiffened. "I'm not sure I follow," she said, nervously fingering the black crystal amulet on her necklace.

I moved in closer to Campion. "I think you do. It's one thing catching Barry having illicit sex with young boys and girls. But if, for example, you had pictures of him committing murder? Isn't that why you set up Peter?"

"I didn't know Barry was going to kill Peter that night. How could I?"

"Of course you did. You just told us — 'when Barry gets upset, people start washing up onshore.' In fact, you sent Sammy to cover the murder."

"But there *are no pictures!*" she pleaded. "I don't have any pictures!"

I held up an envelope.

"But I do, Campion. I have the pictures right here."

Chapter 107

ALL OF THE COURTROOM TECHNIQUES I'd tried
so hard to master through the winter and spring deserted
me in a frantic, anxious rush. I quickly opened the envelope instead of milking the moment for what it was
worth. My heart was pumping. All my senses were razor-
sharp. I held several photographs from the envelope in
my fist.

I riffled through the photographs, then slapped them
up on the wall with the others. They were probably the
last seven shots Sammy had ever taken, and in a terrible
way they were his masterpieces.

Each was printed horizontally on nineteen-by-twenty-
two paper and was as black and murky as Sammy's
pornography was bright. Taped to the wall in a dark
jagged row, they looked less like photographs than ex-
pressionist paintings swirling violently with rage and fear
and death.

Like so much of the pornography, the action was three-on-one. But the lust was now replaced by fury, the pelvic thrusts by whaling fists and feet.

There, I could see the blurred face of Neubauer's platinum Cartier watch as he swung a blackjack at Peter's neck.

And *there,* while two other burly shapes pinned back Peter's arms, I caught the silver streaks of the buckle on Neubauer's loafer as he kicked Peter's ribs.

There was a face half-hidden in the shadows — but I could tell it was Frank Volpi's. He'd lied about being there, but of course, why wouldn't he lie? Everyone else had.

The last picture was the most hellish. I slapped it up on the wall and watched Molly's lens zoom in. I knew it would be engraved on my retina forever.

At the instant that particular picture was taken, there must have been a break in the cloud cover. As Peter lay broken at the feet of his murderers, his face was momentarily illuminated.

It was like a candlelit face in a Caravaggio, the face of a young man who knew that he was down to his last few seconds and that no one was going to save him. The horror in his eyes was too much, and even though I'd seen the photograph before, I had to look away.

"Is there any end to this shameless grandstanding?" screamed Montrose. "In all of these pictures, you can see only a single face, and that's the *victim's.*"

"The prosecutor will approach the bench," snapped Macklin. "Right now."

When I got there, he was as angry as I'd ever seen him. "Montrose is right. These pictures are useless, and you know it. What the hell are you doing, Jack? Do you have a point to make?"

"Fuck Montrose. And Neubauer. And fuck you." I spat out the words. Then I started to cry. I just lost it. "I don't care whether these pictures have value as evidence. They show Peter getting beaten to death on a beach by Neubauer and two goons, one of whom is Volpi. If I have to see it in my head for the rest of my life, then so do they. Peter didn't kill himself, he didn't drown — he was murdered, Mack. That's what it shows."

Macklin reached up and grabbed my wet face with both huge hands. He squeezed it hard as if it were a bleeding wound he was trying to staunch.

"Jack. Listen to me," he said with a heartbreaking smile. "You're doing a fine job, better than that. Don't let it get away from you now, son. Do you have anything to finish off these bastards? Please say yes, Jack."

Chapter 108

DON'T LET IT GET AWAY FROM YOU NOW.

When Peter and I were kids, our father told us a story about a huge rat that got into his and my mother's apartment in Hell's Kitchen. It was a freezing December morning. He had my mother, who was pregnant with me, sit in a coffee shop across the street.

Then my father borrowed a shovel from the super and walked back up the five flights to face the rat. He found it in the living room at the end of the railroad flat, scurrying along the wall, trying to nose a way out. It was the size of a small cat, at least ten pounds, with a shiny orange-brown pelt.

Brandishing the shovel, my father backed it into a corner. The rat tried to get past, making feints left and right, but when he saw that it was no use, he bared his teeth and waited. When my father cocked the shovel over his right shoulder like a Louisville Slugger, *the rat leaped at him!*

With a desperate swing, my father knocked it out of the air like a furry, gray-tailed softball. The rat bounced off the wall hard enough to knock over half the books on the shelves. My father barely had time to recock the shovel before the rat was flying back at him. Again the shovel caught it flush. Again the rat crashed into the wall. My father knocked it out of the air two more times before he could kill it.

When I called Barry Neubauer to the stand, he looked at me the way that rat must have looked up at my father that winter morning.

Without taking his beady eyes off me, he twitched and he seethed. His long fingers were white where they clasped the arms of his chair.

And he didn't budge.

I was starting to breathe a little hard.

"You want me to sit on your stage," he hissed. "You're going to have to drag me up there. But that wouldn't look good on television, would it, golden boy?"

"We'd be delighted to drag you up here," said Macklin, stepping down off his platform. "Hell, I'll do it myself."

After making certain his arms and legs were securely tethered to the chair, Mack and I got on either side of him. We hoisted Neubauer into the air.

As soon as his feet left the ground, he struggled against his restraints worse than the Mudman had in his dying moments. By the time we plopped him on the stand, his face and hair were covered with sweat. Behind his expensive wire-rim glasses, his pupils had shrunk to pinpoints.

"What do you have to show us now, Counselor?" he

asked in an angry, grating whine that set my teeth on edge. It was the same demeaning tone he used with employees at his house. "More dirty pictures? Proving what? That photographic images can be manipulated by computer? C'mon, Jack, you must have something better than that."

Neubauer's last taunt was barely out of his lips when there was a knock at the door at the back of the room.

"Actually, I do have something else to show you. In fact, here it comes now."

Chapter 109

NERVOUSLY LOOKING AT HER FEET, the way any-one might if she found herself walking through a lengthy room with half of America watching, Pauline slowly made her way to the front. I couldn't help feeling proud of her. She had stuck with this all the way to the end.

When she got to my side, she slipped me a piece of paper. I read it with my heart in my throat. It said, *East Hampton, L.A., Manhattan — 1996.*

Then, because she felt like it, I guess, she kissed me softly on the cheek and took a seat beside Marci.

"There is one thing you could clear up for me," I said to Neubauer, gesturing toward the pictures on the wall. "Didn't anyone ever ask you to use a condom?"

His thin slits of eyes narrowed even more. "Is this where you turn this whole thing into a public-service announce-ment? I told them they had nothing to worry about. I have myself tested all the time."

"I see. So, you lied to these people."

Neubauer's eyes grew even darker, and he twisted his neck at me. "What are you talking about?"

"I'm talking about not telling the truth. It's called lying. You lied to these people. Your wife, Tricia Powell, the Fitzhardings. My brother."

"You're crazy. Anyone can see that. This is absurd. You're a madman."

"Remember those blood samples we took when you arrived? We had yours tested for HIV."

"What are you talking about?" Neubauer bellowed.

"You're *positive,* Mr. Neubauer. We ran it through three times. Your Honor, the People offer this lab report as People's Exhibit D."

"You had no right," he screeched, rocking his chair so violently that it nearly tipped off the platform.

"What's the difference whether we had the right? If you had yourself tested all the time, we just saved you the trouble."

"It's not a crime to be sick," Neubauer said.

"No, but it is a crime to knowingly expose your partners to HIV."

"I didn't know I was HIV-positive until this minute," Neubauer snarled.

"I guess that might have been possible if it weren't for the AZT we found in your blood. Then we got your old pharmacy records. The People offer these records as People's Exhibit E. We had no right to do that, either, but you killed my brother, so we did it anyway. We found you've had prescriptions for AZT in East Hampton, Los Angeles, and Manhattan. Since 1996."

Neubauer's whole body was shaking. He didn't want

to hear anymore. Montrose was on his feet, shouting objections that Mack overruled. The Fitzhardings and Tricia Powell were screaming at Neubauer. So was Frank Volpi, who had to be restrained by Hank and Fenton.

"*Order!*" shouted Mack from his chair. "I mean it!"

"Would it surprise you to learn that in the past two weeks," I continued, "we've tracked down twelve people from the photographs on this wall and in this envelope. Not including my brother, who you also probably infected, seven have since tested positive."

Marci wheeled the camera around behind Neubauer. As I spoke to him, I was virtually looking into the lens.

"Your Honor, the People now offer seven sworn affidavits by seven individuals who, based on the timing of the results, all believe they were infected by Barry Neubauer. Most important, they state in their affidavits that Neubauer lied to them about his HIV status."

"This is all a lie," Neubauer continued to scream at me. He was shaking uncontrollably in his chair. "Make him stop telling these lies about me, Bill!"

I slowly walked toward Barry Neubauer. He'd always been so smug and controlled. He didn't believe anybody could touch him. He was smart, he was rich, he was the CEO of a major corporation, he owned people. Only now, his dark eyes looked as doomed as Peter's had on the beach.

"In New York State, knowingly exposing someone to HIV is first-degree assault. It's punishable by up to twelve years in prison. That's on each count. Twelve times twelve works out to a hundred forty-four years in prison. I could live with that."

I bent down close to the bastard's face. "My brother

was flawed; who isn't? But he was basically a good person, a good brother. Peter never hurt anybody. You killed him. I can't prove it, but I got you anyway, you bastard. How about that?"

I straightened up and addressed Molly's lens for the last time. *"The People* v. *Barry Neubauer,"* I said, "rest their case. We're out of here."

Chapter 110

IT WAS ALMOST FIVE IN THE AFTERNOON when Fenton and Hank led our guests out the front door and released them. "Go forth and multiply," Fenton said.

For a while we all stood blinking in the golden East End light, not knowing quite what to do next.

The Fitzhardings, Campion, and Tricia Powell drifted off to one end of the porch. They sat quietly together, their feet dangling over the side, their eyes staring vacantly at the unsodded lot. Frank Volpi found his own spot nearby. "Jeez," Pauline said, "they look like day laborers waiting for a lift home. Maybe clothes do make the man, and woman. I need to rethink everything."

Bill Montrose sat alone on the stoop about ten feet away from the others. Still tethered to the old beach chair, Barry Neubauer sat where Fenton and Hank had planted him after carrying him out of the house. His eyes barely moved. No one came over to talk to him, not even his lawyer.

"That's a nice image," Pauline said. "Barry Neubauer alone and broken. I'm going to hang on to it for a rainy day."

We outfitted Marci, Fenton, and Hank with bathing suits, beach towels, and flip-flops. Then we sent them wandering off in separate directions like three more sun-addled vacationers. Since they had never appeared on camera, there was no one to verify their involvement, except for the hostages. We hoped they'd be too distracted with their own problems to worry about the three of them.

Molly dragged her tripod to the driveway and looked for the best vantage point to shoot the big final scene. Pauline, Mack, and I sat down at the end of the porch away from our guests. We were blown away and as exhausted as they were.

We leaned against one another more than against the wall of the house. We soaked up some sun. Late-afternoon rays always seem the most precious, even at the beginning of the summer, but these were even more so. They felt like, I don't know, affection.

"I love you, Pauline," said Mack, breaking the silence.

"Love you back," said Pauline, too tired to lift her head off my chest.

I cleared my throat ostentatiously until Mack added, "Don't get maudlin, Jack. We're quite fond of you, too."

After a while Mack got up with a groan and walked over to where Tricia Powell was sitting. He reached into her tote and pulled out a chrome Nokia. She was too tired to complain. "Don't worry, Trish," said Mack, "it's local."

"Anyone have anything profound to say before the shit hits the fan?" he asked when he returned.

"Thanks," I said. "I couldn't have done it without you. Couldn't have done a thing. I love you both."

"Anyone want to add something we don't know?" replied Mack as he settled back down with us. "Okay, then."

Mack tapped the phone's tiny rubber pads with his enormous splayed fingers, then smiled with exaggerated delight when it started ringing. "Damn thing actually works."

"This is Mack Mullen," he told whoever picked up at the police station. "Me, my grandson, and his beautiful girl are sitting around with the Neubauers, the Fitzhardings, and some of our other favorite people on earth. We were wondering if you wanted to stop by. We're at the Kleinerhunt place. Oh, one other thing. No one's hurt and no one's armed. There's no need to do anything silly. We'll go peacefully."

Then he snapped the little phone shut like a clam, and hurled it off the porch into the sand. "They should ban those things."

Less than five minutes later, about a hundred cops and federal agents roared up Montauk's Main Street in their various marked and unmarked cars amid wailing sirens that sounded like the end of the world.

Because the Coast Guard helicopters got there just before them, we didn't hear a thing as they arrived to arrest us.

EPILOGUE

Chapter 111

IT WAS ALMOST FIVE MONTHS LATER. Pauline, Macklin, and I were sitting in the far corner of a bar near Foley Square. We were sipping muddy Guinnesses. Except for the bartender and a white cat, the place was empty. Most bars are at eleven in the morning, even in boomtown New York.

"May he rot in jail," said Macklin, dusting off his favorite toast since the start of the summer. For the record, it looked as if Barry Neubauer would. His first manslaughter trial had just begun. And there were twelve more lined up behind it like Mercedes and Audi station wagons at a Route 27 traffic light.

And here was the best part. Because of the likelihood of Neubauer's trying to flee the country, he was spending his nights and weekends on Rikers Island until the last verdict was in the books. The stock of Mayflower Enterprises had dropped to under two dollars. Barry Neubauer was ruined.

As for the three of us, that day would probably be our last day of Guinness-sipping freedom for some time. Our lawyer, Joshua Epstein, the same guy representing Molly and Channel 70, refused to have a drink with us before we headed over to court in another few minutes. He'd already prepared us, though — he didn't think our chances were good.

Mack was utterly unfazed. Then again, he was eighty-seven. He said he wanted to throw a Memorial Day party of his own to replace the gaping Beach House hole in the Hamptons social calendar. "I want to throw a *real* party," said Macklin, wiping the foam off his lips. "Something that will make those Puff Daddy shindigs that everyone gets so bent out of shape over seem like an afternoon tea."

"I feel you, Macklin," said Pauline.

"I don't want to be a party pooper," I told the two of them, "but it's time to go. We have a date in court."

"I prefer *this* bar," said Mack, and grinned like the madman he is.

"Let's go face the music," I said.

Chapter 112

AS PAULINE, MACK, AND I approached the steps of the U.S. district court in Foley Square, we were met by our nervous-looking attorney, Josh Epstein, and a crush of reporters, their lights and microphones and cameras pushing against the blue-and-white police barricades.

"My clients have no comment," Josh said, waving off the press hordes and throwing a stern stare at Mack and me. Then Josh led us on a brisk ascent of the limestone steps, into the column-lined entryway, through the metal detectors, and onto the elevator.

We rode the elevator to the twenty-third floor in silence. As the doors to the elevator slid open, Mack cleared his throat. "In the words of that old Irishman Benjamin Franklin, 'We must all hang together, or most assuredly, we will hang separately.'"

The courtroom of the Honorable James L. Blake

looked not the least like our "people's courtroom" on the cliffs of Montauk. With thirty-foot ceilings, chandeliers, and polished mahogany paneling and benches for the public, it could have been the Old Whalers' Church in Sag Harbor.

We took our seats at the defense table as Josh chatted in hushed tones with the assistant U.S. attorney assigned to our case. Dressed in a plain gray suit, white button-down shirt, and red and blue silk rep tie, AUSA Arthur Marshall was reasonable yet stern, determined to "exercise his prosecutorial discretion" in accordance with the Department of Justice operating manual.

Three months earlier Mack, Pauline, and I had all entered guilty pleas to a two-count indictment, charging us with conspiracy to kidnap and the actual kidnapping of Barry Neubauer, Campion Neubauer, William Montrose, Tom Fitzharding, Stella Fitzharding, Tricia Powell, and Frank Volpi. There had been no point in going through with a trial; we knew what we were doing, and why. At the time we entered our guilty pleas, we were informed by Judge Blake of the price we would have to pay for the justice that we had gotten for Peter: "At the time of sentencing, you will face a custodial sentence of not less than twenty years."

Today was that day.

"All rise!" commanded the bailiff as the Honorable James L. Blake entered the courtroom.

The crowd in the courtroom "pews" rose as the elderly judge lumbered up the steps to the bench, his black robe dragging on the floor behind him. He looked almost as old as Mack, and just as thorny. He took his seat and glared out at the courtroom.

"Be seated," he barked.

"The United States versus Jack Mullen, Macklin Reid Mullen, and Pauline Grabowski," called out the bailiff. "This case is on for sentencing."

Chapter 113

"IS THE GOVERNMENT PREPARED TO PROCEED?" asked the judge.

"The government is ready, Your Honor," replied Marshall, rising to his feet.

"The defense?"

"We are ready to proceed," said Josh, looking a bit green around the gills.

"Well, then, have a seat, gentlemen," said the judge. "We're likely to be here for some time."

With that, Josh and Arthur Marshall exchanged a quick glance and sat down.

"I have been deeply troubled by the actions of the defendants in this case, as I am in every criminal case," began Judge Blake.

"Not simply because of the nature of the crime, an abhorrent deprivation of the liberty worked upon several individuals, but because of the backgrounds of the defendants.

"The younger Mr. Mullen is a recent graduate of one of our nation's foremost schools of law, where he had the benefit of exposure to preeminent legal scholars.

"Ms. Grabowski has spent the past ten years as a private investigator, employed by one of this city's most well-established law firms. She has testified in this very courthouse innumerable times, and has worked with some of our finest practitioners.

"As for the senior Mr. Mullen, you came to this country seeking economic opportunity for yourself and your family. You spent the majority of your adulthood as a hardworking man of your community. True, you have suffered a tremendous loss with the tragic death of your grandson, but this cannot excuse your conduct."

When the judge took a moment to catch his breath, Mack seized the opportunity to whisper an old Irish prayer. For the first time, Pauline looked scared. I took her hand and squeezed it. I loved this woman. I couldn't begin to imagine being separated from her.

"As for the government, young Mr. Marshall here," the judge continued, nodding in the direction of the prosecutor, "and his boss, U.S. Attorney Lily Grace Drucker, have, in their infinite compassion, recommended that I impose only the minimum sentence statutorily available to me, twenty years, in light of the defendants' lack of any prior criminal records. After much consideration, I'm afraid I decline to accept the government's generous recommendation.

"But before I proceed to hand down the sentence of

the court, I wish to comment upon the collateral consequences of the defendants' actions.

"As I am sure all parties are aware, as a direct result of the defendants' investigative work and expertise at 'trial,' Mr. Barry Neubauer, the main 'victim' here, has been charged with twelve separate counts of manslaughter and is on trial as I speak in the New York State criminal court.

"As U.S. Attorney Drucker has announced, the FBI is currently investigating William Montrose, esquire, in connection with charges that he suborned perjury and intimidated a witness — Dr. Jane Davis — at the inquest into Peter Mullen's death, again, as a direct result of the defendants' actions.

"Mr. and Mrs. Fitzharding have left this court's jurisdiction and have refused to assist this court in its presentence investigation.

"Detective Francis Volpi has recently been arrested in connection with the homicide of Sammy Giamalva here in Manhattan. He is also a suspect in the murder of Peter Mullen.

"And Campion Neubauer has been indicted as an accessory in the murder of Peter Mullen."

The judge looked up from his bench, as if to survey the courtroom. "These are dark times for our system of criminal justice. Recent verdicts in so-called high-profile cases have led to the broadly held conclusion that there is justice in this country only for those whose wealth or celebrity can buy it for them.

"I have sat on this bench for the past forty-four years, since President Eisenhower saw fit to appoint me. In all those years, I have never been as distressed by the so-called administration of justice in this country as I am today.

"That said, here is my ruling."

There wasn't a sound anywhere in the court. Pauline's nails were cutting into my palm. Macklin had my other hand wrapped in his.

"The court," said Judge Blake, "on its own motion, chooses to invoke Federal Sentencing Guideline Five-K-One point one. This section, for the ladies and gentlemen of the press, allows the court to downwardly depart in sentencing those defendants whose cooperation with the government has led to the investigation or prosecution of another person or persons. Given the valuable assistance the defendants have provided, I am sure that I will hear no objection from the government on this motion?" asked the judge. He looked over at the prosecution table.

"None, whatsoever," croaked Marshall, looking in his fresh-scrubbed youth like a boy who had just been spared a dreaded chore by a forgiving adult.

"Good answer."

"Macklin Reid Mullen, Pauline Grabowski, Jack Mullen, the court sentences you each to time served and to six hundred hours of community service, to be performed in the Legal Aid Society, Capital Defenders Unit. From now on, the only trials you will be involved in will be on behalf of indigent death row defendants.

"This court now stands adjourned."

As the judge pounded his gavel on the bench and rose to walk down the stairs, the spectator section exploded in applause, cheers, and high fives.

Reporters crowded around us as Mack, Pauline, and I

embraced in a bear hug. None of us said a word to the press.

"Your brother is proud of you," Mack whispered in my ear.

As the three of us were leaving the courtroom, arm in arm, I thought of something, an old sacred memory.

When Peter was just a little kid, after our mother had died, he used to sneak into bed with me just about every night. "I like hearing your heart beat, Jack," he'd say.

I had liked hearing Peter's heart, too. I missed it.

It surprises some readers that When The Wind Blows *(featuring Max and the gang) is my most successful novel around the world. Who knows why for sure, but I suspect it's because an awful lot of people, myself included, have a recurring fantasy in which they fly. They treasure it. On the other hand, there are plenty of folks who won't fantasize or play make-believe. They wouldn't have gotten to Neverneverland with Peter Pan. There is one other thing that might be interesting to those who read this book. When I researched it I interviewed dozens of scientists. All of them said that things like what happens in* The Lake House *will happen in our lifetime. In fact, a scientist in New England claims that he can put wings on humans right now. I'll bet he can.*

So settle in, you believers, and even you Muggles. Let yourself fly.

—James Patterson

PROLOGUE

RESURRECTION

The Hospital; somewhere in Maryland

At around eleven in the evening, Dr. Ethan Kane trudged down the gray-and-blue-painted corridor toward a private elevator. His mind was filled with images of death and suffering, but also progress, *great progress that would change the world.*

A young and quite homely scrub nurse rounded the corner of the passageway, and nodded her head deferentially as she approached him. She had a crush on Dr. Kane, and she wasn't the only one.

"Doctor," she said, "you're still working."

"Esther, *you* go home, now. Please," Ethan Kane said, pretending to be solicitous and caring, which couldn't be further from the truth. He considered the nurse inferior in every way, including the fact that she was female.

He was also exhausted from a surgical marathon: five major operations in a day. The elevator car finally arrived, the doors slid open, and he stepped inside.

"Goodnight, Esther," he said, and showed the nurse a lot of very white teeth, but no genuine warmth, because there was none to show.

He straightened his tall body and wearily passed his hand over his longish blond hair, cleaned his wire-rimmed glasses on the tail of his lab coat, then rubbed his eyes before putting his glasses back on as he descended to the sub-basement level.

One more thing to check on . . . always one more thing for him to do.

He walked a half-dozen quick steps to a thick steel door and pushed it open with the palm of his hand.

He entered the dark and chilly atmosphere of a basement storage room. A pungent odor struck him.

There, lying on a double row of gurneys, were six naked bodies. Four men, two women, all in their late teens and early twenties. Each was brain dead, each as good as gone, but each had served a worthy purpose, a higher one. The plastic bracelets on their wrists said *DONOR*.

"You're making the world a better place," Kane whispered as he passed the bodies. "Take comfort in that."

Dr. Kane strode to the far end of the room and pushed open another steel door, an exact duplicate of the first. This time rather than a chill blast, he was met by a searing wave of hot air, the deafening roar of fire, and the unmistakable smell of death.

All three of the incinerators were going tonight. Two of his night-time porters, their powerful working-man bodies glistening with grime and sweat, looked up as Dr. Kane entered the cinderblock chamber. The men nodded respectfully, but their eyes showed fear.

"Let's pick up the pace, gentlemen. This is taking

too long," Kane called out. "Let's go, let's go! You're being paid well for this scut-work. Too well."

He glanced at a naked young woman's corpse laid out on the cement floor. She was white-blond, pretty in a music video sort of way. The porters had probably been diddling with her. That's why they were behind schedule, wasn't it?

Gurneys were shoved haphazardly into one corner, like discarded shopping carts in a supermarket parking lot. Quite a spectacle. *Hellish* to be sure.

As he watched, one of the sweat-glazed minions worked a wooden paddle under a young male's body while the other swung open the heavy glass door of an oven. Together they pushed, shoved, slid the body into the fire as if it were a pizza.

The flames dampened for a moment, then as the porters locked down the door, the inferno flared again. The cremation chamber was also called a "retort." Each retort burned at 3600 degrees, and it took just over fifteen minutes to reduce a human body to nothing but ashes.

To Dr. Ethan Kane that meant one thing: no evidence of what was happening at the Hospital. Absolutely no evidence of Resurrection.

"Pick up the pace!" he yelled again. "Burn these bodies!"

The donors.

PART ONE

CHILD CUSTODY

CHAPTER ONE

It was being called "the mother of all custody trials," and that might explain why an extra fifty thousand people had poured into Denver on that warm day in early spring.

The case was also being billed as potentially more wrenching and explosive than Baby M, or Elian Gonzales, or O.J. Simpson's battle against truth and decency. I happened to think that this time *maybe* the media hype was fitting and appropriate, and even a tiny bit underplayed. The fate of six extraordinary children was at stake.

Six children who had been created in a laboratory, and made history, both scientific and philosophical.

Six adorable, good-hearted kids whom I loved as if they were my own.

Max, Matthew, Icarus, Ozymandias, Peter and Wendy.

The actual trial was scheduled to begin in an hour in the City and County Building, a gleaming white neoclassical-looking courthouse. Designed to appear unmistakably judicial, it was crowned with a pointy pediment just like the one atop the U.S. Supreme Court building. I could see it now.

Kit and I slumped down on the front seat of my dusty, trusty beat-up blue Suburban. It was parked down the block from the courthouse, where we could see and not be seen, at least so far.

I had chewed my nails down to the quick, and there was a pesky muscle twitching in Kit's cheek.

"I know, Frannie," he'd said just a moment before. "I'm twitching again."

We were suing for custody of the children, and we knew that the full weight of the law was against us. We *weren't* married, *weren't* related to the kids, and their biological parents *were* basically good people. Not too terrific for us.

What we did have going for us was our unshakable love for these children, with whom we'd gone through several degrees of hell, and their love for us.

Now all we had to do was prove that living with us was in the best interest of the children, and that meant I was going to have to tell a story that sounded crazy, even to my closest friends, sometimes even to myself.

But every word was true, so help me God.

CHAPTER TWO

The amazing story had actually started six months ago in the tiny burg of Bear Bluff, Colorado, which is fifty or so miles northwest of Boulder on the "Peak-to-Peak" highway.

I was driving home late one night when I happened to see a streaking white flash—then realized it was a young girl running fast through the woods not too far from my home.

But that was just part of what I saw. I'm a veterinarian, "Dr. Frannie," and my brain didn't want to accept what my eyes told me, so I stopped my car and got out.

The strange girl looked to be eleven or twelve, with long blond hair and a loose-fitting white smock that was stained with blood and ripped. I remember gasping for breath and literally steadying myself against a tree. I had the clear and distinct thought that I couldn't be seeing what I was seeing.

But my eyes didn't lie. Along with a pair of fore-shortened arms, *the girl had wings!*

That's correct—wings! About a nine-foot span. Below the wings, and attached somehow were her arms. She was *double-limbed.* And the fit of her wings was absolutely perfect. Extraordinary from a scientific and aesthetic point of view. A mind-altering dose of reality.

She had also been hurt, which was how I eventually came to capture her, in a "mist net," and sedate her, with the help of an FBI agent named Thomas Brennan whom I knew better as Kit. We brought her to the animal hospital I operate, the Inn-Patient, where I examined her. I found very large pectoral muscles anchored to an oversized breastbone, anterior and posterior air sacs, a heart as large as a horse's.

She had been "engineered" that way. A *perfect* design, actually. Totally brilliant.

But why? And by whom?

Her name was Max, short for Maximum, and it was incredibly hard to win her trust at first. But in her own good time she told me things that made me sick to my stomach, and also angrier than I'd ever been. She told me about a place called the School where she'd been kept captive since the day she was born.

Everything you're about to hear is already *happening by the way.* It's going on in outlaw labs across the United States and other countries as well. In our life-time! If it's hard to take, all I can say is, buckle up the seatbelts on your easy chair. This is what happened to Max and a few others like her.

Biologists, trying to break the barrier on human longevity, had melded bird DNA with human zygotes. It *can* be done. They had created Max and several other children. A *flock*. Unfortunately, the scientists couldn't grow the babies in test tubes, so the genetically modified embryos had to be implanted in their mothers' wombs.

When the mothers were close to term, labor was induced. The poor mothers were then told that their premature children had died. The preemies were shipped to an underground lab called "the School." The School was, by any definition, a maximum-security prison. The children were kept in cages and the rejects were "put to sleep," a horrible euphemism for cold-blooded murder.

Like I said, *buckle up those seatbelts*!

Anyway, that was why Max had done what she'd been forbidden to do. She had escaped from the School. Amazingly, we succeeded. We even got to live with the kids a few months at a magical place we all called the Lake House. Kit and I listened to what Max had to tell us, then we went with her to try and rescue the children still trapped at the lab called the School.

When the smoke cleared, *literally*, the six surviving children, including Max and her brother, were sent to live with their biological parents—people they'd never known a day in their lives.

That should have been fine, I guess, but this real-life fairy tale didn't have a happy ending.

The kids, who ranged from twelve years old down to about four, phoned Kit and me constantly every single day. They told us they were horribly depressed, bored, scared, miserable, suicidal, and I knew why. As a vet, I understood what no one else seemed to.

The children had done a bird thing: *they had imprinted on Kit and me*. We were the only parents they knew and could love.